KAUFERING XII

THE STORY OF A JEWISH SS OFFICER

DANNY RITTMAN

KAUFERING XII
THE STORY OF A JEWISH SS OFFICER

iUniverse books may be ordered through booksellers or by contacting:

iUniverse
1663 Liberty Drive
Bloomington, IN 47403
www.iuniverse.com
1-800-Authors (1-800-288-4677)

ISBN: 978-1-6632-0255-0 (sc)
ISBN: 978-1-5320-9172-8 (e)

Library of Congress Control Number: 2020910242

Print information available on the last page.

iUniverse rev. date: 06/18/2020

בְּמָקוֹם שֶׁאֵין אֲנָשִׁים, הִשְׁתַּדֵּל לִהְיוֹת אִישׁ.

Mishnah

In a place where there are no men, strive to be a man.

Acknowledgments

I'd like to thank Yochanan, who is this story's main hero, for his courage in sharing his story with the world. In addition, I'd like to thank my personal friend Ofer, who helped to gather historical information about the story. Finally, I would like to thank my friend and the editor of this book, Brian Downing, for inspiring support and sound advice.

Author's Note

My father introduced me to "Yochanan Berger" at the London Cafe in Netanya. They are both Holocaust survivors, though in different ways—some would say in opposing ways, though my father would not. The two men became good friends over the years, and my father eventually nudged Yochanan into telling his story. I was fascinated by it and asked permission to put it in writing. He was generous enough to agree, albeit reluctantly.

His only request was that he remain anonymous and that certain names and places be changed. Most events occur at a Dachau subcamp called Kaufering XII. Dachau had several Kaufering subcamps but not a twelfth one.

It took almost two years to gather the story. Almost all of it was given by Yochanan himself at the London Cafe. A few passages were added after talks with his daughter, who recalled events from conversations with her father.

My interviews with Yochanan—Yochi—were long and often painful. At many points, he became emotional, highly so. I wondered if the project should be cut short or shelved altogether, but he wouldn't hear of it. He collected himself and persevered, right up to the end.

Yochanan passed away in 2018. He was found on the doorstep of his home, shortly after he had called emergency services. The death was ruled from natural causes. He was ninety-eight years old.

My dear friend Yochanan, here is your story, rendered with

historical accuracy. May readers come to appreciate your ordeals and understand your life in its fullness. May you rest in peace.

Danny Rittman
San Diego, November 2019

Grim Reality

I watched in horror as one of the soldiers unexpectedly started beating an old woman who stood in the front line in that morning roll call. He lashed out in unexplained anger, beating her with his club. Instinctively, I made one step forward to stop this madness. Then I remembered who I was, and deep fear froze me. I was one of the SS soldiers and officers. One of the staff. As a matter of fact, I was second-in-command. The scene seemed so unreal, and for a moment, I doubted that it was really happening. My heart raced, and I tried with all my power to control my breathing so no one would notice my panic.

My horrific new reality slowly sank in: a young SS officer had beaten an old woman, maybe in her eighties, with his club. I saw her wrinkled face warping in pain as the blows came harshly on her back, legs, and abdomen. She didn't even have the power to scream in pain anymore as she raised her weak arms in the air, trying to protect her face from the repeated vicious hits. For a moment she looked straight at me, and my mouth became dry in panic. I could see the excruciating pain in her face. One of her eyes was closed, and blood gushed out of her nose. When she looked at me for that split second, it was as if she were asking for mercy, but I couldn't do anything. I think I was in shock. A few minutes later, she silently fell to the ground and didn't move. The soldier swore, put his club on his holster, and walked away from the scene.

I just had finished my training in the SS headquarters and had started my service in a working camp, a subcamp of Dachau. Today was my first day. I never imagined that I'd see scenes like this, and I was not prepared for it. My body shook from despair and fear. I had to gather all my power not to pass out.

The old woman's body lay there, reminding me of the inhumanity of the Nazi regime, of which I was a part. I was an SS officer. I had been recruited to the SS against my will, but I held a crucial secret—a secret that could cost my family and me our lives—and I was determined to keep the secret at all costs.

I was an imposter—an Orthodox Jewish man.

1

MY WORLD

Yochanan Berger is my name. I was born into an Orthodox Jewish family in 1920. We lived in Friedrichstadt, a suburb just south of Berlin that is now part of the city. Outside, we spoke German. At home, it was Yiddish, a dialect with a variety of imported words and a highly distinctive accent. It was part of my life, and, as it turned out, it helped save my life in a Dachau subcamp.

A menorah and other items of Judaica had honored places in our home. We had two sets of dishes and followed our faith's other dietary rules. Lapses were too few to mention. My father saw to that.

Our large house was near the heart of Friedrichstadt, not far from public buildings and parks where children played and enjoyed the sight of a glorious fountain, until the cold closed it down, and we eagerly awaited spring. Six months seemed like an eternity to us. My father was a respected engineer in a firm that made locomotives and railcars—paradoxical, given their later use. My mother took care of the house and doted on me, her only child.

Every day, my father and I donned yarmulkes and walked to the synagogue. No matter the weather, it was a sacred duty. *Schul* took place in a building from the late nineteenth century. Not so old back then. Members of our community felt the same duty, especially on Friday evenings. We were a close-knit group. We all knew each other and cared for one another's well-being.

When the day of my bar mitzvah arrived, at the age of thirteen, family and community gathered at the synagogue. It was 1933, and our country already had sensed winds of change. Schoolteachers, tradesmen, doctors, lawyers, shopkeepers, and civil servants came for the occasion of welcoming a new young man into the community. I read the sacred text clearly and solemnly and sang the same way. My parents and relatives beamed. Hearty congratulations and well wishes followed. I must have shaken more hands that day than on any other. The rabbi who'd prepared me for the day complimented me on my knowledge of the Torah and my effortless delivery. He offered that I'd become a fine rabbi myself one day. My father had the same hope.

I stayed on the path for many years, living at home, of course, and attending yeshiva not far away. I studied mathematics, history, literature, and art, but they were secondary to the study of the Torah and Talmud. I did well in all my studies. There was no great urging from my parents. It was simply expected.

My friends were yeshiva classmates and a few children of the congregants who attended public schools. The larger world was strange to us, though not yet menacing.

I had an athletic look; I was much taller than my father and a little stouter too. My friends and I played various games in the parks and fields. We were enthusiastic, but none was destined for athletic achievement. One thing that set me apart from my friends was my blue eyes. Oh, I might also have been more inquisitive than they were. I also had blond-brown hair. I never imagined that these features would help to save my and my family's lives later.

My path in life seemed clear to the rabbi, my parents, schoolmates, and me—perhaps especially to me. The adults knew there were many paths a member could take. I'd continue my studies, both religious and secular; choose a profession; and find a young woman from within the community or maybe from another one in the Berlin area. There'd be another ceremony, one involving a chuppah and a cloth-covered glass. Then my bride and I would raise our children, all within the warm circle of the Orthodox faith. Family, synagogue, ritual, and continuity were central in our lives. And we were sure that nothing could change it.

Berlin was mostly Lutheran but with many Catholics as well. Like us, they had their own neighborhoods, schools, folkways, and places of worship. Their churches struck me as wonderfully ornate, at least from the outside. Naturally, I'd never been inside one.

Not far from the way to the synagogue was a Catholic church. Father and I walked past it on our way to schul. On certain days, we'd see priests and nuns dressed in religious garb I'd never seen before. Solemn processions made their way around the block on holy days. The blues and reds of the church's stained-glass windows caught my eye in the warm glow of late afternoon or bright moonlight. With each day, I saw greater beauty.

Father noticed my interest one evening. "Don't ever go in there, young man! It's forbidden! Absolutely forbidden!"

From then on, my glances had to be short and cautious. But memories last, and a young man's mind wants to know more.

One evening in mid-November 1938, I was worried about a math exam and needed more preparation. Father told me to join him at the synagogue when I could. After an hour of memorization and problem-solving, I put the books down, donned my black suit and yarmulke, and headed out.

It was chilly, and the streets were livelier as the Gentiles shopped for the approaching holiday. Tall pines were sold on every other street corner. Snowflakes flitted down and sparkled in the light of gas lamps.

The sounds of an organ and choir met me a block from the church. I stood outside the engraved wooden doors and listened, only for a moment or two. The lovely music briefly increased in volume and clarity as latecomers hurriedly opened the heavy doors and rushed in. I hesitantly ascended the steps for a peek. A young family walked by and held the door open for me and—well, I found myself inside. Only then did Father's admonition echo within me. I must say it faded and became lost in the music.

I was drawn toward the rear area where the choir stood and heard more musical instruments and individual voices, which from afar had blended into one. The singers were in gowns of deep blue and ivory. I think the hymn was in Latin, but I couldn't be sure, as I had no familiarity with it. Anyway, language was not as important as beauty. Their voices grew in volume and ascended to higher pitches. Male voices added lower harmony.

Then I saw her. Her fair hair, oval face, and delicate lips and eyebrows stood out, and her voice came through. Moments later, she raised a row of brass bells and delicately struck each one. The bright tones easily made it through the choir and instruments. The passage was repeated, and the bells once again brought esthetic perfection. This time, I noticed how they rang across the ceiling and down the aisles.

No one in the congregation that night appreciated her part more than I did. No one.

Her eyes passed from side to side of the sanctuary area, perhaps looking for family members or a special loved one—a notion that unexpectedly worried me. Her eyes came upon mine and settled on them. I thought it would only last a moment and then she'd quickly feel discomfort with a stranger, but the moment went on.

The music was magical. The orchestra moved up in volume and I was amazed to hear the clear ringing of the bells in perfect time. I was transfigured. The musicians fell silent for a moment; then, one instrument after another—cellos and violins, flutes and horns—started in again until assembling into a crescendo.

Our eyes met once more. We remained transfixed as another crescendo built. The music fell silent once again, and the performance concluded with the masterful ringing of bells from her gentle hands. The congregants sat in appreciative wonder for a moment, until a few began to clap and others followed. Soon, the church was filled with grateful applause, including from the young visitor that night.

The congregants began to leave, and the musicians and singers filtered into the rows of pews. I was delighted but a little nervous as she walked my way. Was she on her way to her parents and I was simply on her path, just another congregant? Or had our moment struck her as much as it had me? To my delight she came right up to me.

"I'm Emilie. May I ask your name?" Her voice was as mellifluous as any instrument in the church that night, and her daring was well beyond that of most women then, regardless of community or faith. My reply was undoubtedly awkward but at least it was brief.

"Yochanan," I mumbled after a long delay.

She observed me thoroughly and then smiled, and I melted entirely. Then she noticed the yarmulke on my head. "Are you Jewish?"

"Yes."

We looked at each other for few minutes.

She smiled beautifully, illuminating the world. "Aren't you forbidden to enter churches?" she asked quietly. "I have a friend who told me that once."

"Yes, if my father knew—"

"That's fine." She smiled again, and this time I joined her. "He'll never know, will he?"

I shook my head. "I like your singing. You sing beautifully."

"Thank you. We sing here twice a week in the holiday season."

"Can I come to see you?"

"Of course. I invite you to come. As a matter of fact, I'm singing here tomorrow. Will you come to see me, Yochanan?"

I answered without thinking. "Yes, I will."

She took my hand, and I couldn't believe we were holding hands. Her hand was warm and soft, and I felt heat flashes all over me. My heart was beating so hard that I was afraid she would notice it.

"Promise?" She gave me a smile that melted me.

"Promise."

"Good. I have to go now. I'm going home with my girlfriend's parents. See you tomorrow."

She walked over to a girl her age, and they whispered to each other. Her friend looked my way and giggled.

I couldn't wait for our next meeting.

One cold November night, we sat at the dinner table. I already knew the ritual. After the meal, we'd go to the synagogue for our evening prayer. Mother talked about some new decrees that the city had imposed on Jewish people, but I didn't listen much. All I could think about was how to excuse myself from going to the schul that night. I wanted to see Emilie. My heart beat fast as I told Father that I'd not attend prayers at the schul.

Father wasn't pleased. "Why aren't you coming to schul tonight?"

"I'm going to see a friend to prepare for exams. I'll be there later."

The half-truth was all I could allow just then. He gave me a thorough look. I revealed no particular expression, and he accepted my answer.

"That's fine, Yochi. Learning is important."

I could hardly hide my joy. I finished my meal and nonchalantly went to my room. Quickly, I put on my fancy shirt and Sabbat shoes. My hair refused to behave at first, and I had to wet it to comb it straight. Finally, I put on a few drops of perfume and quietly sneaked through the back door. Down the streets I flew.

When I was half a block away, I could see people entering the church, so I knew I wasn't late. I found a place in a pew only a few rows from the choir. I noticed that the women had scarves or lace over the heads, but the men had removed their hats, so I took off my yarmulke and placed it inside my overcoat.

"Welcome, Yochanan," came a whisper from my left. Yes, it was Emilie! No one else there knew my name. Our gazes locked once more. "Come with me. There are seats for choir members in the front pew." Sensing my unease, she added, "It's all right. You're with me!"

"But I'm not a member of the church. I'm not even—"

"Yochanan," she whispered assuredly, "it doesn't matter. You're with me."

"What was the name of the music you performed last time?"

"It's called 'Carol of the Bells.' We're doing it tonight as well."

She escorted me to her pew and took her place in the choir. A while later, a priest in golden silk robes emerged from a chamber, with an altar boy on either side of him. No mass that evening, though; just more music. More glorious music. The priest and altar boys sat, and the organist and choir recognized their cue.

They began with lighter Christmas songs, followed by a solemn choral work. I had a little knowledge of Lutheran sacred music from the radio. The melodies and hymns that night, however, were quite different—and more beautiful too. Naturally, my senses may have been swayed by my heart. My heart certainly helped in discerning her voice.

To my delight, the program closed with "Carol of the Bells." Once again, I was transported into another world as voices and instruments waltzed with each other. Emilie's moment was approaching. The bells rang out with each touch, reverberating throughout the church and lifting the hearts of all, especially the lovestruck lad with a yarmulke in his coat pocket.

My visits to the church became routine, although I was by no means a regular member of the parish. Twice a week, I'd find a reason and make my way there. We even met at the library and a coffeehouse.

One evening Emilie showed me around the church's interior. Rows of candles flickered in red glasses. More stained glass adorned each corner. Murals gave life to the walls. Front pews had fine detailing on the woodwork. We found our way to a quiet, recessed part, next to a holy water font.

"Did you enjoy the program this evening, Yochi?"

"Yes, very much so. The music was wonderful. And it's moving to see how people of another faith give praise to God."

Her hand held mine. That was expected, at least somewhat. But then she kissed me, and nothing could have been more unexpected, nor could anything have been more welcome or wondrous. My entire being awakened. It would have been all too easy to forget where we were. Only after a lengthy time—and highly reluctantly—did our lips part, and a moment of blissful pondering began.

"Yochi, will you come visit me at my family's country home on Christmas?" She saw my astonishment but perhaps also a little willingness. "You know, it's the twenty-fifth. You will have concluded the eight days of Hanukkah."

"How do you know of our holiday observation?"

"Yochanan! We have Jewish friends. I know about the menorah and even a thing or two about the Maccabees and the temple!"

"Yes, of course. Our worlds are not so far apart, then. But there is one problem. I need to know where you live!"

"It's just outside the city in a rural part of Brandenburg. There are tall trees and a pond that's beginning to freeze over. Oh, Yochi, please say you'll come!"

No one could have refused a beautiful young woman with such joy and love in her eyes, least of all me. The thought never entered my mind.

"Of course I'll be there."

"Wonderful! Thank you. I must be off now."

She gave me a quick kiss and darted away, her feet barely touching the ground. I stood there, blushing, bewildered, and counting the days till the Christian holiday came. And wondering how I would explain it to my family.

The next day, the secret was coursing mightily within me. I wondered if those around me at home and school could see. How could they not? How could a mother not? It was early in the morning when I sat with my mom in the kitchen. My mother was a meticulous person who kept a beautifully organized home. She also loved plants, so our kitchen was full of green planters with colorful flowers everywhere. The wooden floor was always clean, and there was always the good aroma of some dish in the air—a beef stew at dinner or breakfast potatoes early in the morning.

As on every morning, my mother insisted on cooking my breakfast and keeping me company so I wouldn't eat alone. My mom was in her late sixties, plump, with a constant positive attitude. Her eyes always radiated good nature and happiness, not like my dad, who typically was serious and short-tempered. Mom always wore her apron, as if she was in the middle of cooking, and she always insisted that I leave the house with a sweater, even on the hottest summer days. That morning, she watched me as I ate quietly. As a sensitive mother, she could tell that something was different.

"Yochi, what is going on? You are not as usual."

"I met someone the other day." I couldn't hide the truth from her.

"So that's it! I knew it! I sensed something like that! I probably I know her. What's her name? Who are her parents? What does the father do?"

"Mom, it's rather early in our relationship. Please be patient. When I know more, I will tell you."

"You're not going to tell me now? Oh, Yochanan, please! I'm your mother! How does she look?"

As she continued to stare at me, I said, "She is a beautiful young woman, Mother, with blonde hair and green eyes. Her look is soul-penetrating, and her voice is delicate and gentle. I think she is gorgeous."

My mom smiled widely. "It seems to me that you have feelings for this young lady."

"Indeed I have, Mother; indeed I have. But I don't want to get anyone's hopes up yet, Mom. I know the plans you and Father have for me."

"Very well, young man, very well. You know your father and I only want the best for you—and for your girlfriend. Oh, I almost certainly know her parents! Fine people, I'm sure!"

I sank into daydreaming about Emilie until my mother's voice woke me.

"Now eat your potatoes, and don't forget to drink your milk, young man. It's very healthy for you."

I finished my meal and left for school, but a terrible dilemma followed me for the next few days. Mother might be understanding. But Father? The head of the house back then was the father. His word was law, and there was no doubt where he would stand on this. I decided that I wasn't truly committing to anything, and there was nothing wrong with meeting Emilie and her family. I was young but not so young as not to realize that romantic attractions often come and go. A time for this and a time for that, as it says in the sacred texts of both faiths. I couldn't imagine refusing to see Emilie on that day.

In the next few weeks, we became closer. We became best friends. We met almost every weekend when she arrived to perform at the church. We secretly met at coffee shops when her uncle and friends gave her rides back home.

One cold evening, we had coffee at one of Berlin's finest cafeterias. We sat close to each other and couldn't have enough of holding hands.

"It's becoming hard for me to be apart from you during the week," Emilie told me.

We treasured a long kiss.

"For me too, Emilie. I miss you so much."

"I am concerned. My father says that there are winds of war in our country. He doesn't like me going so often to the big city."

"I was shocked when I had to wear the yellow star," I said. "It's crazy. I can't believe this is going on in such a modern and educated country like ours."

"Many say it'll go away with time. Others say it's very dangerous. As long as we are together, I'm not afraid. The people of Germany will not let anything bad happen."

"I hope so. My father keeps telling me that he has a bad feeling about this."

We sipped our warm coffees and hugged. All seemed to be good when we were together, and we couldn't imagine anything else.

Our love had deepened gradually with our long walks in the park at the center of the city and our lingering conversations in cafés, with the steaming-hot coffee as a balm to our souls. When you're in love, time gets distorted somehow. You lose touch with the basics of reality, and you love every minute of it, hoping it will last forever, while knowing in your heart of hearts that nothing, not even love, can ever last forever. Yet in this case, I felt it would last forever. I was already deeply in love with her.

I told my parents that I was going to visit a friend on that day in late December. They were quizzical but let it go. I wasn't a boy anymore but a twenty-year-old man. I met Emilie and her uncle near the church, and after preliminary pleasantries, off we went in a compact Opel for the hour-long journey to the countryside. The drizzle and narrow roads kept our speed low, but that was just fine to the couple in the back seat, holding hands and treasuring the joy of young love.

We soon left the buildings and streets of Berlin and passed forests with sparse foliage, a handful of small farms, and creeks and ponds with frost along their banks. An hour or so later, we reached a lovely village with mostly narrow streets and quaint shops centered in an old quarter.

The family house was a few hundred meters away. It was made from large stones with sturdy timbers, giving support and majesty. A chimney stood atop a tiled roof and sent whitish smoke up to the skies. Pots with hardy plants rested on the windows.

A short, plump woman greeted us with a wide smile. "Hello and welcome! You must be Yochanan! Come in, come in! Now take off your hat and coat, young man."

I didn't know how I'd feel on meeting her folks, but I felt genuinely welcome. I was at home—all the more so with a half dozen logs crackling in the stone fireplace.

The floors were made of oak planks, which announced their age with every step. A table, perhaps three meters long, filled the dining room. The light maple's flame-like markings shimmered as though alive. Cups marked with hunting scenes and filled with hot cocoa awaited us. Emilie promised to join us after freshening up.

Mrs. Hintze resembled her daughter but with a few more kilograms here and there and many more glimpses of life—mostly good, it appeared. As we sipped cocoa, a man in a thick cardigan descended the stairs. A generous waxed mustache came into view in the better light, along with a warm smile.

"Stefan! This is our daughter's gentleman friend Yochanan Berger. And young man, this is my husband, Stefan Hintze."

I stood to shake his hand and searched his face for signs of discomfort. I was put at ease. He might have done the same. After talk of the drive from Berlin and the weather, the fatherly questions came fast. I told him of my plans to attend Berlin University the following semester to study electrical engineering.

He thought it was a fine field that would help Germany. "All of Germany," he added. "Emilie is to enroll shortly after you. As you might already know, she will study art, especially music."

She'd told me that, of course, but I listened politely.

"She has a gift for music," I said. "There's no doubt about that."

"And you have excellent taste!" Mr. Hintze said.

Emilie descended the stairs gracefully in a long red skirt, white blouse, and black jacket to protect from drafts. Her light-brown tresses had been done into braids. The three of us brightened. Mr. Hintze and I stood to greet her.

Upon finishing our cocoa, we settled down on a red velvet sofa in the living room, where a two-meter tree stood in a corner. Mr. Hintze stoked the fire with another log from a neatly stacked pile and positioned it with a wrought-iron poker.

"I chopped our tree down two weeks ago. I didn't have to go far. Just a short walk from the porch."

"And we all decorated it that very night," Emilie added.

"The Hintze household is not the most religious one in Brandenburg," her father said. "Yes, we celebrate the holiday but chiefly as a time of joy and community. Family and friends visit for conversation and refreshments. One has come today, unless I miss my guess."

I knew his next words would come sooner or later. My last name, Berger, means "coal miner" and is a common German surname. Yochanan is less common and more revealing.

"I understand you are Jewish."

"Yes, we are an Orthodox family. And we have been so for many generations. Many in the extended family are followers of the Masorti branch of Judaism, which is more accepting of the outside."

He knew the social implications of that. I knew that some Christian families had similar structures. Oddly, the matter made me realize how much I cared for Emilie. But then I thought of my father.

"Enough about religion!" Emilie said. "I promised to show you around, and I will keep my word, no matter how engaging my parents can be."

"Yes, please. No need to stay and indulge the old folks," Mr. Hintze added. "Look about the place—the woods and hills and cabin."

"We're not that old, Stefan," Mrs. Hintze chided gently, "but by all means, explore the place."

We donned coats and headed for a hilly area covered by pines, her hand warming my entire being. The snow wasn't deep or slippery in the copse. We turned, looked into each other's eyes, and kissed—longer than in the church and much more comfortably. If it had been spring, we would have lain down.

"Come along, Yochi."

Deeper in the woods stood a cabin, its roof dusted by snow. It was straight out of *Hansel and Gretel.* I almost looked for a trail of bread crumbs. The smokeless chimney promised no warmth, but in we went.

"A caretaker once lived here, but it's mostly vacant these days. I stay overnight here sometimes. Oh, the door is so creaky."

The interior was perhaps ten meters by eight. Cooking pots hung next to the fireplace. Happily, there was a cord of wood, and soon enough, a few logs brought warmth. An oil lamp gave us soft light. We must have spoken a little, but our kisses renewed surprisingly quickly, and we lay down on a small bed and covered ourselves with a quilt. Nature took it from there, as our love took over. We kissed passionately, and our hands seemed to have desires of their own. Quickly, we remained in Adam and Eve clothing, as we couldn't have enough of touching, caressing, and tasting each other. Our bodies united, and the whole world was gone, and all that existed was us, holding each other, sweating in the exquisite rhythm of love that fulfilled our entire beings, until an explosion of fireworks drifted us away to an eternal oblivion. It was wonderfully natural.

We slowly and reluctantly returned to the mundane.

"Your parents are not concerned about religious differences?" I asked Emilie.

"Not really. Our relationship was unexpected but not worrisome. They know I care for you, and you for me. That's what's important to them. They are concerned about the growing anti-Semitism in our country. My father keeps telling me that he hopes that Hitler's days will soon end. He is a danger to our country and to the world. We have very good Jewish friends who are strongly concerned about what is going on in Germany now. As a matter of fact, they are going to move to Switzerland in few months. They say that they don't trust Hitler, and things will escalate. I'm sure your parents will come to feel the same way. What if they move away as well?"

"My parents are not going to move away. Although my father is concerned, he is holding a good job, and I don't see us moving out of Germany. As for religion, he is stiffer, and we'll definitely have to convince him about our love. He is a bit narrow-minded when it comes to religion. But I know him. He has a kind heart. We'll get him on our side—eventually."

She smiled. "All will be well, Yochi. You'll see. After all, some things are meant to be! Let's go back into the woods a little deeper. I want to show you something. Something amazing. Come."

We walked hand in hand, deeper into the woods. I started to ask what was afoot but was immediately shushed. We stopped, and she told me to listen carefully. I almost asked what we were listening for, but I feared another shush would come as instantly as the first.

Moments of silence followed, accented only by murmuring pine branches as gentle winds flowed through them. A louder sound came.

Rustling. Louder.

A fawn was inching our way, sniffing the air for signs of danger and finding none. Emilie silently drew an apple from her coat and offered it to the gentle creature. To my astonishment, he took the apple from her hand and darted back into the brush for a welcome treat in the bare forest.

Emilie's face took on a fresh glow of beauty, from what I could only suspect was a frequent communication with the fauna of the Brandenburg woods. It was my first.

"I want to go back to the cabin now." I kissed her.

Soon enough, we were back and cuddled once more on the bed next to the fading embers of the fire. My passion had awakened again, and within seconds, we found ourselves naked in front of the warm fireplace. In the dim firelight, she looked as beautiful as Venus rising from the waves. Her body silhouette reflected on mine as we joined together in the dance of love. Our bodies entwined as one as the climax caught us by surprise and left us breathless and sweaty. After a while, we cuddled in front of the fireplace, wrapped in blankets.

"When I was a young girl, I came here by myself and talked with the birds and raccoons and deer. One day, it came to me—I wanted to be married here. Not long thereafter, maybe a week or so, I decided on something else. When my time is done, I want to be buried here."

"Now, there are plenty of things to concern ourselves with before we pass from this world, don't you think?"

"Yes, I see that. But this is my favorite place in the world. My *being* is here. And I want it to be here for all time." She pressed her breasts to my chest and looked into me. "Do you feel it, Yochi? Do you feel our hearts beating together? Pulse by pulse. They are one! We are one!"

And we became one again. Kisses, caresses, murmurs, pleadings—all under the quilt by the fire in the cabin.

That was my first Christmas, one might say. A memorable one, a cherished one, but one that few religious figures of any faith would have looked especially favorably upon. We returned to the house and enjoyed a dinner of goose, potatoes, and green beans. I admit to being pleased that the Hintzes did not serve ham or sausage dressing that night.

Looking back on that festive December gathering at Emilie's house, I find it hard to understand why we weren't more aware of how the country was spiraling out of control. We Jews were already wearing yellow stars, and yet many of us buried our heads in the sand.

Less than a year later, terror would reign in early November during the Night of Glass, or *Kristallnacht*, when German Brown Shirts went on a rampage.

After lengthy farewells came the drive back to Berlin. The traffic was light until we neared Friedrichstadt. A band was playing two blocks away. As we drove ahead slowly, I could see the musicians weren't from a church or the army—those were common enough sights in Berlin. These musicians wore red-and-black armbands with swastikas. Yes, at the time Emilie and I were falling in love, our country was abandoning generations of reason and law and taking on the hatred and violence of darker periods, thought buried long ago.

Yet it took me a few more weeks until I made the decision to come forward. I summoned the courage to divulge the secret but only to my mother. There was a limit to my courage but no limit to my father's will. At times, there were no limits to his wrath.

My mother's response came in rushed Yiddish. *Oi vey* and *Gewalt* came with every other sentence. A shake of the head came with most others.

"What did you say the girl's name is? Emilie? Why couldn't you find a Rivka or Sara or something more sensible? Emilie! What your father will say? He'll not like it. Not one bit, he won't! *Oi vey!*"

"Mother, please know that Emilie and I love each other. Very much so. We've been together for almost six months now."

"I am happy for my son, of course. What mother wouldn't be? None! But fathers? Fathers are another thing, Yochi, and Benjamin Berger is another thing altogether. It will take some time and persuasion. I've had almost thirty years of practice. Before you were born, I already was persuading him. Yes, it will take time." She sighed heavily. "But my little boy has found his love. Emilie—it's beginning to sound nice. Maybe grandchildren someday?"

"Someday, Mother. Someday. And Mother?"

"Yes, Yochanan?"

"Emilie is a lovely name. It's the loveliest name in the world."

A week or so later, after a good deal of planning, Mother and I decided to break the news to Father. The two conspirators knocked on the study door, where he had retreated following dinner for a glass of wine and a perusal of engineering journals. Mother offered to be the one to tell him, but I insisted it was my duty. She patted my hand, assured me it would go well, and took her place just outside the door. As I walked in, I was thinking all the time of Abraham and Isaac.

"A shiksa! Never! Out of the question! Completely unacceptable! Have we taught you nothing in all these years? You and she are from different religions, different faiths. It's intolerable! In this house, in any house in this community and country, the son obeys the father. You are to stop seeing this shiksa as of this instant! Do you hear me, Yochanan Berger? Do you understand?"

"Emilie and I are in love. We've been seeing each other for many months. It's not a passing fancy based on exploring the forbidden."

"The relationship will only bring trouble," Father insisted.

When I said we were planning to get married and have children, he looked sickened. Another tirade erupted.

I was beginning to despair. Would I have to make a choice? The decision would be painful; the consequences far worse.

Mother came in and took up the cause with the skills and passion of the best Berlin attorney. She said she was convinced that Emilie and I were truly in love and that she supported us and wanted us to be happy. "If you insist on standing in the way of our son's happiness, you will do him, Emilie, and me great harm. What's more, husband of mine, you will be doing yourself great harm. Everyone will be the worse for it. We are in a modern country, Benjamin, not a *shtetl*!"

Father was silent but showed no sign of relenting.

"Father, I'd like you and Mother to meet Emilie. She will be singing in her church on Sunday evening."

His eyes glared, and thunder seemed about to roar.

"It's not a religious service, Father, only a choral concert. You've listened to Brahms's *Requiem* on the radio and thoroughly enjoyed it. I know you did. The concert will be almost as beautiful as that, if not more so. The sounds will amaze you."

"It will be a lovely evening, Benjamin. Let us all go."

Father was silent again.

On Sunday evening, the three of us walked to the church. Families were scurrying in from a gentle spring shower. Father stopped cold as we reached the door atop the steps. He looked at it as though it were the gate to a dank prison that would slam shut behind him and trap him inside forever. Mother stepped in, and Father and I followed. He shook his head and murmured something in Yiddish that I didn't catch. I wondered if it had something to do with Abraham and Isaac.

He looked around at the artwork but seemed unimpressed. It was far more elaborate than anything in synagogues, where austerity is the rule. He looked at a row of sanctuary candles, and I was sure he thought they were not as beautiful or significant as menorahs.

The music started up, and he listened indifferently. He was merely doing his wife a favor. A crescendo at least caused an eyebrow to raise. A softer passage brought a wistful look, as though he was pondering a distant memory. Another crescendo reverberated throughout the church and within the being of a reluctant visitor too. Cellos and violins swept through him, but it was the bells that seemed to play upon his spine and overwhelm him.

A beautiful young woman rang a row of glistening bells with unexpected charm. He stared at her in awe.

"That's Emilie, Father," I whispered. "That's the woman I love."

2

The Cabin

Father climbed into the car and drove us out of the city. He knew the way by then, and a handful of family members—not all of them, by any means—followed closely behind. I sat in the front and tried not to wrinkle my new suit. The trees had full foliage, and bright clusters of cornflowers graced the meadows on either side of the winding roadway. It was late summer 1938.

As we neared the Hintze house, we could see several cars and dozens of guests, all colorfully dressed. Most of the women had bright flowers pinned to their fronts. A man named Rudolph Weber was there too. I'd met him previously, and our paths would cross many times over the years. Indeed, he became central to our lives.

My father was a slight man, and it was almost comical to watch him shake hands with Emilie's tall, outdoorsman dad. The handshake became increasingly warm until the two men laughed and hugged each other.

"Shall we make our way to the cabin, Benjamin?"

"It's time, Stefan."

The two fathers headed up the path, and the entourage followed. The woods were lovelier than on that winter day. More birds, more blossoms, more life. Waiting for me in the cabin doorway, in a flowing lace dress, was my Emilie, the woman I was to marry that day.

It took some doing, but we were able to find a priest and a

rabbi who would cobble together an interfaith ceremony. And after orations and recitals in Hebrew and Latin, I put foot to glass—quite successfully too. Emilie and I were husband and wife. Gasps of joy and hearty congratulations came from all. The proud fathers embraced once more, this time with a little dew in their eyes.

Emilie and I spent the next few nights in the cabin before traveling to an island in the Baltic Sea for our official honeymoon. No marriage began with more love and promise.

We didn't have time for a long honeymoon, as Emilie and I were to start at Berlin University in the fall. Eventually, we didn't start our education as planned but later, since we had missed the fall semester. We rented a small apartment in the center of Berlin. Emilie always wanted to live there. Every night after dinner, we went for long walks, hand in hand, enjoying the bistros, aromas, and sounds. Most of the sounds were pleasant enough, but there was the occasional blaring of National Socialist speakers and the shouts of its fervent hooligans.

Emilie and I had part-time jobs—she in a department store, and I in a radio repair shop. We were comfortable, and by then, 1938, the economy was doing much better.

She continued to sing in the choir. The ensemble had become so accomplished that it was performing in other churches in the city. Sometimes, I joined her and sat back with the unfamiliar congregants of a dozen or more churches.

She studied art and music, and I buried myself in electrical engineering. Neither of us spoke of religion with neighbors or classmates, and I don't think many people knew I was Jewish.

The Orthodox community, or at least parts of it, accepted us. It was clear that we were a cheerful, engaging pair and deeply in love. My father used to make small comments about us here and there, often in Berlin Yiddish, but after a year, he relented.

When we arrived home from work or school, we'd rest on a threadbare sofa, talk of our day, and renew our love. We took turns putting together meals, though Emilie was the better cook by far.

On weekends, we shopped in secondhand stores for furniture and paintings to make our flat a home.

Father and Emilie established a warm bond after our marriage the previous summer. He went to hear her sing several times, even when I was busy with school or work.

The Nazi government was in its sixth year, and its anti-Semitism was more pronounced and menacing. Late in the fall of 1938, Jewish shops were attacked and looted. Jews were accosted in the streets. *Kristallnacht* had come. We got on with our lives and didn't pay much attention to the outside world's events. You might say that our love compensated for all.

We did watch with fear, however, when Germany slowly changed for the worse, but our feeling was that then nothing worse could happened. As a young, loving couple, we felt invincible. Things come and go, people said. That's what Emilie and I thought too. That was even what my parents thought.

My father took ill with a severe lung disease. Specialists were consulted, including a woman doctor in Frankfurt. Prescriptions were brought in from pharmaceutical firms in Switzerland. By the summer of 1939, however, there was nothing more to do. His frame was gaunt; his eyes sunken. The battle was lost. We gathered in the Berlin hospital, and Father called us in, one by one. I was last.

"There aren't many regrets I have, Yochanan, but I am sorry for my objections to Emilie. A shiksa, I called her. She's a wonderful young woman, and seeing you two sharing love has given me great joy. I couldn't love her any more if she were my own flesh and blood." A faint smile came and went.

"No need for regrets, Father. No need at all. We know you've come to accept her and to love her."

"I regret that I will not be here to see your children." He paused, not from weakness but from thoughtfulness. "There's a darkness descending on Germany. I will not see its fullness, only the ominous shadows. Yes, it will get worse. I want you and Emilie to leave Berlin. Get away from this place before the evil comes down on you!"

"The Nazis will come and go. Everyone says so."

"Yes, they will come and go, Yochi, but they will do great harm before they leave the scene. I've read of them since you were a child. Their appeal has grown, and it continues to grow. They're not going away soon." He looked at me with greater clarity in his eyes. "You can continue your schooling in Prague or Warsaw. Not Vienna, though."

"Emilie and I will talk about it immediately." I didn't share his urgency, but the time was not right for debate.

"Good. And you both know you have my blessing and love."

I nodded and rested my hand on his. An hour later, his hand became still, and his eyes slowly closed.

We don't know how much we love and rely on someone until that person is gone. The loss of my father was devastating. The man I'd admired and depended on was gone forever. I no longer had his presence, his will, or his advice. Emilie, of course, was there to console me and urge me on. Without her, I have no idea how I would have gotten by. I continued my studies and my job at the repair shop, but there was an emptiness.

My father's counsel about fleeing Berlin was put aside, but it came back to mind with every street beating we came upon. We discussed leaving but concluded that the German people were decent and committed to law and order. They wouldn't stand for Hitler much longer. He and his Nazis would soon be gone. Later that year, the war began.

My mother took my father's death very badly. Naturally, we visited her every weekend, took her to restaurants, and discussed memories and current events. She talked with us and went out with friends, but there was a void. Time would bring her back, we thought. It didn't. She was losing weight and losing interest as well. Her appetite diminished, and she soon enough fell into depression.

The doctors detected heart trouble and had her hospitalized. Emilie and I visited and encouraged her as much as we could. One night, however, her warm heart gave out.

Father and Mother were gone in the course of only a few months.

Emilie's parents consoled us but stayed in the countryside and avoided the city. Whatever lay ahead, Emilie and I would have to face it alone.

The war was on. Poland fell quickly, and so did France the next year. Most Germans were thrilled by the early success, and nationalist exuberance soared. The Nazis would be in power for some time, and anti-Semitism would worsen. It had been building since the 1920s, and some thought it had peaked with Kristallnacht, but with nationalist fervor often comes hatred toward those deemed not of the nation. Most Jews I knew were proud Germans, but that mattered little to the Nazis.

Scores of decrees and regulations restricted Jewish lives, both public and personal. Some of the government acts were national; others were done by local officials who sensed the changing times. It would pass, insisted the older people. Germany was a cosmopolitan land, not a stretch of backwater in Eastern Europe.

Emilie and I had good news. We were to have a child. Protecting my family undergirded my every thought from that moment on.

Hearing someone at the door shortly before midnight is unsettling in the best of times. In the winter of 1940, with the war underway and oppression rampant, it usually augured nothing good. However, it was Rudolph Weber, the friend of Emilie's family who was a guest at our wedding. We were puzzled by the nocturnal visit but asked him in and told him to take off his wet coat.

"No, thank you. I don't have much time. I don't know if you two know, but I work at the government records office. We oversee birth records, education certificates, and the like. Your life is on file with us." Anguish came over his face as he stood just inside the doorway, rain dripping from his coat. "With the new decrees, the Gestapo is taking custody of all the records and searching for Jews. Every Jew is being flagged for special attention."

Emilie and I pondered the meaning for us and for the baby on the way.

"Yochanan, I took the liberty of destroying your file and creating a new identity for you. From now on, or at least for the foreseeable future, you are 'Johan Ludwig.' That is your name from now on. You were born in Vienna to Catholic parents. Both of them passed away in Austria before the Anschluss, and their records cannot be located. You, Johan, are a Roman Catholic, as are most people from Austria. You and Emilie are now both Catholics. It's vital that you remember this at all times. It must be instinctual, reflexive, matter-of-fact. Not second nature but first nature."

We tried to form questions and demurrals, but we were overwhelmed.

"I am sorry for heaping this on you suddenly and without warning," he said, "but this is the only way to protect you. And Emilie, you too must be on guard. The Nazis do not look favorably on Christians who marry Jews. In their fevered minds, it dilutes the German race. I must tell you more. At the office, we are increasingly coming under the scrutiny of dozens of Gestapo officials. They are being placed everywhere in the state. Everywhere. More of them every month. They are a vengeful lot."

"This is nonsensical!" Emilie protested.

"It is indeed nonsensical, Emilie, but every action is perfectly legal. The orders are signed by lawfully appointed people, and for most people in our bureaus, that's enough. Like many people, they believe the Nazis are a passing aberration. But for now, they are signing the orders, and the bureaucrats are obeying them, as their parents obeyed the kaisers and kings. Some of us, however, do what we can. So I am here on this rainy night to do what I can."

We thanked Rudolph and asked him again to sit awhile. He declined once more and then looked behind him.

"I've taken the further liberty of printing these identity cards for you. From now on, you are Johan and Emilie Ludwig. If someone calls you Yochanan, you must not respond. If someone calls you Johan, you must answer instantly."

Emilie and I looked at our new papers with both gratitude and dismay.

"Look through your wallets, purses, and records. Get rid of anything with your former names. Burn them! I'm afraid I must add that you must get rid of any Judaica. If you feel you must retain them, hide them very carefully. A menorah or tefillin could mean your lives. Please excuse this unexpected visit and sad news. I must be going. *Guten Abend, Herr und Frau Ludwig.*"

With a gentlemanly bow, he left.

It's a startling thing to be told you have to become someone else—not for a school play or parlor game but for years and years. I tried to fathom what it would entail but could not. My father's warning echoed in my soul.

We remained in our old apartment, which had been leased to the Hintzes, but with new names and uncertain futures. We discussed eliminating any sign of my Jewish faith and with little debate began packing away the Judaica into a box. A few days later, Johan Ludwig buried Yochanan Berger and his memorabilia near the cabin in the forest. It was a private ceremony.

For the next few days, we created new stories of my parents and relatives and the days in Vienna. I gave names and occupations to four grandparents. We noted that the dear folks never got to see their grandson, Johan. We allayed our fear for a moment by joking that part was true.

I even practiced the distinctive dialect, though the Ludwigs had left Austria when their boy was quite young. I looked at maps of Vienna to know prominent places. Magazines showed me pictures. The library had books that were helpful, and so did a bookstore nearby.

My readings informed me that the government was constructing a large camp for political prisoners near Munich to the south of Berlin. The term *political prisoners* referred to anyone who opposed the Nazis and people deemed inferior. That included Gypsies, the disabled, homosexuals, and, of course, Yochanan Berger's people.

On April 11, 1940, Herr and Frau Ludwig had a baby girl.

They entered her name in the government records office as "Sophia Ludwig" and her religion as Catholic.

We cradled Sophia in our arms as we heard mobs breaking into stores and beating people, only a few blocks away. It went on and on. Jewish doctors and lawyers had their practices identified and limited. Jewish admissions to universities and professional schools ended. In many cities, the Jewish populations were herded into ghettoes. Luckily, no one paid attention to me and didn't noticed that I'd stopped wearing the yellow star. Overnight, I became a devoted Catholic, but I watched in fear as more and more classmates disappeared. Common to all of them was the yellow star.

As a married man who worked part-time, I didn't have many friends at school. The ones I knew undoubtedly were aware of my new identity and must have kept the secret, some of them until their deaths not long thereafter—some in Auschwitz and Treblinka; others in North Africa and Russia. So many perished, one way or another.

I had aunts and uncles who were not able to change their identities. Some of them were fortunate enough to get out of the country, but others were not.

On Sundays, we went to church—the same church where I first set eyes upon Emilie, the same church where Sophia was baptized. That Catholic church was as much my refuge as my identity. I wasn't a believer. Baptism wasn't for me. But I did feel comfort there and found some hope in believing there was one God above us, silent and distant though he was just then.

We were startled a few months later by the sound of men ascending the stairs and stopping at our door. Loud knocks came a moment later. We both immediately wondered in fear—had we been discovered? Did this mean bad news for us, this time bearing urgent word of trouble at the records office?

Emilie and I looked at each other in alarm. There were too many stories of late-night "visits," leading to detainment, arrest, and disappearance into the dark night. I feigned calm for Emilie. The knocks became insistent, and we knew whoever it was would not leave without seeing us. At least the door wasn't being kicked down. I went to open the door as Emilie went to Sophia's bedroom.

A man in a military-like tunic and kepi stood next to another in civilian clothing. I knew immediately they were from the Geheime Staatspolizei, better known as the Gestapo.

"Guten Abend. My name is Hauptsturmführer Otto Kaiser. I've come to ask a few questions. May we come in?"

It wasn't a request that could be denied or put off. It was as polite as could be expected, but it came with unmistakable superiority and implied danger. I motioned them to the living room and even offered tea.

"No, thank you, Herr Ludwig. I apologize for the late-night visit, but we are quite busy, what with enemies everywhere; I'm sure you understand."

In a way, I did.

They looked around the room and saw a crucifix and a statue of the Virgin Mary.

"There is no need for fear," Kaiser said. "We are here to help secure the fatherland during time of war."

"That, of course, is something every German wants," I said.

"Yes. Is Frau Ludwig at home this evening?"

"Yes. She's asleep just now—with our baby."

"Ah. I am sorry to burden you, but can you bring her out now? The matter is pressing."

His ingratiating demeanor was unsettling. I entered the bedroom. Emilie was already donning a housecoat. Sophia was sound asleep. Emilie and I went back to the living room without disturbing little Sophia's sleep.

"Frau Ludwig, I apologize for this matter so late at night." Hauptsturmführer Kaiser smiled, as though at a social event. "But it is regarding a matter of some importance. It has come to the Gestapo's attention—through one of your neighbors, I shall add in passing—that you have connections with Jews. As you undoubtedly know, our job is to deal firmly and decisively with Jews and also with any matters harmful to the German Reich." He once again scanned the room.

We became on edge.

His eyes were cold and determined, single-minded, and lethal. "Frau Ludwig, we are convinced you are Catholic. It is you, Herr Ludwig, who concerns us. I've looked into you—very thoroughly, in fact. Yet information about your family is limited. Very limited. And we find that interesting, even worrisome. Your eyes are blue, but so are those of many Jews. Please be so good as to ease our worries."

We'd prepared for this, as actors would have for their most important performances. We knew our parts and lines.

"My parents were from Austria—"

"Yes, I know that," Kaiser interrupted. "Catholic from Vienna. Yet no further information can be found!"

"Well, then. I shall give you all details that I know."

"Indeed, you shall." He removed a notebook from his coat and flipped through several pages, which I presumed were filled with information about Emilie and me. "Let us hear these details, shall we? By all means, tell me all that you know about your family. Let's begin with your parents."

What followed was the background of my departed, nonexistent parents—their names, mothers' maiden names, occupations, schools, attire, addresses, household items, pets, churches, and Christmas presents. I'd even prepared anecdotes about my father's service in the Austro-Hungarian army and his time on the Galician front—he'd complained of the weight of his Mannlicher rifle.

It was when I relayed the story of our faithful dog's sad end that Kaiser waved his hand for me to stop. He revealed no sign of belief or disbelief. Cold and calculating, he was.

"That will be enough for now. We have sufficient material to look into, but there is the matter of searching your apartment."

"Why, yes, but—"

My approval wasn't necessary. They stood up and rummaged about.

"Please, we have a baby girl. She is sleeping. Can we do this another time?" Emilie asked in a steady voice as she looked fearlessly into the eyes of Nazi officialdom.

Kaiser was annoyed but undeterred. Emilie was undeterred as well.

"Storming about a house with a young child in it! How can you be so inconsiderate? There will be a complaint filed about this!"

Kaiser smiled. "I'm quite sure your child will forgive us. She'll also want to help us in any way she can. It is, after all, important for her future that no stone is left unturned today."

I remembered something, and cold sweat built across my back. I hadn't buried every aspect of my past out in the Brandenburg woods. I'd recently found a miniature menorah in the back of a dresser drawer. It was still there, mixed in with socks and handkerchiefs. Judging by Emilie's face, she had the same realization.

Kaiser headed for the bedroom. His uniformed accomplice watched over me in the living room as he looked about the shelves and beneath the seats before going through the pantry and kitchen. He then opened the drawers of my desk and unceremoniously emptied the contents onto the floor. Poor Sophia was bawling by then. Emilie brought her out to the living room.

Kaiser emerged from the bedroom and offered an insincere apology. "It's all for the good of the Reich."

"There is no justification for waking up a baby girl!" Emilie was upset.

The powerful hand of the uniformed man came down on my shoulder and took hold.

Kaiser walked toward me slowly. "It may seem to you, Herr Ludwig, that you and I are equals here, but it only seems that way. And the Reich always has justification for its actions. Always. *Versteh*?" Kaiser returned to the bedroom.

We listened nervously as drawers were yanked open, and object after object clattered to the floor. Emilie and I had one thought.

Ten minutes later, Kaiser emerged, keenly disappointed. "Again, I apologize for the intrusion, Herr *und* Frau Ludwig. As unpleasant as it may appear to you, it is absolutely necessary. You have my word on that. That will be all for now." He motioned to the guard, and they left.

It was almost one in the morning. Emilie and I embraced. She was near tears. So was I.

"I hid it in the back of the closet earlier today, Johan. We should have never kept it here."

The three of us sat in the living room in silence for almost an hour until drowsiness finally came.

We continued with school and work. Home became a haven from the outside. The sound of the door as we closed it gently behind us was most welcome, though the Gestapo had made clear the limits to our security. We discussed getting out—picking up a few belongings and heading for another country. Switzerland was the only option, as every other country around us was at war with Germany or occupied by it. Had we tried for Switzerland, however, it would have signaled Kaiser and his ilk that something was amiss with the Ludwigs. Only the guilty flee.

Rudolph Weber visited from time to time. We told him of the Gestapo's late-night search, and he was relieved that nothing had come of it. He recommended not trying to get away and shared our concern that an effort to leave would raise alarms in the Gestapo. He mentioned camps being built and plans to build more. The Gestapo had free access to government records, and it was busily going through every file cabinet and archive packet, ever searching for someone who was getting away. I mentioned the name Kaiser, and he recognized it.

3

CONSCRIPTION

I'd just come home from the radio repair shop, and Emilie and I were enjoying the amazing sight of Sophia crawling across the old Persian carpet in the living room.

More loud knocks.

The three of us turned our heads. Sophia had learned that we were wary of visitors. It was Kaiser again, this time in Gestapo tunic and with two similarly attired hoodlums. No sooner had I opened the door than they pushed by me and stood imperiously in the living.

"Guten Abend. I hope all is well. I bring news for you all, though mainly for you, Johan Ludwig. You, a proud German patriot, are willing to serve your country, are you not?"

I struggled to comprehend what he was getting at but had to form a reply. "Yes. Of course."

"Fine, fine. Then come with me now."

"Wait!" Emilie cried. "Where are you taking my husband?"

"Please have no concerns, Frau Ludwig. Your husband will be back home in only a matter of days. So I must advise him to bring additional clothing."

"But I am attending Berlin University. I also work at—"

"Yes, yes. We know all that. Please give us more credit. School and work will have to wait. Germany is at war, and your country needs you. No more of these petty complaints. You are coming with us!"

I packed up and said goodbye to my wife and child. For where and how long, I didn't know. It was unusual to be inducted by a sudden visit from the Gestapo, and that only added to our concern that my past was not above suspicion and that protest would worsen things.

In the morning, I was put in the back of a truck with several other young men—some bewildered, some eager—and driven south. There was little talk. The trip lasted several hours, and in the late afternoon, we came to a halt.

I looked about at a sprawling installation with scores of official buildings in orderly rows behind a tall barbed-wire fence. Kaiser and an aide got out of a car that had accompanied us, presumably not to enjoy the scenery.

"Welcome to Dachau!" Kaiser said.

Oh God, I thought. *Kaiser's found out about me and sent me to the internment camp for political prisoners.* I'd read about it. I knew I had to remain outwardly composed as we stepped out of the truck, but my heart thudded in my ears. I felt sick to my stomach, and I began to sweat. My mouth became dry, and I made efforts not to panic. A strange, sickly sweet odor hung in the air, one I couldn't identify. *Is this my fate?* I wondered. *What about Emilie and Sophia? I'll never see them again.*

We were led inside the barbed wire by a guard. He had a Luger on his side but never took it out, though I'd see him use it in the future. We were taken to a warehouse, where we were issued military garb, and then to a barracks with cramped rows of cots. There were a couple dozen guys there. Some smoked and played cards; others lay on their bunks. While not a hospitable place by any means, it wasn't a row of dark cells either.

"These are your quarters for the night, young men!" barked Kaiser. He turned specifically to me and said, "We have business with you in the morning."

With that, he left.

Most puzzling. I thought I was being imprisoned, but there I was in a barracks of some sort, quartered with men who looked like the sort who smashed the windows of Jewish shops and beat my friends on the street. What was Kaiser up to, and what was this business in the morning?

For now, I had to hold fast to my assumed identity. If these men knew who I really was, the business with Kaiser would never come. My life depended on playing the part Rudolph Weber had begun for me in the records office.

I nervously introduced myself to another fellow, and he gruffly told me to pick one of the empty bunks.

"The blankets are thin and cheap. Quite shitty, in fact. But that's what it's like in the service." He lit up a pungent cigarette and asked to be dealt in on the next hand.

No one else was interested in the new guys.

I picked out a cot. The mattress was thin but reasonably soft, as it lay on rows of taut rope. The blankets were as I was told—thin and made of coarse wool. *So things are rough here*, I mused. I lay there, wondering why I was there. *I'm a student of electrical engineering and am not cut out for the service—if that's what I'm in.*

I was sure Kaiser was on to something. Maybe I was there for interrogation. *Are these guys also suspects, or are they here to trick me into giving myself away?* Maybe after some paperwork or a slip of the tongue, I'd be hurled into a cell. I was, after all, behind barbed wire. Then I thought the military wanted my technical skills.

I lay there and pulled up the blanket. It reeked of disinfectant. I thought of Emilie and Sophia. How were they doing? Were they sitting in some other camp, or were they safe at home in Friedrichstadt, wondering where I was? Sometime after midnight, I managed to drift off.

"*Raus! Raus!*"

Angry cadres rudely awakened us. We had to get out of our bunks, don our uniforms, and assemble in a field for roll call and calisthenics. I was still in civilian clothes, but I followed them out to the yard. A familiar voice called me over.

"Ludwig, Ludwig, Ludwig—no need for you to get involved in all that nonsense. Let's have breakfast in the officers' mess."

It was Kaiser, out of uniform that morning. He took me to a building a short walk from the yard. Inside came the aroma of bread and hot food. It didn't seem like a lead-up to imprisonment, so I took a tray and walked down the chow line with my Gestapo escort.

The staff heaped generous portions of food onto our trays. It was a welcome sight to a young student with a part-time job and a family. I took a ration of sausage for appearances.

Kaiser took only bread and ersatz coffee before leading me to a table on the side. Removed from the context of a midnight inspection and rough search, he looked like a nondescript German, someone I'd pass on the street without even noticing. *Banality*, it was later called.

He lit up and studied me while I ate. "I see you have a good appetite after our little trip."

"Yes, I do. The food is quite good. Better than the university's dining hall." I tried to come across as cooperative and not a guilty party.

"Ludwig, you must have asked yourself why I've brought you here. Unless I'm wrong—and I rarely am on such matters—you wondered that very thing on the way down here and into the night."

"Yes, I did, well into the night."

As Kaiser continued to lecture me, my eyes briefly scanned the officers' mess. A picture of Hitler, along with, I guessed, another Nazi officer hung on the wall. SS officers were getting food, socializing, or reading a morning newspaper. Workers, who were dressed in striped pajamas, were cleaning the tables and refilling the buffet with new food.

My eyes focused on one of the workers, as he looked very weak. His eyes were sunken into his skull, and his uniform looked ripped. He limped. To my horror, I noticed that he wore broken wooden shoes without socks. I knew the temperature outside. He looked like a human ruin. Then I saw the yellow star on his uniform, and my heart raced.

My fork fell, and I picked it up, gently wiping it with a napkin as I tried to organize my thoughts. *I am a Jew. This can turn into my death in a split second.*

"Ludwig, we are at war. It's going splendidly under the leadership of the Führer, but alas, it will not be short. There are enemies all around us and even inside the Reich. Bolsheviks and Jews are the best-known ones, but there are others. We have a long list."

"I agree entirely." I took a long sip from my coffee and secretly observed Kaiser.

He seemed deeply involved in his speech. "Everyone must serve the Reich in some manner, great or small. I've been chosen to work for the Gestapo. Others serve in the Wehrmacht. Having given the matter some thought, I feel you can serve the Reich best in this place."

What does he mean by "this place"?

He saw my puzzlement. "Here at Dachau, I mean."

"It's very good to know that you have such a high regard for me, Hauptsturmführer. But I'm a student. My skills are in electrical engineering, and such men are needed elsewhere."

"We'll make you a soldier, Ludwig. A fine one—and in the SS. Dachau is a large place and a growing one. It will have a dozen or more subcamps soon. Most of them are designated to make war matériel. One of the newer subcamps is being built not far from us now. It will need resourceful men. Men like you."

More puzzlement surely must have come across my face.

"You have the qualities of leadership and resourcefulness, which will make for a fine officer."

"An officer? An officer in the SS?"

"Yes, an officer in the elite SS. It's grown tremendously since its days as the Führer's bodyguard detail. Combat units are being formed to serve alongside the Wehrmacht on the Reich's frontiers. It's building its own factories and entire industries. It's taking charge of internal security as well. The Gestapo and SS are partners in that. Johan, a young man like you can grow with the SS!"

I was sure it was all a dream. I was eating eggs and sausage in a mess hall for officers in the dreaded *Schutzstaffel.* If I remained calm, it was a miracle. Was this another ploy to get me to reveal my past? Was there anything the Gestapo wouldn't do to hunt down a Jew? I thought of the phrase *Oi vey.* As fitting as those words were for the moment, uttering them would mean losing all.

Kaiser took a final drag from one cigarette and lit another from its glowing stub.

"I'm honored. Of course. But how—"

"You'll begin training in Berlin. Oh, the usual basic-training regimen but with a welcome amount of education. You will better know our nation's proud past and limitless future. A handsome, athletic young man with blue eyes in a smart uniform—you will be envied by all your friends."

"But I have a wife and child."

"Yes, yes, I know all about them. Remember? Ah, here comes the good news. You'll get much better pay with us. As an officer, your income will be far better than at the radio shop. You have my word on that."

He probably knew my pay down to the reichsmark. And my rent and grocery bills too. It was probably written in his notebook and copied into a file in Berlin.

"The fatherland needs you now, and with the power of my authority, I've selected you."

There was no mistaking the power relationship. He wasn't asking my permission; he was ordering me. A smile formed on his roundish face. It was neither sincere nor entirely false. I think he wanted me in the fold. It would have been more than just impolite to refuse him; it would have been foolish. It would have been very risky. Refusal would have brought suspicion and probably deeper investigation. Rudolph was able to do only so much.

"Come, Johan. Come and see. A little north of here."

He drove us out of Dachau and down a country road. The sun

filtered through tall pines. Trucks occasionally came from the other way. In twenty minutes, we arrived at a construction site. Work crews were pouring concrete foundations and nailing wooden frames together. The workers all wore the same nonmilitary uniforms of striped pajamas.

"This, my friend, is Kaufering XII, one of many subcamps in the Dachau system."

We walked about a hundred meters and came to a large, long building. Machinery was being unloaded onto loading docks in the rear.

"And this is the heart and central purpose of K XII—an ammunition factory with the finest lathes and engineering equipment Germany has to offer. It will produce 88 mm rounds for the mighty guns of the Waffen SS and Wehrmacht. More will come. Much more! The Führer has a keen eye for new weaponry. He has teams of scientists working night and day. Germany will be all the stronger!"

"Where do you find workers?" I asked. "This site is well out of the way, and there are labor shortages throughout the fatherland."

"That's the best part of it, young man! The sheer genius! The genius of it all! The workers will be Jewish inmates from Dachau. Other inferior types too and the odd political prisoner, but mostly Jews. Think of it! People who've done the fatherland nothing but harm for many years will now make amends. Everyone gets what they deserve. So the sign reads at one of our other camps."

The dream was becoming nightmarish.

"Johan?"

"Yes, sir."

"Johan, this is where your resourcefulness will be best utilized. After proper training in Berlin, you can bring this subcamp into production. And you can be in charge of it one day. Think of it, young man! Look around you, and think of it! You, a virile, talented man, will be helping the Reich—and proudly wearing the uniform of the SS. Yes, Johan, you are to be one of us—the honor, prestige, tunic, and insignia!"

It was no dream. I'd convinced myself of that hours ago. But now I felt I was in some afterlife for the damned, tricked into serving the devil and punishing my people for all time. Refusal could bring death. I would face my own death, but I would do anything to prevent harm coming to Emilie and Sophia. I'm not sure if I nodded or simply looked receptive.

"You'll go home for few days and then report for duty at the SS headquarters in Berlin on Prinz-Albrecht-Straße. You'll undergo an intense training period, about ten weeks, and then come back to Dachau and Kaufering XII. It will be your new place of business and home. Johan, I'll see that you get splendid quarters. By the time you return, we'll have a full complement of workers—*Jews*."

The emphasis on *Jews* was thick and intentional. He was looking for my reaction to see if I shared his notion that Jews were enemies to be worked hard—very hard.

"They deserve it. Don't they, Johan?"

"Everyone gets what they deserve, sir. Everyone."

Kaiser found my reply inspiring.

Emilie cried for hours. "They'll find out sooner or later, and then you'll be imprisoned or worse. Much worse. They'll think you tried to make fools of them or were a spy. Much worse, much worse. You've heard the stories of their cruelty."

"I can keep the secret," I assured her. "And I can provide for you better as well. My papers are in order, as they say. An officer in that outfit will be above suspicion."

"They'll be all around you. You may make a slip, and all will be lost. There will be another knock at the door. Maybe they'll just kick it in next time. You hear what's happening! Terrible things. Unimaginable things. Think of Sophia!"

"I am thinking of her and of you! By playing my part, I can protect us. We've been practicing for over a year. I know it by heart. It's second nature."

Yes, it was second nature by then. It was second nature to leave my people behind.

A week later, I reported to the SS headquarters on Prinz-Albrecht-Straße, where I was issued uniforms, boots, and belts and assigned a bunk and locker in the cadet barracks. It wasn't far from home, and I thought I'd be able to spend weekends with my family and meet for a meal in the evening.

The SS had other plans. I was not allowed to leave the site for almost three months.

I was immersed into the military world—the SS world, actually. I'd heard of military life, as a few neighbors had gone in, but it was harder than I'd thought it would be.

We were roused every morning at five o'clock, very much in the manner I'd experienced during my brief stay at Dachau. A quick meal at the mess hall was followed by being rushed outside for physical training, all under the eyes of angry cadres determined to intimidate us, break us from our civilian lives and identities, and mold us into fervent knights of the Third Reich. They knew their jobs well.

We marched and performed close-order drill for hours. We learned how to fire weapons, such as the K98k rifle, Luger and Walther pistols, MP-40 machine pistol, and the MG-34 machine gun. And, of course, we had to clean them afterward and pass a thorough inspection. Basic infantry tactics followed—maneuvers, infiltration, infantry-armor techniques. I'd already learned a few things about infiltration.

There was a great deal of indoctrination: the history of Germany and the Third Reich's importance in it; the elite nature of the SS and its mission; and the loathsome enemies around us and within. Unsurprisingly, the Jews figured highly in the latter lectures. None of our ancestors could be Jewish, and we could only marry with the permission of our commanding officers. Our individual thoughts and concerns had to be separated from our duty. "Loyalty is my honor" was the motto.

All this took place within the view of stately baroque and classical buildings, not far from conservatories where the works of Beethoven and Mozart were performed.

I shared a room in the cadet barracks with four young men. Each of them was a true believer, took diligent notes, and became misty-eyed during many lectures.

Fear of giving myself away was with me at all times. I was concerned I might use a Yiddish expression or utter a few lines from the Talmud in my sleep. I was considered a bit of an outlier—not very sociable but determined nonetheless.

An officer interrogated me from time to time, asking about my parents, grandparents, and the like. Emilie and her family had to endure more visits from the Gestapo. Emilie made sure our apartment had crucifixes and statues of saints in prominent places, even though her family was not religious, and ours was the same. I worried that I was being singled out, but in conversations at the mess hall and in the bunks at night, the other cadets said they and their families were undergoing the same routine.

I did get to know one of the other guys. Karl was my age and thoroughly devoted to National Socialism. His bunk was directly above mine. He hated Jews and was determined to eradicate them from his country. I'm not sure he knew exactly what that meant just then—Auschwitz and Treblinka weren't known to us—but if he had, he'd have supported those death mills and been among the first to volunteer to work there.

When he said he was from Berlin, I was alarmed that he might have known me or my parents or of my untraditional wedding. But Berlin was no Bavarian village. His father had been a colonel in the German army and had served in the First World War. I mentioned my deceased parents—the ones from Austria, of course. I came to know him, how he thought, and what he hoped to do once out of the academy. We helped each other in our studies and in the more difficult parts of physical training. It was strange to see human feelings, such as loneliness and hope, in someone like that.

From time to time, Hauptsturmführer Kaiser came by SS headquarters and the cadet school. He was pleased that I was doing well and had befriended someone as dedicated as Karl. I was doing well in school. It wasn't due to any great effort on my part. You might say that most classmates were not University of Berlin material.

I was eager to see Emilie and Sophia as soon as possible, but we were isolated from families for many weeks. I wrote them twice a week. Emilie and I would place phrases such as "with Saint Joseph's help" in each letter. The administration read everyone's correspondence, of course.

After two months, we were allowed a weekend pass. No time to let Emilie know in advance, so I just took a bus down to Friedrichstadt and knocked gently on the door. She was astonished, speechless, confused, and elated. Her kisses showered upon me and her embrace pressed sweet tears onto my face. To my amazement, our little girl was crawling my way. The regimen had not destroyed my ability to feel joy or shed tears.

Emilie put together a wonderful meal on short notice. We sat at the table and dined once again as a family. We didn't see any point in mentioning that our ability to share meals together was uncertain. Nor did we mention the absence of the traditional candles. Nor did we begin with a Friday-night prayer. We said grace, but it wasn't out of religiousness.

We didn't know for certain that we weren't being spied upon by an agent of Kaiser or a nosy neighbor, seeking to curry favor with the authorities. That was no way to live a life, but we were no different from most other Germans in feeling such concerns, even during family moments.

Emilie asked about training, and I gave her an outline of the curriculum and calisthenics. I mentioned conversations with Karl and how intriguing it was to get to know a true believer. She naturally cautioned me about making a slip, but I assured her that talking with Karl was building my confidence in being able to keep up the deception. Words flowed more smoothly and spontaneously. I was playing my part well. I had to do so. More demanding performances would be required. After dinner, we said another prayer.

Sophia stayed up with us as long as she could. After she was put to bed, Emilie and I held each other silently and then adjourned to the bedroom for long-awaited intimacy.

Afterward, I couldn't sleep. I looked out the window onto the streets of Friedrichstadt. They were quieter and less inviting than before. Maybe it was because so many men had been conscripted or gone away to war jobs. Maybe everyone knew they were being watched.

For the first time in a long while, I felt the need to pray, to ask the heavens for hope and guidance and for a shield to protect Emilie and Sophia. I'd not said prayers in many months, but I said Shabbat prayers that night in the darkness and silence. I wasn't sure they were heard anymore.

Weekends go by more quickly when you're a soldier on leave; ask anyone who's served in any army. On Sunday night, I was back in the barracks. The next morning began with the familiar ritual of loud shouts, hurried breakfast, and arduous calisthenics. It was becoming easier for us. The coursework shifted away from leadership, weapons, and history to the danger posed by Jews.

The lectures were delivered by an especially hateful officer named Kruger, a *Sturmbannführer*, the equivalent of a major in other armies. The instant the tall, powerfully built man entered the classroom, all conversations and jokes ended, and attention was fixed on him. He stared at us intently for several minutes, as though he thoroughly disapproved of us. No one dared say a word or even look to one another.

His eyes had an unsettling intensity. He had no humor or decency, only hatred and dedication. He'd found himself in the SS. Finally, he spoke.

"Cadets, you are here because you want to become part of the SS, the elite of the Third Reich. You want to be the best-trained and best-motivated soldiers the German nation has ever produced. There are only three things that matter in this world—the Führer, the Reich, and the SS. The foreign dangers are being dealt with on the frontiers, but there is a more sinister enemy within. And dealing with this one will not be easy. The methods employed will not be pleasant to learn, let alone put into practice. But with me, you will discover new things. You will do new things—things you never could have imagined yourself doing. You will find powers within yourself that you never dreamed were there! Only then will you become a true SS officer and a loyal instrument of the Führer and the Reich."

At times, he spoke with great passion, but more, often his voice was cold and even monotonous. When he turned to one side, I'd quickly look around. My classmates were in awe—frightened and intrigued, eager to listen and obey, desperate to find those undreamed of powers and put them into practice. This Kruger was more fanatical and dangerous than his peers. I knew what was coming.

"The Jew has always been Germany's enemy. They are more dangerous than other enemies for they are *inside* the fatherland. They live among us. In some cases, right next door to loved ones. Insidious! But things are changing."

Pens scratched down notes. Kruger went on to outline, in great detail and in a cold voice, how Jews had betrayed Germany in the First World War and brought defeat and dishonor. Afterward, they continued to control the economy, taking jobs and businesses away from "true German." Everything that was wrong with the country was laid at the doorstep of "the Jew."

"They have to be eradicated from Germany. That is our task. Nay, it is our sacred duty. Do not be fooled by appearances, young men. An old, enfeebled Jew has been responsible for countless grievances against Germany in his long life. A Jewish boy will grow up to do more. A Jewish girl will breed a new generation of them."

I'd heard those stories before, of course, but hearing them spoken with such conviction and passion was nonetheless alarming. My classmates nodded their heads dutifully and took notes. Their faces told me they found the lecture truthful and even inspiring. The anti-Semitism in German life was amplified by Nazi ideology. How many classes of eager young men had come before ours? How many more would come in the months and years ahead?

I too wrote down notes—I had to do so in order to pass exams. Johan Ludwig's name was high on the grade list posted on the *kommandant*'s door.

Kruger informed us one morning that we would face an important test later in the day. It would not be taken at a desk with pen and paper, and it wasn't a matter of demonstrating physical fitness. He offered no details but said the test would make us stronger and more able to perform the duties that lay ahead. The barracks were abuzz with speculation. We joked about Kruger's lectures and demeanor to ease the anxiety.

That evening, we were marched to an adjacent building and into a dimly lit classroom with many desks but no lectern or chalkboard. We were too nervous for the usual chatter. Unidentifiable sounds came from a few rooms away. Kruger strode in, and we snapped to attention.

"Tonight, each of you will be put to the test—one closer to the ones awaiting you. I will call each of you into a room down the hallway. The rest will wait here."

Kruger called a classmate's name, and he walked down the hall. Ten minutes later, another cadet was summoned, and he too went down the hall. We heard only occasional scuffling and stifled voices. The process continued, and the room became emptier. Cadets went out and did not return. I whispered to Karl that they were probably exiting from a back door. He made no reply.

"Take it easy, Karl," I said. "It's probably a ridiculous secret ritual. That's all."

Karl's name was called, and he rose nervously. I nodded to him, and off he went. There were only a handful of us left, and one by one, they left. I sat alone in the room, wondering if they knew about me, wondering if the others were being told about me in the room down the hall.

"Ludwig!"

I entered a smaller room with two doors beside the one where we'd come in. I stood at attention as Kruger seated himself at a small table. A pair of gloves lay on the dark wooden surface.

"Cadet Ludwig!"

I stiffened and replied, "Yes, Sturmbannführer!"

"Cadet Ludwig, in the next room you will find a cat. It is an adult and has considerable strength and wiles. I order you to kill it." He then looked at the gloves and began to speak in his characteristic monotone. "Capture the cat, and kill it in your bare hands. Some of the cats are domesticated and friendly. Others are feral and spirited. You will soon see which category your animal fits. It's entirely up to you how you accomplish your mission. Strangling is one method. Bashing its head against the wall is another. Some opt to break its neck." With that, he made a breaking motion with his hands. His face showed no more emotion than his voice. "Any questions?"

My mind raced, and I became unnerved. Was my performance about to fail? "Sturmbannführer, may I ask what principle lies behind this test?"

I immediately regretted my words, but Kruger wasn't annoyed.

"An understandable question. We all love pets; we all love animals. This task is to prepare you for your work in the field. An SS officer must deal with many situations—some of them simple; others more challenging. Ludwig, an SS officer will have to kill—and I'm not talking about small animals. As extreme and puzzling as this test may seem, it is an essential part of training, and it will serve both you and the Reich well. Now, Cadet Ludwig, I order you to kill the cat in the room next door."

I tried to search for excuses in my head but found nothing.

My boots clicked, and I exclaimed, "*Ja wohl!*"

Kruger saw it as a sign of enthusiasm and smiled. He thought I had the right stuff, as Americans say, but it came from despair and outrage.

"Well, Cadet Ludwig, proceed then. Here are the gloves; there is the room. When you have executed my order, leave by the back way. The others are assembled there." He heaved a sigh. "And Ludwig, the hour is late. Ten minutes."

The room was small and empty but brightly illuminated by institutional lighting on an overhead rack, which emitted an unnerving buzz. A doorway at the other end had a red exit sign—one way out. In the corner sat my prey, calmly licking its paws. It was a gray tabby, probably quite young.

I walked slowly toward the cat in a friendly manner. Clearly, it was not feral. It came up to me, perhaps thinking I'd brought food and that it had found a friend in a strange place. I thought of cats that came to the cabin for the milk that Emilie and I put out at night.

"Ludwig! The hour is late," came the voice, as if through a loudspeaker. "You have your order."

I patted its head and pondered the best method and optimal angle. The poor creature deserved a swift end. I owed him that much. My mind rebelled at the idea of killing anything needlessly. But what would it mean for my family and me? Why should the life of a cat impact the lives of loved ones? If I failed to execute the order, the game might be up.

The door behind me came open suddenly, and Kruger walked in, his boots hitting hard on the wooden floor.

"Sturmbannführer, I was just—"

"You were just hesitating! You were just refusing to follow orders!"

The cat trotted over to him. I wouldn't have thought any creature would do so.

"You have failed, Cadet Ludwig. Your orders were simple and clearly expressed, but you failed to obey them."

He picked up the cat, stroked its head, and then violently snapped its head back. A short screech was all it had time for before going limp. Kruger let it fall to the floor with a soft thump.

"Not so hard. Not so hard at all. Ah, such soft-hearted boys we have today. You will learn, though. Out there, you will learn."

I passed out. My last recollection was seeing the lifeless cat not a half meter from my face.

Emilie was horrified. Had she not heard the account from me, she'd never have believed it. Sophia was asleep by our side in the living room.

"Luckily, I wasn't the only cadet who failed. Ten out of a class of thirty couldn't go through with it either."

"Why would they want people to do such a thing? It's not human."

"The cat isn't human, dear." My attempt to allay her ire fell flat.

"They can't prosecute you for this."

"I think you're right," I agreed. "I hope you're right. These SS officers are not ordinary people, by any means. To think that out of uniform they simply go for walks in the park and dine at restaurants next to decent Germans."

"Can't you tell them that you simply aren't made for this organization? Maybe they'll release you, and you can get your old job back at the radio shop."

"I've raised the subject with Kaiser. He comes by the school periodically. He insists I see it through. Maybe he still thinks I'm Jewish, and this is a creative way of punishing me. I can't think of a more sinister punishment. There's no way out at this point."

"Will there be more tests like that one?"

"I don't know. But the other guys think there are more like it coming our way. Maybe worse."

As it turned out, there weren't any more such tests. The harder tests came out in the field.

Kruger paced back and forth at the front of the classroom. He placed hand to chin in a thoughtful pose and then suddenly presented a problem. "You are in charge of a detail of prisoners that carries heavy rocks. You instruct them to bring them to a plant, where they are ground into gravel for the war effort. You see an old man who can barely walk with his load. He is lagging behind and causing the entire group to lag behind. You have a schedule to meet. The war can't wait. Another thing—the old man is a Jew. What do you do?"

A few hands went up in an instant, and Kruger called on a young man.

"I'll shout for the old man to move faster."

"Ah, but he can't. He's simply too old and weak at this point."

"I'll hit him a few times to encourage him to find the strength!" another student answered with a hopeful look.

"No, no. That won't help. If you hit him, he'll fall, and the work will be slower for it. Not an easy situation, all things considered."

I knew from the start what Kruger was looking for. I raised my hand, probably less crisply than my fellow cadets. "He should be shot. Shot right there on the spot. His usefulness has come to an end, and he is in the way. Better he die so that our fighting men do not want. The war can't wait."

"Very good, Ludwig. Very good indeed. The war certainly can't wait. You are an excellent student here in the classroom, but you need work in the practical applications. And the same goes for many of you others. A Jew in the way is a danger to production and the war. He cannot be allowed to continue holding things up."

I sat back in my chair and felt a secret shame. Anger soon welled up.

Kaiser called me in for a meeting. I walked in and saluted smartly. He returned the salute and chuckled. He lit up a cigarette and offered me one, but I declined.

"At ease, young cadet! They are training you well here, I see. You are becoming a fine SS officer, one who will serve the Third Reich well. And as I thought, you look quite dashing in uniform."

"I'm pleased to hear that."

"I called you today, Johan, because in a few weeks you'll complete your training and receive your commission. You're doing well, even better than I hoped. We discussed a position at Kaufering XII. Construction is going well, and the munitions will soon be pouring out from its factories." He sat back in his chair and exhaled as he sized me up. "I'll be honest with you, Johan. I'm always honest with my staff and protégées. I am not convinced you don't have some Jewish blood. I can't prove it, though. Some investigations take longer, and often the results are rewarding and helpful in future work. You are clever, Johan, but not as clever as I am."

My dismay might have appeared to him as puzzlement.

"K XII will utilize forced labor—criminals, political prisoners, but mostly Jews. We treat Jews the harshest. After all, they are the most dangerous. Gypsies, homosexuals, and Bolsheviks are criminals, but their numbers are small—the same with their minds. I'm sure you've already received a solid grounding on the Jewish peril here.

Kruger is highly knowledgeable on the subject. What's your opinion of Jews, Johan?"

"I'll do whatever is necessary to serve my country, sir."

"Yes, yes. But how do you *feel* about the Jews? They will work for you. You'll have to punish them. Maybe even kill them if they don't listen to your orders."

"We are at war. We must do whatever it requires to win."

"Even if it means killing Jews?"

"Yes!"

"Elderly Jews?"

"Yes!"

"Jewish children?"

"Yes!"

"Look at me, Johan. Look directly at me. Not off to the side or at my forehead. Look directly into my eyes."

His eyes were cold and devoid of humanity. I stared into them and tried not to blink. He stared at me for what seemed like a couple of minutes. He broke the contest and put his cigarette out in the ashtray. "We shall see. We shall see."

The final segment of school was what one might call on-the-job training. We boarded a train for Munich, as Kruger was leading the tour. A bus took us to the Dachau main camp, where we were to observe methods in maintaining discipline. Every SS trainee went through this at Dachau. We watched morning roll call, the march to the mess hall with bowls in hand, and the orders for work assignments. It was well organized. My colleagues were impressed—and proud.

We were shown the camp's crematory. Deaths, we were told, were quite common from illness, malnutrition, and beatings. Cremation was the most efficient way to dispose of the remains.

So Dachau was designed to systematically overwork and underfeed prisoners, especially Jews, in order reduce their numbers in Germany and the lands coming under its control through conquest.

We were told this in clear terms. There was a calculus of food intake and work output and of the declining utility of workers in poor health. Summary beatings and executions were part of camp policy. Many prisoners were ill-behaved and had to be made examples for the benefit of camp discipline and output. Kruger made no mention of personal pleasure involved. He didn't have to.

A few mornings later, we witnessed a "selection"—a cursory look at the health of inmates to determine their fitness to continue. The inmates, most of whom bore Stars of David on their grimy uniforms, stripped naked and stood in an assembly yard. Classical music broadcast over loudspeakers. The reasonably healthy continued to work, but those judged as no longer fit were boarded onto trains. It was fairly clear what that meant. Some who were too sick to travel were shot and sent to the crematory. If the ovens were backed up, there was an open pit nearby. I hoped I hid my dismay. I hoped the other cadets felt horror too, but I doubted that many saw anything but efficiency, justice, and opportunity for advancement.

Slowly, the reality sank in inside me. I realized that the Third Reich was going to humiliate Jews, take everything from them, including their human rights, and probably murder many of them. I was not aware to the upcoming horrors yet. I felt horrible. How would I be able to sustain this ordeal? I was an orthodox Jew. Then I thought about my family. In my imagination, I saw my beautiful daughter, Sophia. Then I saw my wife, the love of my life. *I can't let them die*, I thought. *I must survive. I must pretend to be one of them. One of the Nazis. I'll do anything for my family. Anything.*

After a month, we returned to Berlin. It felt like a reprieve.

Shortly before finishing cadet training, I spent a weekend with Emilie and Sophia. Not long before dinner, a knock sounded at the door. In came Kaiser with a uniformed man and a civilian.

"This is your neighbor, Herr Böhm," Kaiser said. "He is certain that he remembers Jews visiting you here."

I knew the man, though not well. He lived on a lower floor, not far from the entrance. If there was one thing I'd learned as a cadet, it was to think fast and react with authority.

"Jews in my home? That's an outrageous claim! It soils my honor and that of my family!"

"I remember seeing Jews visit you. I saw them in the stairway," Böhm insisted. "It was a long time ago, and I don't know if they were friends or family."

"Hauptsturmführer, in two weeks I will receive my commission in the SS," I said. "I will wear my uniform proudly and defend my nation fiercely. How dare this man enter my home and present such outrageous lies! We are devout Catholics who were brought up knowing Jews for what they are. Aryans, we are! And we would no sooner allow a Jew in our sacred home than a diseased rat!"

Böhm was taken aback, exactly as I'd hoped.

Emilie spoke up, which startled me. "Look around our house! Look anywhere you wish! Do you see anything Jewish? No, of course not. There never was. You'll never find anything connecting us to Jews. My husband is dedicating his life to the Reich. We, as a family, will endure great hardships, but we understand it's for Germany. Now, please stop this nonsense immediately! It's disgraceful and upsetting!"

I glared at Böhm. "I will soon be an SS officer. If you'll not retract these monstrous lies, I'll personally make sure that we investigate your ancestry and associations. Who knows? Maybe you yourself have Jewish blood polluting our race, and this is your way to win favor."

Old Böhm was on the defensive. In fact, he was unnerved. I can't be sure if he saw the pride on Kaiser's face as I launched into my speech, but I did.

"Johan, Johan, Johan. Let's not be too hard on this fellow. He's just doing his duty as a citizen of the Reich." He patted Böhm on the shoulder patronizingly and signaled an exit.

The moment the door closed behind them, Emilie and I sighed and sat on the couch.

Two weeks later, I graduated with honors, the second in my class, and received the rank of *Untersturmführer*, which was higher than most graduates. My colleagues heartily congratulated me. Naturally, I feigned pride.

Graduation brought a diploma, the sort of thing one framed, showed the folks, and perhaps hung in an office. Graduation from the SS academy brought another sort of diploma. It wasn't a sheepskin or plaque or ring. It was a tattoo showing our blood types that was inked into the fleshy area on our lower left biceps. My religion forbade tattoos, but I could hardly apply for an exemption.

We lined up outside an office and waited our turns. Almost everyone was elated that they'd have a mark of honor for all time. A few guys joked nervously, as the procedure was known to be somewhat painful. I felt nauseated—in part because I'd break a religious rule; in part because I'd be forever branded. How could I ever return to my community—or anyone's community, for that matter? I'd be like a prisoner in older times, whose punishment was mutilation or branding.

When my turn came, I lifted my arm and closed my eyes. Each prick of the needle felt like the devil's searing bite, and I grimaced. It was over in a few minutes, and I was forever marked. Convict Ludwig might walk the earth for the rest of his days with it.

Even the SS academy had a graduation ceremony with dignitaries and families. In late 1941, I took part in such a ceremony. There was an SS general or two, who spoke of duty and honor. Many faces beamed as they listened, cadets and families alike. A general pinned our officer insignias on us, one by one.

Emilie came but left Sophia with a neighbor for the day. I was thankful for that. It would have been painful to see my precious child impressed by Nazi pageantry.

The ritual made most cadets feel like true men and true sons of the Reich. It made me feel a greater ability to protect wife and child, but with it came deep shame.

Karl was assigned to Buchenwald, about 150 kilometers southwest of Berlin. I never saw him again. That's how it was in the military. I always hoped that he survived what was in store. And I also hoped he had a moment of realization too. Terrible things awaited SS officers during the war and after it—terrible but mostly appropriate.

I had to come home in uniform, as civilian clothing wasn't allowed in the academy. It was a dark uniform with metal accoutrements and a thick belt. The tunic and trousers had been especially well pressed for graduation. I'd become accustomed to wearing it, but Emilie was repelled. She insisted I change clothes the instant I stepped inside. I looked in the mirror and became confused and disoriented. Powerful whirlwinds swept inside me—memories of my parents and schul, kommandants, and barracks. I had to sit down for fear of losing consciousness.

Over the months, I'd learned a thing or two about Kaiser. He was keenly interested in me, so I would have been unwise not to have looked into him. Kaiser was what the Gestapo and SS (the two organizations had effectively merged by then) liked to call a "bloodhound." He was someone who specialized in finding Jews who were hiding in monasteries and Christian homes and living under assumed identities.

He knew his way around Berlin bureaus and was well connected and even feared, but he'd soon be stationed in Munich. He enjoyed his work and was frighteningly good at it. I was determined to outmaneuver him.

4

SECOND-IN-COMMAND

A few of us were sent into Bavaria, not far from the old border with Austria. Of course, Austria had become integrated into Germany with the *Anschluss* of 1938. There was in-processing, where I received additional uniforms, a Luger, and an installation identity card.

There was also an orientation program. A young officer standing before a large map proudly noted that Dachau was more than one large camp; it was the hub of a system of camps, dozens of them; each assigned to produce war matériel; each run by the SS. Just as a large firm has smaller offices stretching out from a center, so did Dachau and the other large camps.

Kaiser was present at one of the orientation lectures. Afterward, he spoke to me. "You are an exceptional young man, Johan. We'll see if your resourcefulness includes the telltale shrewdness." With that, he patted my back and told me to walk with him. "As we discussed in your civilian days, you will be at K XII, not far from here. But you have to know Dachau proper. It's divided into two sections. All around us is the main area, and far off is the crematory. It's kept at a good distance for reasons that should be obvious. We've just left the administrative building. That is the brain of the Dachau body."

What proceeded was something like a tour of a small town, given by a proud city father. There were kitchen facilities, bakeries, dining halls for prisoners and staff (separate, of course), laundries, several workshops, row after row of barracks (blocks), and a large assembly yard for roll calls.

"The yard is also used, at times, for executions. They instill discipline and fear—absolutely essential for proper operation. You've been taught this in Berlin. Now you'll see it in here."

He pointed to a group of buildings that he said were used for medical experiments. That sounded like the camp had a good side. All around us were high barbed-wire fences with immense, grotesque electrodes atop them.

"Some inmates choose to end it all by grabbing hold of the wire. Every few mornings, a detail comes around with a cart to pick up the bodies. The electricity has to be shut off before the hands can be pried off."

We passed guard towers with searchlights and MG-34s every fifty meters or so. I'd trained on those rapid-firing guns at a range outside Berlin.

There was more truck traffic on the way to K XII than before, most of it departing. Inside, I could see that there were many more buildings than there had been on my initial visit, and still more were being put up. The buildings were almost slapdash compared to those at the main camp. The barracks were partially dug into the earth, presumably to save time and money.

Kaiser asked a guard at the administration building where we might find the kommandant, and we were directed to the officers' mess. It was small and primitive, little more than a hut. Kaiser ordered a laborer to bring hot drinks.

"There's still much construction to be done here, but thankfully, they have coffee. Well, as you know, it's actually made from acorns and grains. In time of war, Johan, in time of war. You take yours black."

I wondered if that little piece of information was in a dossier somewhere.

No more than fifteen minutes later, an officer strode in, and I snapped to attention. It was reflexive, as anyone who's been in any military knows. Obersturmbannführer Ernst Osten, the commander of K XII, had come to meet his second-in-command.

He returned my salute, and we sized each other up, although I did so furtively. I expected a fearsome face of evil, but it wasn't the case. I saw an even disposition. Take away the uniform, and he would look like an engineer or businessman. That was not the case with Kaiser—he always looked wary and eager to pounce.

Osten was tall, meager, and, above all, meticulous. His uniform was crisply pressed, well tailored, and spotless. His wooden cigarette holder suggested an upper-crust emulation and a way with women and nightlife.

"Well, Hauptsturmführer Kaiser, you've spoken so well of this young man before us now, and Dachau has made an excellent choice. I'm sure he'll serve us well here."

"Thank you, sir," I said. "I'm sure I will learn much from you here."

"We will watch you learn. You have my word on that," Kaiser added.

"Top of your class at the academy; impeccable background." Osten seemed impressed with my records. "Yes, you are what we want here. Your arrival is timely. This week we will receive a large shipment of workers—Jews, for the most part. Production of 88 mm rounds is only the beginning. We will also manufacture other types of ammunition and uniforms. After that, we will undoubtedly expand further. So much work to be done."

"I'm proud to be a part of the Dachau and K XII, sir."

"What we do here is important and rewarding, but it isn't for the faint of heart, Ludwig." Osten lit a cigarette.

"I will do whatever is required of me, sir."

I suspected Osten had high standards for those who worked under him. I would come to learn that his expectations were that those under him would carry the load.

An enlisted soldier showed me to my quarters. Though essentially another fairly primitive hut, it was an improvement over the cramped barracks of cadet school. I had my own "apartment"—a private shower, a full-sized bed (not a cot or double-tier bunk bed), a living room with a sofa, and a compact kitchen. A portrait of Hitler hung on a living room wall—mandatory in SS quarters and offices. His stern presence was supposed to convey senses of duty and loyalty. To me, it meant I was being watched.

I sat on the sofa and took stock of the situation. My quarters were both prison and refuge. I mused how one of our family paintings would look in the room—it depicted three venerable rabbis discussing a passage from the Torah. But of course, that painting was long gone, and items like it were buried near the cabin in Brandenburg.

We decorate our homes in a manner that reflects who we are. My quarters had to convey who I wasn't. A crucifix hung over the bed, and a Christian Bible lay on the night table. I leafed thorough it after duty hours. Naturally, I'd read the Old Testament several times and knew the stories of Ruth and Jonah almost by heart. I took to studying the New Testament. I read the parables of Jesus, accounts of his suffering and death, and the correspondence of the early Christians who had to live in hiding.

I had been an engineering student at Berlin, but the religions of other people interested me. I sometimes looked through class listings and syllabi on comparative religion and the rows of books on various faiths in a bookstore I passed on the way to school. But calculus and physics were very demanding so I didn't have much time to further study religion. Years later, I found myself researching Christianity—in Dachau, of all places.

The following morning began with a physical training regimen for officers. It was quite early, of course, and subsequent sessions began promptly at the same time. Everything at K XII began and ended at precise times or at least tried to do. It was Osten's passion or idiosyncrasy, and it wasn't questioned, not even by his second-in-command. Day-to-day operations were handled by others. In time, that would be me.

There were twenty guards and another five officers, all of them SS. They were assisted by inmate trustees, or *kapos*. We assembled and awaited Osten. He didn't keep us waiting.

"We are going to maintain a smooth-running camp," Osten told us one morning. "We will have regular meetings to ensure this, and we will be the envy of the Dachau system. Each of you will perform your duties faithfully and completely. If you do not, I will let you know it, quickly and harshly. I know each of you wants me to look upon you favorably, as I want to look upon you.

"This morning, a train will arrive from Dachau with a consignment of inmates. They are from many parts of Germany, and you know who they are. In coming months, more consignments will arrive on a regular basis. Some will bear prisoners from other parts of Europe—areas that our troops have valiantly conquered."

If Osten could have controlled the train crews, they would have arrived at exact times. He didn't, of course, so we stood by the track just outside the wire and waited. No station or platform, just a spur running from the main tracks.

An hour later, we heard a whistle about two kilometers away, followed by a growing rumble. Everyone took his place. The train slowed to a noisy halt. Bursts of steam came from the locomotive's brakes. A hundred prisoners were herded out, placed in rows and columns, and marched to an assembly yard by menacing guards.

Kommandant Osten introduced the new inmates to the camp. He stressed full cooperation and a work ethic. He promised good treatment in return for hard work.

Somehow, I didn't believe any of his words. Yet many inmates that morning probably thought K XII wouldn't be such a bad place after all.

The men and women were separated. Each group was then led to a warehouse-like hut, where K XII's older inmates handed out blankets and meal bowls. They went on to tables set up outside, where SS personnel made a quick assessment and assigned them to various sections of the camp—general labor, arms factory, sewing shops, kitchens, and the like. Men and women were ordinarily not to work the same sites.

With discipline instilled and work assignments handed out, production could begin. Workers got the knack of lathes, assembly lines, and stamping machines. The deadly 88 mm rounds would soon come off the line and head for artillery pieces, antiaircraft guns, and panzers.

A few evenings later, Osten gathered the SS personnel in the administration hut. Smoking was authorized, and most of us lit up as we socialized and wondered what was up. I sat off to one side, pretty much alone, partly out of personal aloofness; partly out of my position as Osten's second. Soon enough, he strode in. We snapped to attention, and he stood at the lectern for a full minute before giving us the at-ease.

"The work here is progressing. I expect my production schedules to be read carefully, committed to memory, and met. *Met,* gentlemen. *Met!* You've been taught the methods of ensuring discipline and productivity, and you will put them into effect with full force. Berlin has sent us new guidelines. They insist that materiel shortages be eliminated. Punishments are left to your discretion. Always remember, though, that should you feel that duty requires you to use the most extreme form of punishment, you must relay the information so that a replacement can be brought in quickly, and production can proceed seamlessly."

Most looked on in silence and awe.

Here and there, Osten slurred a word, and the closer I looked at his eyes, the more glazed they seemed.

"These are not valued German workers. They are Jews and criminals—mostly Jews now. An inmate life means nothing. Producing weapons for the Reich, everything." More slurred words. He'd been drinking.

A few others must have noticed but, of course, held their tongues.

Osten paused and smiled, evidently pleased with his presentation and fawning audience. "Sanitation, gentlemen. Sanitation is essential. Without it, disease and vermin rise up, and productivity and spirit fall. Other camps are having trouble with typhus and cholera. That will not happen here."

He paused again and seemed to struggle to recall something. After a few moments, he asked if there were any questions. There were none.

"Then let us march forward. Heil Hitler!"

"Heil Hitler," came the immediate response.

I was among the first to stand, and my voice might well have been the loudest.

K XII was put to work in the next few days. Osten had brought in experienced guards and kapos from Dachau for the start-up. To say they were experienced meant they were hardened, insensitive, and sadistic. Moreover, they took their work seriously and enjoyed cruelty. Osten thought they'd be useful, not only in intimidating the inmates but in showing the newly minted guards and officers how things got done.

Inmates shivered in the winter cold during morning roll call, or *Appel*, as it was called. A woman in her fifties or sixties fell, and a few women went to help her up. An SS guard ordered them to step away. He sauntered over to the woman, who'd managed to get on her knees, and struck her with a baton. Blow after blow came down on her shoulders, back, and skull as the woman pleaded for help. Most of the SS watched with no more interest than if they were watching a truck being loaded or a conveyor belt roll by. It was all part of the process. After no more than two minutes, the beating stopped. So did the pleading.

I stood in numbed silence. Osten told the guard to report a lost worker. I skipped breakfast. I might have nibbled on some bread, but I wasn't able to eat more. The corpse was left there all day and remained for evening assembly—a testament to the nature of the place and the latitude given guards and kapos.

That evening in my quarters, I couldn't shake those dreadful images, nor could I shake my position there and my reasoning for taking it. We can control every event around us—at least that's what we're told. But I wasn't in Friedrichstadt or a village in Bavaria in normal times. I was in a Nazi labor camp during the Second World War. Nonetheless, the insignia on my uniform meant something to the guards. Anxiety overtook me.

I lay down and listened to a classical music broadcast on a radio housed in a wooden cabinet. The dial glowed softly in the dark as Furtwängler conducted the Berlin Philharmonic. I imagined rows of prominent Nazi figures and their wives in the audience, lavishly attired, displaying their appreciation of high culture.

My lot was far better than that of the thousands around me. I was one of them but in league with a self-professed master race. Sympathetic toward the thousands, yet oppressing them. My father used to say that everyone has a purpose in life that is determined by God. We don't know what that purpose is until it comes. It may arrive when we are young or old. We have to look for it, and, more important, we have to summon the courage to act on it. What was my life's purpose?

Morning came. I breakfasted with an officer named Hauser with whom I'd attended cadet school but knew only vaguely. He came from a prosperous Berlin family that owned several businesses and had sent him to the best gymnasium in the city. Athletic, handsome, and dedicated, he was the SS ideal. He could have appeared in recruitment posters and propaganda films. Yet he joined the SS only because of his father's wishes. He would have preferred a good-paying job, perhaps with one of the family businesses, and playing the field with the women of Berlin. Nonetheless, there he was, far from the good life and in charge of one of K XII's shops.

"Ach! This is a waste of time, Johan. I could be driving out in the country in my Mercedes with a buxom girl. Or skiing the Tyrol with another. There are so many available women in the cities these days."

"We all have to make sacrifices."

"They have enough soldiers and officers. I haven't seen a good-looking woman since I got here."

I smiled and pointed to my wedding band.

"There is one aspect of military life that attracts me," he said.

My look suggested he go on, but I sensed reluctance. It passed, though.

"I've always wondered what it would be like to kill someone. You recall the lectures. All that talk of the inferiority of Jews and their ilk. The importance of instilling discipline and fear and meeting production levels. And the part about finding powers within. Those words reached something inside me. Something that in other times I'd have to hide."

Across from me stood a product of the times—the vicious, Nazi times. Twenty years earlier, someone like him never would have revealed this, let alone acted on it. Maybe he was like those soldiers who were attracted to killing. Maybe he secretly would have murdered a young boy or an unwilling girl.

"That's no way to talk! You cannot take a human life simply because something inside you urges you on." I spoke with the chiding tone of a superior officer. He noticed. I went on. "You didn't understand our training correctly. Let me explain it to you so there are no costly errors here. We are at K XII to serve the Reich, not to explore the dark depths of our souls. We have schedules and quotas. Discipline, even harsh force, is only a means to those ends."

I realized that day that Hauser wasn't very intelligent. He was from a wealthy family and had graduated from the finest schools. Money can take you places, and that was the case with him, maybe even at cadet school.

My authority had come across. Hauser was embarrassed. He stared into his meal, regretting his words, though not what lurked within him.

"If you are so eager to kill, please request a transfer to the Waffen SS. Himmler is building countless divisions, some of them elite panzer units. Perhaps you would be better able to serve the Reich on the frontlines. Killing for your country in time of war is one thing, killing for personal pleasure quite another. Don't you agree?"

"Yes, Johan. I'm sure you're right. A Russian soldier in the steppes is quite different from a fellow German on a dark street, I suppose." He finished his meal and went off to his workplace.

I looked around the mess hall and out into the rows of buildings. I shook my head and finished my meal.

That moment formed a template for my responses to a slew of problems that would confront me. I'd use the SS's own productivity concerns against it. I had the rank, vocabulary, and delivery to pull it off. Yet I had to face many acts of cruelty without being able to interfere. After all, the methods of the Dachau guards had been adopted at K XII. Humiliations, beatings, and killings took place routinely. I couldn't be everywhere, and I could never make K XII a respectable place.

I could only stop cruelty on a limited basis—a highly limited basis. Timetables and schedules, timetables and schedules—that caused a vicious guard or kapo to back off and think twice the next time. Word spread, and the guards and kapos were wary of me. The inmates might have wondered about me, but I doubt many wanted to thank me. And I'm certain no one thought I might be sympathetic toward them, let alone that I was one of them.

Sleep didn't come easily, though, and I could see the wear on me when I looked into the mirror to shave in the morning. After only a few months, I had to go to the clinic for sleeping pills. Hans Tauber, the camp physician, was helpful in many matters.

The eager young officer with the murderous heart soon enough transferred to the Waffen SS. It seemed one of my many duties was career counseling.

Every month or so, I was able to get leave for a short visit to Emilie and Sophia. Most of the SS personnel were granted such breaks; most eagerly took them. Perhaps I wasn't the only one being worn down. I thought I saw unease in a few faces, but it was not a subject one ordinarily pursued, especially with the second-in-command. It might look bad in an efficiency report, and everyone was watching for loss of faith.

I sent enough money home for Emilie to stop working and stay with our daughter. We discussed the war and the continuing investigations in Berlin. Kaiser had not visited in a while, and we hadn't heard from friends and neighbors of any visits from him or his office.

I told Emilie that fellow officers had passed around word of numerous more camps and subcamps being built in Germany and elsewhere. I explained to her that their purpose was to gradually work the inmates to death. Briefings by officers from Berlin boasted of immense new camps in Poland.

"The Reich is unstoppable, Johan. It just goes on and continues spreading across Europe."

Living in the capital, she was better able to follow events than an officer in the Bavarian countryside. It was early 1942, and the Third Reich was taking more of Europe and sending more people to the camps. If an end to the war seemed likely then, it was because the Reich was conquering a vast empire and consolidating.

5

LIFE AND DEATH IN K XII

By early 1943, the camp was producing war matériel and grinding down the population. Workers toiled and persevered; guards intimidated and killed. The machinery was working well, just as the designers in Berlin had intended. And, it must be made clear, I was part of the machinery—a smaller one than the engineers but not a mere cog.

Several thousand inmates had died by then. Malnutrition, overwork, and beatings had taken a toll. The same things went on in the other subcamps in every other camp system. There were about fifteen thousand of them across Europe. Many prisoners chose to end their lives rather than live another day. They'd goad a guard or allow themselves to fall into a downward spiral.

The inmates had a term for prisoners who'd lost hope and moved about almost lifelessly. They were called *Muselmänner.* They were easily recognizable, even from afar. Listlessness was a bad sign. They'd soon enough die in their sleep, fail a selection, or kill themselves.

The K XII population grew far beyond the ten thousand it was planned to hold. Roll calls became larger and took longer. Inmates were out in the elements and more susceptible to exhaustion and disease. The blocks were more densely packed. That too meant depletion, but of course the railhead was nearby. Everyone heard the whistle in the distance.

There were initially three munitions plants. A fourth came on line that used only women laborers. A principal part of my work was to inspect these plants and see that the shells continued to roll off the line.

I also inspected the blocks on a regular basis. Each time depressed me. In the morning, there was a stack of bodies—people who had died in the night. Work details brought corpses to a mass pit. Some were taken to a crematory, but it was unable to handle them all. I gave orders to keep the blocks as clean as possible and ensure sanitary washing areas.

Kaiser came by every few months. We'd have lunch or dinner to talk about the camp. He told me what I'd already suspected from dealings with Kommandant Osten—I was performing my job well. Discipline and production were good. Kaiser patted me on the back more than once.

Osten too appreciated my work. He was leaving more and more matters to me. His predilection for order and schedules was giving way to women and drink. How often he remained in his quarters or locked in his office, I cannot say. Bottles of beer and cognac were hauled away by an obliging enlisted man. Osten didn't favor the more expensive labels. He occasionally walked about the camp, and it was clear he'd been drinking, though not falling-down drunk or even tipsy. He was able to move crisply and look determined. But the hazy eyes and pungent breath told the tale.

Such people often dress sloppily, as drinking is part of a pattern of deterioration. Not so with Osten. His uniform and grooming were always excellent. An aide saw to it.

We established a measure of cordiality. We talked about more than just the camp. We spoke of family and travel and restaurants in Munich, which was not far. He'd probably raised a glass or two before entering the SS. Most Germans did. But I came to see his drinking as a retreat from the dismalness surrounding him. I learned to take advantage of his weakness. It helped me to save inmates' lives.

Every month, Berlin sent a functionary to lecture us. Some of it was war news. Naturally, the speaker asserted all was well, despite temporary adversity in Russia. Most of the lectures stressed racial superiority and the need to eliminate inferior people—Jews, homosexuals, the handicapped, and others. Evidently, Berlin felt the need to strengthen the ideology at places where its logic led to its conclusions.

One of the most frequent lecturers was Oberführer Backe, the equivalent of a full colonel. He was of average height and beefy build. He all but waddled as he entered the room in the administration building and stood at the podium. Osten was there. That was unusual.

Backe took on a look of severity. "The Führer is taking an extraordinary step to ensure the strength of the Reich and solve one of the most important dangers to it. I am proud to say that he has chosen Reichsführer Himmler and our SS to lead the way."

The audience was intrigued. That wasn't always the case for these presentations. Most of them were listened to as a chore.

"The Reich's leadership has given great thought to the matter of the Jews and other *Untermenschen*, and at last, a decision has been made! A plan has been formulated! It is called the Final Solution!"

He looked out into the audience of two dozen men and appreciated the intent faces. I was probably not the only one who thought the process of dealing with the Jews and other supposed subhumans was already well underway. The cart and pit ably attested to that. Still, greater enormity was in the offing.

"The Final Solution will be of a larger scale than anything seen before. Until now, the process has been slow and limited in scale. Yes, the Dachau system is large and doing its work well, but the problem is too vast, too immense. Stronger measures are needed. Larger camps and more decisive methods."

The room fell silent.

"Camps in Poland are being expanded. Jews and the others from all of Europe will be transported there by rail. Those in reasonable health will work in factories, as here in the Dachau system. As for the unfit, extraordinary measures await them. They will be directed to large rooms, doors will close, and they will be put to death by means of lethal gas."

My mind reeled. The idea was shocking. *This is an intentional elimination of an ethnic group. This is policy now.* In my mind, I could see the crowd butchering Jews just because it was allowed. *Can it be? Am I hallucinating?* The concept was so unimaginable that I had hard time believing it. *We are Germany, an educated culture, an enlightened country. It's simply can't be happening.* Yet there I sat in that classroom, listening to the Nazi officer psychopath talking about killing millions just because of their beliefs. It sounded absurd.

I'd gradually seen things get worse, but a massive, systematic murder of millions of people was incomprehensible to me. The worst came at last to my mind. *I am a Jew. I am an imposter. I am hiding in the devil's nest in order to save my family.* Would I be able to handle that?

Osten spoke up to express his objection, of sorts, waking me from my fearful thoughts. "Oberführer Backe, will this not affect our supply of labor? What of production for the war?"

"Ernst, my friend, be not concerned. The Führer and Reichsmarschall have naturally given this considerable thought. The numbers have been gone through, and they indicate that the numbers of *Untermenschen* are astoundingly large and thus sufficient for factory work to last over three years. I've seen the tables myself!"

Osten leaned back and drew from his cigarette holder.

My mind conjured up images of the schools and synagogues from my upbringing and friends and neighbors. Where were they? Where would they be in three years?

"The process charged to us is challenging and vital to Germany's future. Sending people to their deaths may weigh heavily on some of us. We realize that. But let us not shrink from our patriotic duty! Let me quote from Reichsführer Himmler:

"'How is it with the women and children? I decided to find a clear solution here as well. I did not consider myself justified to exterminate the men—that is, to kill them or have them killed—and allow the avengers of our sons and grandsons in the form of their children to grow up. The difficult decision had to be taken to make this people disappear from the earth.'"

I gasped for air. With these quotes from Himmler himself, especially mentioning murdering children, I realized that madness had overtaken Germany. I felt cold sweat crawling down my back, and my heart raced. *How will I be able to perform?* I wondered. *I'm not capable of shooting people—definitely not children. I'll fail. I'll be exposed.*

Then thoughts of my family brought me back to reality—my reality, the reality of a survivor. I took a deep breath. *I'll have to work on a plan, something that I can live with until the end of the war.* I was sure that type of madness would not exist for long. Someone would stop it eventually. My father's words floated in my mind. Yes, this madness would come to an end, but how many would lose their lives in the process?

The men around me were honored to have Himmler's words read to them by someone who'd sat with him in Berlin. There might have been more from Backe. There might have been a few questions. At this point, I already was tuned out of the situation. I returned to my quarters and turned on the radio. Classical music filled my room, but I couldn't listen. My mind went on searching for a logical explanation for all this, but I couldn't find any. All seemed unreal. I had to push my thoughts to the side in order to continue. *I'll cross that bridge when I come to it*, I thought.

What had begun with smashing windows and street beatings was leading to extermination. I don't think the word *genocide* was well known then. If it was, it referred only to the Armenians and Turks.

I couldn't sleep at all that night. I feared for my family and friends and prayed for them as well—in Hebrew.

Things started to move faster. Not long after the lecture, the selection process that separated the able from the infirm, that separated those who'd live a while longer from those marked for death, became stricter. A fever, limp, or hoarse cough meant being sent to the side and then by train "to the east." That meant Auschwitz or Treblinka or one of the other camps built specifically for mass murder. Backe promised trains with more Jews and others, and they arrived more frequently.

Inmates were required to stand in the cold and rain for longer periods. Minor disciplinary infractions led to swift responses, sometimes with a burst of MP-40 fire. The distinctive staccato report became more common. In places, the sounds reverberated off buildings and caused everyone to pause—almost everyone, anyway.

This interfered with production. Experienced workers were sent away or shot. When I mentioned this to Osten, he shrugged his shoulders.

"Berlin is aware of that, Johan. They have priorities. Right now, the priorities are killing off the Jews. It's hardly in our hands, old boy."

"Ernst, this will reduce supplies reaching our troops in Russia and Italy."

"Berlin has always made the proper decisions. You'll see," he said, although his voice lacked conviction.

Such were Berlin's priorities. My priorities were my helping where I could. I'd reprimand a guard for beating a good worker, but the guards were vicious thugs to begin with, and as guards, they felt emboldened. I tried to stop the killings as much as I could, but I wasn't a hero or guardian; I was part of it.

I had enough will to stride confidently about the camp on inspections and socialize at the mess hall and administration building, if minimally. The other SS men, for the most part, had the faith. Most believed in the Reich and the mission it laid before them in lectures and film clips. A few lost the faith and drank heavily or transferred to combat units. I never had the faith. The only faith I had was that if I played my role, my family would survive. It was enough.

Osten and I became collegial—not friends, just friendly. He called me Johan, and I called him Ernst. He depended on me to manage the camp and hide his alcoholism from Dachau and inspection teams. Collegiality gave me a friend in high places.

During chats, I'd talk about my Catholic upbringing. My patron saint was Johan—the apostle, not the baptist. I had a rosary that my grandfather in Vienna had given me. I looked forward to my daughter's First Communion in a few years.

Osten said Kaiser often asked about me, over the phone or in conversation. Osten gave me high marks. I never shook the idea that Kaiser retained suspicions about me and treasured the idea of having placed me in a paradoxical hell. Perhaps the urgency of the Final Solution gave him less time to run down hunches. Yet later, I thought that luck was on my side because the German army actually needed our camp's production. That's what allowed for fairly low execution of the Final Solution policy, as compared to other camps, where Jews were expendable.

Osten let me use his personal car for visits home. What a relief it was to exit the gate and see the wire and towers in the rearview mirror; ahead of me, green forests, winding roads, and loving family. I could make Berlin by dawn.

As an officer, I received gasoline rations, so Emilie and I drove out into the country to enjoy a respite. We wanted to go to the cabin but feared we'd be followed. Neighbors might recall an interfaith marriage a few years back.

Seeing Sophia walk through tall grass and point to ducks brought immense joy. No trucks, roll calls, or angry shouts.

A day or so later, I had the sickening drive south and the sight of barbed wire and guard towers in my headlights.

Duty required me to inspect the factory that exclusively used women laborers. It produced tunics and boots and was slated to expand. As a sergeant and I entered—unannounced, as was my practice—the female SS overseer (*Aufseherin*) jumped to attention and stayed in that position as I walked down the aisles. I stopped occasionally at a few stations to take a look at the workmanship. The workers, naturally, were fearful.

I stood outside a room off to the side, where a few women were chatting. They had no idea I was nearby. If they had, they would have continued doing their work, heads cast downward. There were always side rooms in the factories where the workers didn't feel watchful eyes. I knew most of the places and made a habit of going by to get an idea of the workers' lives. I'm not sure if I thought it was important for camp operation or if I felt sorry for them. Probably both.

That day, two women were talking about a wedding. After a few moments, it was clear they weren't talking about one in the past. It was to take place in a few days and somewhere in the camp.

"Hannah, is it really possible to get everything we need?" one whispered as she folded and stacked tunics.

"Not everything. But we're all taking a little food from the mess hall. Added together, it'll be a banquet. Mendel and friends are trying to fashion a makeshift chuppah from wood and wire."

"Rosa will try to take some bread from breakfast and dinner. We'll manage."

"It'll be wonderful! A little wine would be nice, but I'm afraid that is far beyond our means just now."

They giggled girlishly—a lovely sound. Humor and even love were flourishing behind K XII's barbed wire. I knew that men and women were allowed to mingle most nights in a common area near the mess hall. The guards weren't close by—they were off smoking and reading mail. They knew the inmates weren't going anywhere. The period lasted about two hours and was followed by a shrieking whistle and a somber march back to the earthen blocks. Courtships took place; sometimes proposals.

I quietly turned and left.

A few days later, I returned and came across the same two young women in the storage room. They immediately fell silent and looked downward. I wanted to talk amicably with them but knew they'd not feel at ease.

"It's my understanding that a wedding is being planned. One of you is to be married?"

They froze.

"Please! Have no fear. I have no objection. None at all. In fact, I can be of help—perhaps with a bottle of wine."

They didn't know if it was a trick of some sort, and I couldn't blame them.

The following day, I returned with a canvas sack and handed it to them. "You'll find that a well-wisher who insists on anonymity has sent you some gifts for your wedding. Go ahead and look, if you like."

The women nervously opened the sack and found a loaf of pumpernickel, fruit, and a bottle of red wine. They were amazed and puzzled.

"I only ask that you enjoy them surreptitiously and not divulge the donor's name, should you learn it. Versteh?"

They nodded.

"May I ask the date?"

"Next Saturday. On Saturdays, the guards are fewer in number and less watchful."

An astute observation. Many guards had weekend passes. The others often stayed in the dining hall and chatted with the mess sergeant to get a little extra food.

"If you look deeper in the sack," I said, "you'll find a glass and napkin."

One of the women smiled faintly, probably wondering how I knew of the Jewish wedding rite. With that, I continued with my duties.

The food was from the officers' mess. The wine came from Osten's personal stash. He'd never miss it.

The Saturday arrived, and the duty roster called for only one guard for the evening. I told the man to head back to the barracks or, better yet, to find a ride into Munich for a night on the town. He was out the gate in half an hour.

I paced casually near the mess hall until I saw a gathering of people about seventy-five meters away, just behind the building. An older man with a long beard was presiding—one of a handful of rabbis I knew to be in K XII. They had indeed put together a serviceable chuppah. Buried memories arose. I recalled the joy of my own wedding, and for a moment, I wanted to take part in this one. I considered going over to congratulate the young couple but thought better of it. It was risky for all and might cast a pall over the occasion. I'd made my choice two years earlier, and in so doing, I'd placed myself outside the community.

The rabbi spoke and sang, and the gathering laughed and clapped. I presumed the groom's foot came down on the glass. I'd worried about that part of the rite when Emilie and I married.

Emilie.

The celebration continued for a half hour, and the thought to congratulate the young couple returned, perhaps because I needed a moment of community. Anyway, I walked slowly toward the couple, who were wearing grimy pajamas. Heads turned, and many people took their leave. I approached the young man and woman, and in the old Yiddish dialect, I whispered, "*Mazel tov*," before continuing my rounds.

I glanced back and saw the newlyweds staring in my direction. The woman waved briefly, her hand never rising above her shoulder. I nodded and turned away again.

Another guard came on duty to herd them back to their blocks. I sauntered to my quarters and closed the door.

I'd done something good that day. There weren't many nights when I could say that. I smiled and hoped they enjoyed the wine. Sleep came a little earlier for me that night. In the middle of atrocities, there had been an opportunity to help—and I did. It made me feel good. It made me feel normal. It gave me a strong sense of to which side I belonged. I vowed to continue helping, wherever I could. *I will do my best to help the inmates in here*, I thought.

I saw the husband and wife, here and there, over the next few months, but I could hardly ask how they were enjoying married life—nor could I tell them why I'd helped.

6

SELECTION

Roll calls in the autumn of 1943 often took place under gray skies and light rain. The same held for selections. I initially would steel myself for those summary, pseudo-medical processes that decided who'd live a while longer and who'd be sent east. No longer, though; I no longer felt deep concern for those faceless souls who shivered in the cold and tried to look as healthy as they could. They were unfortunate extras in my performance.

Standing fifty meters or so from the medics, I saw men and women walk before the desks and learn their fates. Waves of relief came to most. Some of the others protested—futilely, of course. Some accepted the sentence as a way out.

By then, word of the gas chambers in Birkenau and Treblinka had spread throughout the SS, including the staff at K XII. It surely had made its way to inmates as well, probably though cruel taunting. They might not have known the precise way the end came, but they knew what lay ahead as they trod over to the condemned group and awaited the train whistle.

Not everyone in the selection process was faceless, though. Some I'd seen in one of our factories, or a mess hall, or on an outdoor labor detail. One face stuck out that morning, and in a moment, I placed it; it was the man who had been married a few months back. He'd been sent to the side for the next train.

With the selection over, the fortunate put their pajamas back on and headed for another day of work. I walked toward those who were staying behind and saw the poor man. He was looking toward the groups marching to work, probably hoping for a final glimpse of his wife. His shirt was stained with blood, and his face had numerous cuts and bruises. One eye was swollen shut. It was a familiar enough sight. A guard had beaten him for one reason or another or for no reason at all. Beatings led to weakness, fever, and a walk to the group on the side.

I told the guard that I'd take care of him. Naturally, he had no objection. I took the bridegroom with me.

"Your name?"

"Mendel Rosenstock."

"Which guard?" I asked.

The bewildered man kept his eyes ahead of him.

We entered the infirmary, and I sat Mendel in front of Hans Tauber, the camp doctor who gave me sleeping pills. He had finished medical school in Stuttgart a few years ago. At meetings, he displayed none of the zeal or sadism that was routine in the camp, even among medical personnel. Discussions of malnutrition and death brought a somber look to his face, albeit briefly and faintly. He saw the same things in me. There was no question of discussing the horror of the camp, let alone the Reich, but we understood how we felt. He once mentioned how paradoxical it was for a doctor to have so little to do with the countless sick and injured all around. The treatment, he once mordantly observed, was no treatment.

"I'd like you to see to this one, Hans. He's an excellent worker. He just ran afoul of one of the guards the other day and that caused him to fail selection. I want him back on the line."

"You took him out of the deportees?" he asked with a look of incredulity.

Hans was moved when I nodded. He examined Mendel for broken bones and abscesses but found nothing. He dressed his wounds and gave him aspirin. Mendel probably needed stitches, but that would have invited suspicion. In half an hour, the hospital visit was over.

"I hope you know what you're doing, Johan."

"I think so. In any event, I know what *we're* doing."

"I know that too."

As I led Mendel to his factory, he kept his eyes straight ahead. "My wife's name is Hannah."

"Lovely name. It means 'grace.'"

"I compliment you on your knowledge of Hebrew."

I told the *Aufseher* to ease him back to work and to make sure the guards didn't let their work interfere with mine again.

The couple came to my attention once again. Inspections of the women's factory that made uniforms and boots allowed me to see Hannah every now and then. She briefly would make eye contact and smile before returning to work. It allowed me to feel human for a moment. One morning, her eyes showed worry. When she went into the back room to do some folding, I followed her.

"I don't know if I should involve you in this," she said, "but there's no one else to turn to."

I motioned for her to go ahead.

"I have a problem, sir. I'm going to have a baby. Can you please help us? Help us again, that is? You know what they'll do."

Indeed, I did. My mind reeled. I sat on a table to ponder the situation. I felt like an enraged father on hearing the news. "How could you two have been so irresponsible? How could you have let this happen? You are not a lovestruck couple in Frankfurt! You know full well where you are!"

"I don't want to die! I don't want our baby to die! Please!"

"How far along?"

"About three months. That's what the women tell me."

Knowing that my ire wasn't helping any, I calmed myself. Officers were supposed to assess unexpected situations and formulate ways ahead. So were enraged fathers. "I'll have to think about this. There are many things that go on here that I cannot control. You have to realize that."

She nodded tearfully.

Not long thereafter, I visited home. My family welcomed me, as always, with warmth and love. I couldn't sleep the first night. On the second, Emilie noticed my disquiet.

"Do you remember the couple that got married a few months ago?" I asked her.

"Yes."

"The woman is pregnant."

"Oh no!"

"It's worse than you know. When her condition becomes known, she'll be sent to a death camp on the next train. Most of the trains go to a place in southern Poland called Auschwitz. Those in reasonable health are put to work, as in Dachau and K XII. The rest are sent immediately to a dark room, where poison gas kills them in about twenty minutes."

"Poison gas?"

"Zyklon B. The extermination program is diligent and thorough."

"Oh, dear God! Oh, dear God!" Emilie wailed. "Can you help the poor girl? You have to!"

"I want to help. Believe me."

"And if Osten or someone else finds out?"

"I'll be sent to prison. Part of Dachau holds SS prisoners. It might endanger you and Sophia as well."

My wife lay down and wept. Late into the night, however, we formed a plan.

On my return to K XII, I led Hannah to the infirmary and told her to wait silently while Hans treated a guard. Afterward, he lamented that several guards drank too much and were coming to him with ulcers and liver trouble. When he looked at me, I could tell he sensed I had a special case.

"Yes, I have a request," I confirmed, "a very important one. I've brought a young woman—an inmate. She's in a family way. About four months now. She's beginning to show, as the women say." I felt uneasy. We were friendly, yes, but the matter was extremely dangerous.

He sighed wearily, uncertain of what I was going to ask. "You want me to—"

"No, no. I hope not, anyway. I want her to have the baby. I want you to keep her here for the next few months. You have small rooms in the back; I know. I run this camp and know more than you might realize. Hans, I want you to hide her here and see that she gives birth to a healthy baby."

"Johan! I want to help. You know that. But this is dangerous—for all of us."

"You may consider it a medical experiment—for the good of the Reich. I'll give you further details in coming weeks and back you up, should anything come of it."

"The medical experiments are at the main camp. I know Dr. Rascher, and I know of his interest in fertility. Why, then, not send her to him?"

We both knew of Sigmund Rascher. Everyone in the system knew of him. He conducted experiments involving oxygen deprivation, freezing, wounds, and, yes, fertility. His work had more to do with sadism than science.

"Hans, I have a keen interest in this particular experiment. Let us leave it at that. More information is forthcoming. We need not bring Rascher in. He might get jealous and jeopardize things. No one needs to know about this but you and me. After she gives birth, I'll take the baby somewhere else for further treatment—not Dachau or any subcamp but a place near Berlin that specializes in such cases."

The good doctor seemed less concerned but wasn't buying my story.

I took on a more official tone. "Now, see here, Hans. I run K XII. Osten is in command, but I run the place. I have connections from my academy days, and they work throughout the SS. They want this matter done, and they want it done my way. Other people in Berlin do as well—names you would know."

He was in line and complied with my peculiar order, but he wasn't buying the experiment story. "Why, exactly, are you doing this, Johan? The real reason, that is."

"I have my reasons, Hans. We all have our reasons. It's for the greater good. You will have more information in a timely manner."

"It's for the greater good of Germany, then?"

"Oh, Hans. It's greater than that. I'm sure you see things like that from time to time."

"Very well, Johan, very well. I'll see that she's cared for. And I have your word that it's all for a greater good."

"I'm certain it is, Hans, my friend."

He examined Hannah and confirmed that she was well along. He also determined that she was in reasonably good health, all things considered.

He placed her in a private room and forbade the staff to mention her presence, warning them that she had an unusual condition that might endanger the camp and that he—and he alone—was administering promising treatments. He also made it plain that the assistant kommandant had given orders for absolute secrecy and that the orders were to be followed to the letter. If they were not—well, the consequences would be fearsome. Everyone knew that the war in Russia wasn't going well and that winters in Bavaria were to be preferred.

Hannah was reasonably safe for now, but worry continued. If discovered, I would be investigated, perhaps by Kaiser. But what would happen a few months from now? The birth of a child should not be feared. Fortunately, I had a helping hand in Hans. He outlined the plan, and I found it promising.

On my next leave, I learned that Emilie had met with success in her part of the plan.

"I spoke with Rudolph about Hannah," she told me. "He can help. If you can bring the baby to Berlin, he can place it in an abbey just outside Berlin. The abbess has agreed not to ask where the baby came from."

"Wonderful news!"

"The abbess made one request—no, it's a firm stipulation. Hannah can never know where her baby's been taken. She can never see her baby again. The abbess insists on this. The baby will be raised as a Catholic orphan and will never know its parents or place of birth. Neither you nor I will know the abbey's location."

"Only Rudolph will know, then."

Emilie shook her head. "I'm not sure even he will know. He spoke of an intermediary."

I pondered the arrangement. The stipulation was understandable, given the Gestapo bloodhounds. I couldn't say how amenable Hannah would be. She initially, of course, would not like the idea.

"Can you convince her?" Emilie murmured.

When I left home that weekend, I was determined to do what was necessary to save the child. The next morning, I entered the infirmary in an official stride and headed for the back room. Staff, patients, and a guard or two fell silent and looked the other way or scurried off. Rank has its advantages, especially when doing something out of bounds. I started to open the door but decided to knock gently first.

Hannah looked relieved. She was about a month away from delivery.

A heavy sigh came from my chest before I spoke. "Hannah, I've found a way to get the baby out of here."

Her face brightened—prematurely, I thought.

"It isn't all you might have hoped it to be, but in these times, it's the only way. A day or so after you give birth—no more than that—we can spirit the baby out of the camp. A convent will take the child in, feed and clothe it, and raise it safely. In the eyes of the government, the child will be an orphan. The records office will enter it as a foundling."

She began to speak but I stopped her.

"No, Hannah. No, I'm afraid not. You can never see the baby again, and you will not know where it is, nor will anyone here, including me. Perhaps someday, when all this is over, it can be looked into, but for now, I must tell you that you will be parting with the child forever. It's the only way we can save you and the baby. Such are our times."

She lay back on the pillow and wept. She knew how to do so quietly by then. Her hands reached for her belly, and the tears fell all the harder. I was able to maintain an official composure.

"Afterward, you will return to the women's block and resume work. Naturally, you are to keep silent on this matter. Completely silent."

Hannah thought it through and calmed herself better than I could have hoped. "I understand, sir. And I will keep my silence. One small favor, though. May I name my baby before giving it away?"

"Yes, you may do that. And the name will be conveyed to the convent."

She sank back in the bed and wept more.

I blotted a tear with my tunic sleeve, and she caught me. Her soul penetrated mine, asking why all this had to happen. I shook my head and sighed. I had no answer. I still don't.

I wouldn't be the only SS officer to take a baby away from its mother in what became known as the Holocaust, but I take consolation in being the only one who did so with both remorse and hope.

Hans sent an orderly to my quarters. I immediately knew why. I put on my tunic hurriedly and walked briskly to the infirmary; then down the hallway to the back room. Along the way, I did my best to appear intimidating. That came easily.

"Her water broke," Hans said as I entered. "The baby will come soon. It's premature but only by five weeks. The baby already has good size, enough to make it through. Johan—"

"Oh, Hans, not that."

"Yes, that. I'll need your assistance."

The first thing was to put wet towels beneath the door to keep the noise down. The screams of an inmate were common enough, not so for those of a newborn.

Labor started, and Hannah gave it her all. Hannah bit down on a towel. Mercifully, it didn't last long. Two hours later, a baby boy came into the world. Healthy and spirited, he lay in his mother's arms. The hardest thing lay ahead.

A few days later, Hans and I wanted to proceed with the plan, but Hannah pleaded for a few more minutes. We could not refuse her. She held him close and began to nurse him.

"I love you more than you will ever know, Adam, and I want my love to be with you forever. I want you to feel this moment at all times, especially hard ones."

The infant soon fell asleep in his mother's arms.

"Hannah ..."

She nodded. "I know. Yes, I know. Adam was my grandfather's name. Please see that he knows his name."

She took him from her breast, and I gently lifted him up, just as I had done for Sophia a few years ago, as Emilie had looked on beatifically. The scent of a newborn child filled my being. Such innocence amid such evil. How dare I hold anything so pure? He knew nothing of his birthplace or what lay ahead for his mother and father, whom he'd never know. I hoped the best for him. Once again, I wiped a tear.

Hannah was on the verge of breaking. I feared she would scream or try to take Adam and make a run for the gate. Hans comforted her and administered a sedative.

"I'll see that he knows his name," I told her.

She nodded.

I wrapped Adam in a blanket and placed him in a leather valise I used on trips to Berlin. A phone call to the main gate, and I was off to my car. The guard at the gate saluted crisply as the second-in-command drove off on pressing business. I thought of Pharaoh's daughter and a basket in the Nile.

"You're out of K XII, Adam. May you have a long life ahead of you in a much better world."

The drive to Berlin went without incident, and my little passenger voiced only small protests every hour or so. If he had cried more, there was nothing I could have done.

Emilie opened the door, saw me with my friend, and joyously

welcomed us. A glass of white wine and a milk bottle were waiting for the weary travelers.

"His name is Adam, dear."

"Welcome, Adam. Enjoy your meal. You are a beautiful little boy. I wish you could stay with us longer. Maybe forever."

I wrapped up Adam once more in my valise and headed across town to a small house near Potsdam. Rudolph was expecting us. I made the introductions.

"We live in heartbreaking times, Johan. We tear babies from their mothers and hide them away. He will have good care. The mother knows this, yes?"

"She does, at least at some level. She has one request, though. She has named him Adam and wants him to go by that name. It was her grandfather's. It's a Jewish tradition."

"That will be relayed to the abbess."

"I have a request as well. I want to say a prayer for Adam."

Rudolph bowed his head as I softly recited a prayer I'd memorized as a boy with my father's help.

"יְבָרֶכְךָ ה׳ וְיִשְׁמְרֶךָ: יָאֵר ה׳ פָּנָיו אֵלֶיךָ וִיחֻנֶּךָּ: יִשָּׂא ה׳ פָּנָיו אֵלֶיךָ וְיָשֵׂם לְךָ שָׁלוֹם."

Our heads remained down for several moments.

"Beautiful, Johan. May I ask what it means?"

"It's a traditional blessing that means, 'May the Lord keep you safe and healthy.' It was given by the great priests of Israel to their people."

"Amen."

"Thank you for all your help, Rudolph. May Adam grow up to be a fine man in a better world. Until then, we pray in secret."

"In secret, in shadows, and in fear."

The next morning, I drove back to K XII. I felt good. Throughout the drive back, I imagined little Adam growing up and living a happy life—life without the Third Reich, a normal life without the madness. *He'll be nurtured, eat well, have a girlfriend, and maybe go to the university one day*, I thought. Tears formed in my eyes, and I wiped them quickly.

What had happened to the world as I knew it? Sometimes I was not sure events really happened. I believed this was true reality only because I did what I felt was the right thing to do. An image of my daughter, Sophia, rose in front of me. I missed her.

The guard saluted crisply as I drove through the gate, and I returned it. The camp had gone on in my absence. It was a machine that could be left to run on its own for small periods. Gears turned, trucks came and went, men and women lined up, matériel shipped out to receding fronts.

A few days later, I saw Hannah at her workplace. She was frail but able to work. She'd pass the next selection. After that, who could tell—not the second-in-command, only someone higher up. I told her in general terms of the successful mission and of my instructions to the abbey regarding the boy's name. I'm sure she thought of the basket in the Nile too. How could she not? As I turned to leave the back room, I told her of the prayer I'd said over Adam. She smiled, and a flame of life came to her eyes.

"I wish I could do more, Hannah. Everything in my soul wants to do more."

She looked at me with her fragile being. "You did a wonderful thing. You saved Adam, and I'll be forever grateful to you. I'll tell Mendel this evening. No names, of course."

"Only the name Adam." I bowed slightly, gave her a faded smile, and left.

I returned to the admin hut and looked at the morning reports, including the number of deaths. My eyes went through the document, but I saw only long lines, grim faces, and endless stretches of barbed wire. I closed the reports. That morning, I refused to feel sad. That morning, my heart rejoiced, for a little baby boy was saved.

Adam.

7

School Reunion

More prisoners arrived every week or so. Many came in from foreign countries now. How many more were still in their homes, or in ghettoes, or in hiding? I couldn't know. They came in with no more dignity than the reams of fabric and hides of leather. Most left with less.

One morning after roll call, as the inmates were trudging off to work, I saw a guard beating an inmate. He knocked the poor fellow to the ground and continued hitting and kicking him. I headed for the scene. As I got closer, my suspicion of the guard's identity was confirmed. It was *Soldat* Kunder, an especially sadistic man, the sort who was a schoolyard bully and who found himself, so to speak, in the SS. Outside, his behavior would anger neighbors and lead to arrest. Not so here.

Osten wasn't present, for one reason or another, and I was in charge. I hadn't used my authority on behalf of an inmate in a while. My authority came readily by then.

I saw the helpless inmate writhing on the ground, as blow after blow fell. When his face became less distorted, I recognized him. It was Juda, a young man I'd gone to school with in Friedrichstadt. He himself had been a schoolyard bully who intimidated and fought classmates for spite. He'd run afoul of a counterpart.

It wasn't a matter of helping an old friend. I disliked Juda and thought—at least for a moment—that he'd done something to deserve it. Truth be told, I even felt satisfaction. I pulled the collar of my overcoat up and the brim of my cap down.

"Soldat Kunder!" I shouted.

He stopped immediately and stood at attention. "Herr Untersturmführer!"

My voice shifted from angered authority to chastening principal. "Don't kill this Jew. He's a good worker in the factory. Perhaps not the best, but he's needed now. We have schedules to meet, and your personal appetites are not to interfere with them. *Klar*?"

"Klar, Herr Untersturmführer!"

"I'll take this one to the factory myself. Back to the others, Kunder. And be forewarned!"

"Ja wohl, Herr Untersturmführer."

Juda lay on the ground, facedown, until I ordered him up; I stood behind him, of course. "*Schnell!*"

Juda limped in front of me toward the factory.

"Name!"

"Juda Kaminski."

"Judging by your accent, you come from Berlin."

He nodded.

"Get to work. And I want no more trouble from you."

He nodded again and entered the factory.

"Get to work!"

As I turned to head back to the administration building, I saw him surreptitiously look my way. I instantly regretted helping him.

While making my presence known later in the same factory, Juda again looked at me—longer this time and with discernible interest. As he loaded a crate of ammunition on the dock, he again looked my way. This time, he approached me—that was unheard of.

"Yes, we're both from Berlin," Juda said. "You're Yochanan. I don't recall your last name right now, but you are Yochanan from the yeshiva. You in the SS? And an officer? I don't understand that at all!"

He wasn't happy to see me, not in the usual sense. He was sizing me up. His face was bruised and swollen, and he grimaced as he walked, but he was the same obnoxious kid from school. And he had no doubt about who I was.

"This is neither the time nor place for talking old times. I have a position here that allows me to help people. You, above all, should see that—and appreciate it as well."

"So they don't know about you, do they? Yochanan, the quiet bookworm, is now one of them! This is a joke! Ha!"

"It's not a joke at all. You should recognize the advantages of the situation."

"It *is* a joke. You should be here with us, Yochi. You're one of us, not one of them. No matter what clothes you wear, you're one of us. But you are most certainly right. There are advantages to this situation. Clearly, there are. I want you to take care of me, my friend. I want food. Good food. The food they give guys in those uniforms, not that crap we get."

"Juda, I remember more than just your name. I know who you are and what you are. It won't work here. Not with me."

"What are you going to do, Yochi? Kill me? We're all dead here anyway. Sooner or later. It's just a matter of time. I want that food. Every day, my friend. Every day. Or you will be wearing *shmattes* like the rest of us very soon." He spat the last words, his face inches from my own. "What a joke! An Orthodox Nazi! Ha!"

"Get back to work!"

Despite my obvious anger, he held his ground in front of me. "Think it over, Yochi. I get food, or you get what you deserve. Shalom, my friend." He smirked and headed back to his station.

I sat in my quarters. I could have shot him on the spot or ordered someone like Kunder to do the job for me. Many would do it gladly, and there would be no more consequences than if they'd stepped on a bug.

But I couldn't do that. Although I had to play my role in a long tragedy, there were certain scenes in which I would not take part. And Juda could see that—hence, his power.

What if Juda told someone, and it reached Osten? Well, he would take my word over an inmate's any day. But what if word reached Kaiser? He came down periodically and probably had someone inside my camp. Juda might tell him the names of rabbis or fellow students who knew me or where bar mitzvah records were kept in the old synagogue, if it hadn't been burned to the ground yet. Or the records might be sitting in an SS warehouse. The SS was good at keeping records.

Juda again approached me at the factory.

"No food for your old friend? I'm disappointed, Yochi. Very disappointed. You have to help an old friend from yeshiva. Don't let me down again."

"Now you listen to me, Juda. You do not grasp the situation here. I can help you. I already have. I'll even help you with food. But on my terms. *My terms!* If I go, you go too." I rested a hand on my holster. "And I can go on my choosing. You, on the other hand, face other methods."

"What a joke! Don't think that I'll hesitate a minute to expose you. I have nothing to lose. You have a lot to lose. Food, Yoshi! Do not let me down again. Food this evening, or I report you at roll call."

"On my terms. I'll bring you food, but don't ever threaten me again."

There was a selection scheduled for the following morning. Inmates would line up naked in front of a row of medics. Classical music would play over the loudspeakers. Images of those things plagued my sleep. I saw friends and relatives standing before faceless medics at a small desk, trying to demonstrate their health, despite the cold and malnutrition and beatings. Sometimes, I'd envision Emilie and Sophia waiting their turns, and I would be standing to the side in silence. Sometimes, I too was naked; sometimes, I was in uniform.

I needed to plan a response to any charge that might come against me. Should I angrily deny it? Laugh at its absurdity? It could be all over in a moment, one way or another. After all, I had a pistol.

That morning, I saw Juda step up to the desk. He still showed signs of Kunder's beatings. Sometimes, internal bleeding took its toll in a few days; sometimes, inmates simply started a downward spiral. The medic told him to raise his arms, breathe in deeply, and cough. I'd seen enough of those procedures to know he didn't look good, so I wasn't surprised when he was sent to the group that would board the next train out.

He looked at me in fear. If he blurted out the secret now, he'd be laughed at or shot on the spot. His eyes pleaded with me, made an unspoken pact with me. My eyes broke contact. My family and I were safe.

After the selection, I walked over to the condemned, made a few cursory looks, and then pulled Juda out and ordered a kapo to take him to the factory. I picked out a woman who looked reasonably healthy and sent her off to her detail. Then I went to the ammunition factory.

"You will have to make a better effort to look healthy, Juda. I want you here, at least for now. Be thankful."

"Don't think for a minute anything's changed between us," he sneered. "You only helped me because you knew I was about to give you away. The SS likes people who help them do their work. Food, Yochi. Food!"

Juda's ingratitude enraged me. I didn't know what to do. The next selection wasn't for a week or more. But the camp's machinery of death operated around the clock.

Two days later, I saw a guard drag a man from the ammunition factory, hurl him to the ground, and then kick him and club him with his machine pistol. The man cried out in pain. I know who part of me hoped it was—and it was indeed Juda. He was writhing in pain and looking around for me. I thought it best that he die right then and there. I told myself he was a danger and not really that good a worker in any case. How our minds work.

I ordered my feet to go away from the scene, but they refused. Instead, I walked toward Juda to save him again. I looked down at my feet in dismay—and then heard a burst of MP-40 fire. I saw

Juda's body fall to the ground. Anxiety threatened to overtake me, and I walked away.

I felt shame. I felt guilt. His life had been in my hands, and I'd let it slip away. Juda had been a danger to me, but he was a human being nonetheless, albeit a foolishly ungrateful one.

Emilie listened as I recounted the episode on my next visit home. She cried for her husband's ordeal and Juda's fate. We both cuddled with little Sophia, finding a reason to move on.

Conditions worsened throughout 1943 and into early 1944. That was true at K XII, the Dachau system, and the camp system across Europe. With so many people coming in on overpacked trains and then being worked hard, fed poorly, and crammed into fetid blocks, the death toll rose. Reports went to Osten, then to Weiter at Dachau, and then up to Himmler in Berlin. Orders came back to Weiter, then Osten, then me. We were to take no steps to reverse rising death tolls.

Osten and I discussed the directive. We knew it would hurt production, but that wasn't what we discussed just then. We looked for the reasoning. We suspected the directive was based on Berlin's concern that the war wasn't going well, and it was important to liquidate the Jews and others as fast as possible. It still made little sense, as the directive imperiled the war effort and put Germany at risk of defeat. Osten felt the Führer et al. had it all planned out. New weapons would soon turn the tide. All was well, he claimed, though I didn't think he really believed it.

I went about my duties. I enforced discipline and met quotas but also tried to limit cruelty where I could. I ordered the guards and kapos to see that the blocks and mess halls were cleaner. More showers and larger rations were beyond my abilities. I left food in certain spots in the factories and was pleased to see it gone an hour later. My experience with Juda made me more cautious. Who knew how many other Berliners there were?

A new factory came online. It made machine parts for automatic weapons—bolts and receivers. Civilians came in to train the workers, as production required skilled lathe operators. I walked up and down the noisy shop floor as the training went on, learning something about the skills and machinery. A man in his forties or so, with a long dark beard and intelligent eyes, caught my attention. He didn't look familiar, but his essence did. I'd seen men like him in my boyhood. For a moment, I was transported back to Friedrichstadt in the early thirties, and it caused me to reel momentarily. But soon enough, I was back in the present, and I continued down the shop floor.

A week later, I was walking through the same building just before the power sent the machinery into motion. I came upon the same man near a lathe in a recessed area. He had a book open on the machine's tray, and he was obviously praying. On closer view, I saw the book was a *siddur*, a Jewish prayer book. Such things were *verboten*, of course, but I'd come across mezuzahs and tefillin and let it go.

He saw me. A moment of fear came and went in an instant, replaced by resignation. His eyes were a clear blue and conveyed intelligence. It confirmed my earlier suspicion. He was a rabbi. I was transfixed by the sight. Memories stirred and assumed a greater presence in my being than they'd had since the interment near the Brandenburg cabin.

"Do you know what I am doing?" he asked gently.

"You are reciting the morning prayer."

He was surprised and looked into my eyes. "Have you seen others reciting this prayer?"

"Yes, I have. I am aware of what goes on around here."

My words were confusing to both of us.

"May I complete my prayer, please? I've done it faithfully since my bar mitzvah."

I nodded, and the fatalistic look came back. He might have thought his prayer would end with a pistol shot to the back of his head. He turned to the *siddur* and began to pray. It wasn't the kaddish. I closed my eyes and found myself saying the morning prayer with him. Initially, I did so in silence, but I found myself murmuring a few Hebrew words. I suddenly stopped and opened my eyes.

He'd seen me. He closed the book and stared at me in puzzlement. "You know Hebrew. How can that be?" He studied my features and nodded slowly. "I see. You are Jewish. Blue eyes, a large frame, but you are Jewish."

"Yes."

"Yet you wear that uniform and dine with those men. Indeed, you command them. I've seen many unusual things in my life. Now this, now this."

The goodness in his soul shone through and brought joy to my own—a little concern too but mostly joy.

"Yes, I am a Jew. I must ask you to keep this information between us. I know what goes on here, but you and the others do not know my soul and how it orders me to help in small ways, when and where I can."

I confessed my story—an Orthodox boyhood, the encounter with Emilie in her church, and my friend's help with my new identity. Either time and place or caution kept specific names and addresses out. I wept and felt relief.

He listened keenly, as though I was a congregant with a vexing problem about his marriage or a dispute with a neighbor. He remained silent for a while as he tried to comprehend it all. I expected a rebuke.

"Extraordinary. This must be very hard on you, young man."

"My name is Yochanan."

"I am Rabbi Yitzchak Rosenblatt. I once led a small congregation in Dresden. I hope to lead it again someday."

"Perhaps I could join you in prayer from time to time. It will have to remain our secret—and circumstances do not permit me to wear the proper religious items."

"No, they certainly do not. You are most welcome to pray alongside me. And few of us wear attire of our choosing here." We enjoyed a moment of humor. "We live in vexing times, Yochanan. You've been placed in a challenging situation that allows you to help. How many of us could have helped others in Berlin or Dresden, yet we did not?"

Lights flickered on over the shop floor and machinery whirred to life. I needed to get on with my duties, and he with his.

"Oh, Yochanan? Remember you are here to help all inmates, not just those of us. You are here to help all here."

I nodded and returned to my position.

Rabbi Yitzchak and I developed trust and friendship and appreciated each other's decency. I left a half loaf at his workstation from time to time. Other times, we prayed there together. Only the two of us. No one else knew. We'd have been great friends in normal years. His kind words and loving eyes told me that my secret resistance was for the good. It was wonderful to think I wasn't entirely a pariah.

I looked out for him at roll calls and selections. I told the guards and kapos that he was an exceptionally skilled lathe operator. I didn't have to elaborate. They knew it meant hands off. The guards and kapos thought it was a sign of my attention to detail and devotion to the Reich. I enjoyed that ironic part of my deception.

One morning Rabbi Yitzchak coughed harshly at roll call. The inmates next to him noticed and avoided any sign of concern. Fortunately, none of the guards noticed. Everyone knew that coughs often degenerated into serious, contagious illnesses. There was a directive for such people.

Later, at his workplace, he coughed more as we prayed. I told him I had valuable workers treated at the infirmary, but he wouldn't have it. A little food was one thing, but receiving medical treatment violated his sense of justice. Besides, he said, it would endanger me.

I went to the infirmary to see Hans, and I noted the large number of sick inmates who should have been selected for the death camps. I told him what I wanted, and he gave me the medications that Rabbi Yitzchak needed to survive.

Rabbi Yitzchak took the medications, though with reluctance. "Why not give some to the others?"

"I only have enough for one right now," I told him. "Others are getting treatment at the infirmary—many others, I assure you."

His cough worsened. I convinced the rabbi to let me take him to the infirmary, where the conditions were better, the food more nutritious, and the treatment better administered.

Hans admitted him.

One evening, I made one of my increasingly frequent inspections of the infirmary. Much to my dismay, Kaiser barged in with two henchmen. I felt my power drain. The doctor and rabbi knew something was wrong, even though they wore no uniforms. No one needed to be told these men were trouble.

"Johan, Johan, Johan," Kaiser said. "Excuse my informal address, but we are old friends. And friends do not keep secrets from one another, do they? I've been informed—reliably, in my view—that you have been deviating from orders, making exceptions. I'll get to the point, Johan, as we are both busy men. I believe you have been helping Jews get around Berlin's directives."

By then, I had developed an air of authority. I knew how to convey power and mastery. It came in handy. I also needed to protect people. I stared at Kaiser. "I only help the Reich, old friend. As do we all. I come here to check on workers and communicable diseases in my camp. Are you aware of how well this camp has grown under my leadership? If you do not, there are people in Berlin who can alert you to this. You would know their names."

It was true. K XII was well respected up north. I'd seen to that.

Kaiser looked at Hans and saw his name tag, medical insignia, and officer rank. "What are you doing here at night, Dr. Tauber?"

"A doctor's work does not come to a halt at the end of the day. We have contagious diseases here, and we need them contained so it doesn't interfere with the camp's mission. I'm sure you understand."

"And how is your work proceeding?"

"We send many of them back to work. Some die, of course, but that's a small matter. More will come."

"I see, I see," Kaiser said before turning his attention back to me. "But you, Johan—there may be many things I don't know about you and your upbringing, but I know you are not a doctor. I have no doubt, however, that with a little preparation, you could pass for one, at least to some people. My information is that you are helping Jews in a manner far beyond what is needed to keep them making 88 rounds and tunics."

"I do my job. I serve the camp, the SS, and higher."

"You and I were both in the administration building when Obersturmbannführer Osten gave word to accelerate the process here."

"Yes, we were. We also received instructions to maximize productivity, to produce material quickly and efficiently, and to get those arms to the men at the fronts. As second-in-command of Kaufering XII, I exercise my judgment. My judgment is sound, and it is respected. My camp is the envy of Dachau. I will not waste my time on idle rumors. Who are these people who dare speak ill of me?"

"My sources are confidential—and reliable."

Before I could open my mouth, Hans told Kaiser rather heatedly, "I've not encountered you before, but I can assure you we care nothing for the lives of Jews here. As the camp medical officer, I can attest to that. We care about schedules and productivity, evidently more so than you. A lost worker has to be replaced by a new inmate, and that inmate has to be trained."

"It isn't an easy process," I said. "Oh, it might seem that way from an office in Munich or Berlin, but it takes time to get a laborer to use a lathe properly. Sometimes, I wonder if everyone in Germany is as concerned with our men at the fronts as we are. Many people strike me as almost treasonous. Look wherever you must. Talk to whomever you want. Then kindly let me and my camp get back to work!"

"I can do that without your permission," Kaiser said. "And I've even spoken with Osten."

"He knows I'm as dedicated to Germany as anyone."

"So he says, so he says. Yet you are sympathetic toward Jews. The reports are clear."

"Lies!" Hans shouted. "Outrageous lies! Johan is a devout

Catholic. He despises Jews for what they are. And as a German of pure Aryan stock, he knows what they have brought down on the nation in the past!"

Hans had no idea of Kaiser's intermittent suspicions. His spirited defense disarmed Kaiser, but the Gestapo bloodhound was more evil than I'd suspected. He paced noisily up and down the ward, knowing the sound of his boot heels unnerved most there. He came upon a man who appeared to be the embodiment of the faith he despised.

"Prove it to me that Jewish lives have no value." He pulled his Luger from its holster, placed it in my hand, and pointed to Rabbi Yitzchak. "Kill him. There's a round in the chamber. I always keep one there. It saves time."

My heart sank; fortunately, I'd separated facial expression from emotions by then. It would have been easier to shoot almost any other inmate than Rabbi Yitzchak. He was my friend in prayer, and through him, I had decency. Now, he lay before me, only half-conscious from fever.

"Release the safety first, Johan," Kaiser instructed. "You know the procedure from the cadet school I placed you in. Think of the cat, Johan. Think of the cat and don't fail me again."

Hans erupted again. "By God, no one kills sick people in my infirmary! The kommandant's authority stops at the doorway, and so does yours. By God, you will obey my orders in here!"

"At ease! The security of the Reich takes precedence over the rules of this or any other camp. I need to test this man. Otherwise, we will have to take him back to Berlin. Sources tell me our friend here shrinks from his duty. He fails to enforce discipline. Naturally, this calls into question his fitness, sense of duty, and perhaps even his ancestry. I myself do not believe every rumor I hear, but the doubts can be laid to rest here and now."

Everyone in the ward froze.

"Now, Johan, show your allegiance to the SS and the Reich—and to all of us."

"Hauptsturmführer Kaiser, you are quite correct about the nature of Jews. They are not humans. They are an enemy to be destroyed, as Berlin has instructed. Nevertheless, I decide who lives and dies in K XII, and I decide who interferes with the proper running of the camp. I do not need a cheap show of force to prove my loyalty." My thumb ran along the safety lever, and I tossed the Luger into the hands of one of Kaiser's aides. "Bah! I have my own!"

I pulled my Luger from its holster and pulled the slide back. I aimed at the man lying next to Rabbi Yitzchak and fired twice. Both rounds struck him in the forehead, causing his head to jerk back violently and his blood to splatter on the bedding and walls. The report boomed down the ward, people gasped, and dust fell from overhead lights. Kaiser flinched.

"Hauptsturmführer Kaiser, I am a proud SS officer and devoted to the Reich. I have duties at this camp. Please be so kind as to never again interfere with its operation. And try to pay more attention to sound evidence than to idle rumor."

Kaiser stood in awed silence. He had his answer. It wasn't exactly how he'd wanted it, but there was no mistake as to what measures I'd take to run the camp as I saw fit. He motioned to his men and left. Only then did I reholster my Luger.

Rabbi Yitzchak and everyone in the ward stared at me in horror as the clacking of Gestapo boots diminished and the door slammed shut.

Hans sat down on a bed and looked at me warily. "Johan, I can only hope you knew that man had breathed his last twenty minutes before those goons came in."

"Yes, Hans, I did. But I saw no reason to tell Kaiser and his associates of that."

"Nor do I, Johan. Nor do I."

Hans and I realized something that evening. We already knew we were more decent than the SS personnel. We now knew that we were more clever than they were too.

As for Kaiser, I'd passed his test, even though I'd cheated. I could run the camp as I saw fit. More important, he now was a little afraid of me. And as the story spread among the guards and kapos, so were they.

Back in my quarters, I enjoyed a glass of Osten's cognac and aimed my Luger at the portrait of Hitler on the wall. I'd won a small victory.

Nonetheless, I knew Kaiser had eyes in K XII.

8

The Medical Experiments

I requisitioned new shoes and blankets. There wasn't anything I could do about the meager food rations, but a few workers found a little bread and fruit as they entered a factory or returned to a block. Rabbi Yitzchak recovered. He and I prayed together as often as I could risk. I prayed for deliverance and mercy.

Hans and I became friends, and we listened to music and the news in my quarters. We spoke about what the end of the war would bring and what life would be like then. We both knew the war was going badly. By mid-1944, the Allies had landed in France and were moving east. The Russians were coming from the other direction. What would they do to the people who had started the war? What was in store for those in charge of places like Dachau or the ones in Poland? Whatever good I was doing would not count for much amid so much suffering and death. Besides, almost no one knew about it.

One evening, Hans came to my quarters. He did so often enough, but his ashen look told me something was wrong. We sat down with tea—no radio just then. He looked weary, sickened. It took a while before he could talk.

"I go to Dachau periodically for medical staff meetings. Not everyone there is doing regular medical work."

I nodded. "Yes, I've heard of experiments."

"And what have you heard?"

"The experiments concern freezing, burns, and wounds. The subject seems out of bounds. That leads to all sorts of rumors."

"I've heard them too," Hans told me, "but I never believed them. I thought that things were bad enough at Dachau without letting one's imagination run wild to create monstrous nonsense. People are frozen to death. Deliberately, Johan. They are placed in ice water until they die or come close to it. Others are put into compression chambers; then rapid decompression takes place."

"They let guards do this?"

"It's done by doctors. Medical doctors. Rascher's in charge. It's his part of the camp. They call it medical research, and maybe some of it is but very little. It's mainly cruelty, sadism, and savagery, with the false halo of science hovering uneasily over it." He hung his head. It was clear he wasn't finished. "In Poland, it's worse. We received a briefing, complete with photographs. People are cut open while still conscious and sewn together with other people."

I tried to visualize this but couldn't until years later—after the war ended, I saw the photos that Hans saw at Dachau.

"It goes on, day in, day out," Hans said. "More are brought in. There is such a darkness over our country today. Vengeance will come down hard on us."

"I hope when this is over, the people who brought this upon our country will face justice. But you're right, Hans. It will probably be vengeance. Bullets, nooses—"

"We could once be proud of Germany. It has a magnificent past. I don't know our future anymore."

"I hope we have one," I said.

"Johan, please listen to me. There's something we can do about those poor souls in Dachau—at least some of them." He must have seen caution cross my face, but he went on anyway; I owed it to him to listen. "I spoke with a man who administers Rascher's section.

They have numerous people who managed to survive the experiments and are slowly recovering or are near death. They are of no further use, and their fates are assured. He said that we could take some of them. I can requisition them for research here. If they recover, we can put them to work at our factories. As bad as things are here, they're far worse in Rascher's little hell. Osten will never know the story. You know that."

Hans looked at me with an earnest, hopeful look, but I was reluctant at first. We'd already risked our necks and barely stepped away from the ax. Sometimes, however, decency overwhelms caution.

Words came to me. "In a place where there are no men, strive to be a man. In other words, act as a decent person when none is around you."

"*Especially* when none is around you."

"Hans, you astound me at times."

Hans made routine trips to Rascher's section in Dachau and returned with one or two people each time, sometimes more. In time, the numbers totaled several dozen. Many already had been injured and had to be treated at our camp. Despite Hans's efforts, many died from brain damage or infections. Others returned to a measure of health and went to work. Hans and I listened to their stories of what went on at Rascher's building and tried not to reveal our dismay and anger.

There were too many people to remember adequately, though Hans took one boy away from Dachau before he underwent any experiments. He was exceptionally emaciated, even by Dachau's "standards." In fact, he was near death. His listless eyes were sunken into his skull, and his paper-thin skin was a ghastly white. I wanted to know about the poor boy.

"What's your name?"

Silence.

"My uniform doesn't cause many to trust me. They mostly just fear me. But I want to talk to you."

"Jakob," he replied warily.

"How old are you, Jakob?"

"Sixteen."

Hans came to stand beside me, but Jakob's fear remained. Hans examined the boy, and the grim prognosis didn't need any words.

The boy looked at his physician. "I think I'm going to die."

I'd seen many people lose weight and hope before going into the descent. It was especially hard to see this in a boy who should have been going to school and playing football.

"You're doing well, Jakob," I told him. "I want you to keep up the struggle."

"You are young; you can make it," Hans added.

"But I am very weak. I can hardly speak."

"We're going to give you better food here," I said. "In a few days, you'll be better."

"Will there be—"

"No experiments here, Jakob," I assured him.

"What then?"

Instead of answering, I changed the subject. "Where are you from?"

"Dresden."

"What did your father do in Dresden?"

"He was a rabbi."

I didn't think it likely, but I asked anyway. "Was his first name Yitzchak?"

Jakob looked at me with recognition and hope.

I walked up and down the shop floor in the usual manner, asked a few official questions of the Aufseher, and then found Rabbi Yitzchak at his station. Amid the din, I asked if the lathe was working properly.

He said it was, but he knew something was up.

"Do you have a son named Jakob?" I asked.

He motioned with hand to ear that the noise was too much.

I leaned over and shouted as loud as I dared. "Jakob! Jakob! Do you have a son by that name?"

His eyes told the story.

That evening after roll call, I ordered a guard to bring Yitzchak to the infirmary. I finished a few administrative matters and headed there too. Yitzchak was sitting beside his son in joyous reunion. The entire ward was riveted but quiet. Jakob soon tired and lay back listlessly. His eyes closed.

"Coma," Hans said.

The word fell hard on the father. He told of being separated from his family in Dresden. He'd diligently asked about them from other inmates, especially those just in from other camps. I knew of those inquiries and hoped the best for all of them.

"I have to stay with my son. May I stay?"

I looked to Hans. He made a cursory checkup and placed Yitzchak on an adjacent cot.

I returned the following day. Jakob was still unresponsive. His father prayed in Yiddish a traditional prayer for the sick. I knew it by heart, in Hebrew and Yiddish, and I stood next to the rabbi.

A moment later, Hans motioned me into his office and closed the door. "You were praying along with the boy's father. How is it that you know Jewish prayers?"

I thought I'd been saying the Yiddish to myself, but evidently, I'd moved my lips. "I took a course in comparative religion at university a few years back. Most Yiddish words come from German. I might have been just echoing what I heard from the old man."

"You have to be careful, Johan. We see eye to eye on many things, but we cannot be too accommodating. Not me, not you. Too dangerous. We must act within limits at all times."

"We both know what's going on," I said. "Senseless killings. Cruel experiments. These are stains on our country."

"True enough," Hans agreed, "but my question stands. How did you come to know Hebrew?"

"I also know a few Lutheran hymns. There is no treason in knowing other religions. It might do us all good."

"I suppose. It was just baffling to hear you speaking that tongue. Frankly, it was disconcerting too."

"As Germans, we are obliged to help where we can. Who knows? It may go easier for us after the war."

"Perhaps. One last thing, Johan. Be more careful from now on. Watch what you say and which language you say it in."

Hans brought a Catholic priest from Rascher's section. Father Jon had been sent to Dachau for hiding Jews on church property. His faith also told him that the Lord had delivered him from Dachau and that we were all in God's hands. What went on at the main camp and at K XII did not undermine his faith. It was all part of God's plan, a test of our faith. I didn't know whether he had such beliefs beforehand, or they came to him as a refuge from insanity.

Yitzchak and Jon, rabbi and priest, Jew and Catholic, prayed for Jakob. Hebrew intermingled with Latin, Yiddish with a southern German dialect. I was reminded of my thoughts on hearing Emilie sing that first night in her church. People of different faiths united in common purpose, praying to the one God, praying for the good. It seemed like a dream—or my own refuge from what was around me, but it made me feel good and have hope.

I bowed my head for a moment and then left for roll call.

The next evening, Jakob was still in a coma. His father sat nearby. Father Jon prayed over the sick boy, though he too looked exhausted.

A commotion at the entrance alerted me—heavy boot heels, two men. It was Osten, accompanied by a guard hefting a machine pistol. Osten was usually in his cups by that hour, but he'd occasionally head out for an inspection, sober or not, to keep everyone on their toes and convince himself that he was the kommandant. I'd encountered the guard before. He was crueler than most of his peers and eager to please superiors. He brandished his MP-40 with a clear swagger, as though it was a mechanical extension of his dark soul.

The sick lay in fear. I had to snap to attention and think of a way to explain the scene.

"Untersturmführer Ludwig, a good evening to you," Osten said.

"Obersturmbannführer Osten."

Osten came up to the priest. "What's the meaning of this?" The question was laced with sarcasm and ill omens.

"The Lord and his son, Jesus, will forgive you all for this," the priest said. "This young man is in a coma because of your kind, and I am praying for the Lord to save him." His words were true and courageous but also costly.

The guard was angered. "We do not allow prayer for Jews! And I know how to stop it!" He raised his MP-40 and fired a short burst into Jakob. Two or three 9 mm rounds hammered into his frail body and ended his struggle. His father groaned and slumped back in despair.

Osten was annoyed that the guard had acted without his order but not overly so.

Father Jon was enraged. "That was one of God's creations! You are a murderer, and you will be judged for it! I shall pray for this poor boy. You should pray for mercy when your time comes, as it inevitably will."

He knelt and wept as he prayed, unaware the MP-40 was being trained on him now. Another burst struck the priest in the back of the neck and head. He crumpled to the floor, blood spread across the floor.

Hans gasped. I did as well.

Osten became angry, something he did not ordinarily do. "Damn you, that's enough! I give the orders here, do I not?"

"Herr Kommandant, these Jews—"

"Soldier, if I don't keep you on a shorter leash, we'll have no one to work here." Osten then turned to me with a puzzled expression. "What has been going on here? A priest, a sick Jew, and my second-in-command are all here in this room. What drama was playing out in my camp?"

"I only just arrived. I allowed the priest to visit the sick. It helps get a few people back on the assembly line."

"He was also a criminal who hid Jews," the guard snarled.

I glared at him and summoned my own rebuke. "Soldier," I said icily, "never again speak impertinently to me or any superior. You should not have shot that man. The Jew, yes, but the priest was a German. Misguided and criminal but not an eternal menace. He was a Catholic—as am I! You will refrain from killing people without a direct order from the kommandant or me; otherwise, you'll be severely punished, versteh?"

The guard was embarrassed and cowed. Osten was impressed and a little cowed himself.

"I have to agree," Osten said, almost meekly. "Now let's be on our way to the perimeter. And do put the safety back on your weapon. Enough shooting for the night. Good evening, Johan. Please return to whatever it was you were doing."

The ward was silent, save for the inmate orderlies who cleaned up the gore and began to place the bodies on a gurney.

"Not yet," Rabbi Yitzchak whispered. His eyes were tearful but strangely accepting. I knew what he wanted. "I must say the kaddish for my son and for this brave priest."

I motioned for the orderlies to wait and the prayer began. I said the words in my head and at the conclusion said *amen*. So did Hans. The orderlies placed the poor souls on a gurney and took them to a pile of corpses behind the infirmary. The next day, they'd be taken to a crematory and sent to the sky.

I filled out a report of the incident and had the guard sent away from K XII. I wrote that he lacked discipline and respect for superior officers. Osten read the report and sent it up to Weiter at the main camp. Weiter, for one reason or another, wanted the guard out of the entire Dachau system.

Osten later told me that the guard had been sent to Sobibor—an extermination camp in Poland. I knew about the place in general terms. I learned more about it over the years, and I'm still learning. That guard belonged at Sobibor.

Rabbi Yitzchak remained in the infirmary for another day on my instructions, but he did not regain his desire to pray, eat, or interact with those around him. He and I spoke about religion, which I explained to Hans was related to my college interests. I wasn't a medical doctor, but I'd seen the downward spiral before, and the signs were clear in front of me. Hans's professional view was no different from mine. He also thought that atrocities were being done in the camps and was determined to help inmates in any way he could.

Hans continued rescuing inmates from Rascher's medical experiments at Dachau. He showed me a twelve-year-old girl, newly arrived from the main camp. Her head was swollen to an alarming size and sickeningly misshapen. Her face was badly bruised, and her eyes bulged from their sockets. She lay listlessly on a cot. She looked at us, but whatever emotions she had were hidden by swelling and discoloration. I'd seen many bad things in the last four years, and this ranked high.

"Tzivya was in a decompression experiment," Hans explained. "She was placed in a chamber; air was pumped in and then rapidly drawn out. Blood rushed to her head. Too much, too fast. Dachau thought she'd die soon, so I offered to bring her here. Naturally, they had no objection. I'm trying a series of medications and therapies to ease the swelling."

"Our own experiments, then," I said.

My words were ill-advised; my rebuke wholly deserved.

"God dammit, that's unfair, Johan! It's experimental, but it's designed to truly help her. That's more than Rascher can say. Bear in mind that by treating people experimentally, I'm protecting us from charges of helping inmates—helping Jews. As you know, that's frowned upon these days. Remember your training? Bear that in mind before you ever again compare me to Rascher!"

"I am truly sorry, Hans. I am just so angry about what's going on in Dachau." My mind searched for a way to do more about the Dachau experiments but nothing came. I could only hope for a day of judgment. I wanted to speak with the girl and comfort her. "Tzivya, can you speak? How do you feel?"

"My eyes hurt. I can't see," she answered. Her voice was frail but had the sweetness of a young girl. "Everything is so dark and blurred."

"The swelling is coming down, Tzivya," Hans said soothingly. "You're actually doing well. We're helping you get better."

"I'm going to live?"

I spoke in as fatherly a voice I'd ever uttered within those fences. "Yes, you are. I'll see to it. Rest, Tzivya. Get some rest."

She nodded quietly.

In a few days, the swelling and discoloration on Tzivya's face had gone down considerably. In time, Hans determined that there was no brain damage. She was eating better and was occasionally heard giggling as she spoke with others.

I found her standing beside Rabbi Yitzchak one day. He was still listless.

"What's happened to him?" Tzivya asked me.

"His son was murdered before his very eyes. Dr. Tauber can't get him out of this."

"What's his name?"

"Rabbi Yitzchak Rosenblatt."

As she leaned over the rabbi's cot, his eyes opened grudgingly, and she smiled sweetly and consolingly. "I am Tzivya. My father is a rabbi. I haven't seen him for a long time, and I don't know if I'll ever see him again. I hope I do, though."

He didn't respond.

"I am sorry you lost your son. My father's name was Rabbi Nachman. I enjoyed going to schul with him every Friday night for Shabbat prayer. I liked watching him in front of his community. I miss those times. Will you say the Shabbat prayer for me someday, please?"

His eyes showed comprehension, but he offered no reply.

"My father said our faith is the strongest thing in the world. No one can break it, and it doesn't matter what has happened to us. When my mother was murdered, I cried out loud. An SS man pulled his gun and shot her. She fell to the ground, bleeding. My father held her to his heart and, with tears in his eyes, said, 'Ha Shem gave, and Ha Shem took away. May the name of the Lord be blessed.' I know your son was taken away. He is with the Lord now. Don't worry anymore. You're needed here."

Rabbi Yitzchak's eyes showed life. He tried to form words, failed, but tried again. "You are a very wise young girl. Your name again?"

"Tzivya."

"Yes, Jakob is with the Lord now. There is no reason to be sad. Thank you for reminding me of this. I promise to pray with you soon."

Tzivya lay her head on his shoulder.

Amazing things happen in even the darkest places. Rabbi Yitzchak lost a son but gained a daughter. They spent as much time as they could together and talked of family and religious passages. On Friday, he conducted the Shabbat for her and a few others.

I wondered if Sophia would ever have the experience of a Shabbat again. There was a time when I thought the Reich would see its campaign of destruction through, but its end was on the horizon.

Tzivya healed rapidly and, as best as Hans could tell, completely. This was welcome, but it presented problems. She'd leave the relative safety of the infirmary and enter the work camp. Fortunately, she had a friend in high places.

I placed her in the women's factory. She helped the seamstresses by bringing material and taking completed tunics and the like to a storage room. Rabbi Yitzchak had been a tinkerer of sorts back in Dresden, so I put him in the same factory, where he kept the rows of Pfaff sewing machines in good working order. I cautioned him about showing excessive attention to Tzivya, as it might encourage abuse from the *Aufseherinnen*. This opened two places at Dr. Tauber's infirmary for the victims of experiments at Dachau.

Other camps were losing workers and productivity because of typhus and other diseases that came from cramped, unsanitary conditions. K XII fared a little better. Our prisoners were in somewhat better health than those in nearby subcamps, but my pride was tempered by the knowledge that we were producing more war matériel.

Osten and I were highly regarded. We were exemplary servants of the Reich. I was promoted to *Obersturmführer.* I knew Osten was crocked half the time, but reports sent up to Berlin made no mention of it.

In the fall of 1944, we received weekly briefings that boasted of great tactical decisions and impending offensives, but we saw the maps. Each week, the Allies moved ahead. The Siegfried Line had been breached. Aachen had fallen. New guards came in from Waffen SS units. They'd been wounded too badly to return to combat. Their pained limps and stricken faces told the tale.

Only true believers thought the war was still winnable. Those who'd lost the faith kept their mouths shut or whispered in private.

The war dragged on, and K XII continued to expand. More workers, more blocks, more supplies. And more work for the kommandant and me—mostly me. We received more guards and kapos who had been criminals. I made it clear to them that arbitrary killings interfered with production. In time, though, they could see that Osten was laxer in that regard, and periodic lectures on the Final Solution were a green light. It all depended on who was present and who was not.

Poor Hans had to make grim decisions about new prisoners—the elderly, the sick, and, of course, the children. It became a weekly ordeal for him, and his faculties suffered. Sleep did not come easily most nights; not at all on many of them. We talked about a way to prevent people from going through the ordeal of a train journey to a death camp in Poland. He mentioned a store of lethal substances and looked to me. I authorized him to act as he saw fit.

The only things I could look forward to were the short visits home. Sophia was an absolute delight. She was beginning school and learning to write. On some visits, we'd go to her church for a recital. My darling Sophia would sit by my side as we watched her mother sing with her choir. Many of the singers and musicians were older men by then.

One night, not long after we arrived home, a blackout came, and sirens wailed. Allied bombers were on their way. We scurried to basement shelters as Flak cannons started to fire, perhaps using 88 mm rounds that had rolled off the line at K XII. Powerful booms were soon heard as the bombs fell. Thankfully, none fell too close. Sometimes, though, the very ground shuddered, and windows were on the verge of shattering. From then on, I had to worry about my family paying for our country's evil.

My inspections were intentionally unpredictable, of course, lest the guards and kapos let things slide. I paid special attention to the women's factory. One afternoon, the Aufseherin greeted me fawningly and offered to accompany me. I told her to stay put. Not everyone there could hear me coming amid the noise of feet trundling rows of sewing machines.

I saw a girl struggling with a male guard, Soldat Horst—a stocky, slovenly man. His vile nature had caused him to run afoul of me in the past. He'd beaten and even killed inmates, but Osten never supported me against him. That afternoon, he was trying to have his way with a young girl—Tzivya. I flew into a rage.

"Soldat!" I shouted from right behind him.

He let her go and snapped to attention. "She wasn't working hard, sir. I was merely trying to get her to do her work properly."

"I've warned you about this before, have I not?"

"Yes, sir."

As I slowly drew closer, trying to convey authority and wrath, I could smell cheap schnapps. "You are drunk!"

"Sir, I apologize. But this one's so pretty. I wanted to have a little fun. You're a man. Surely you understand!" An idiotic smile formed on his face, as though he and I shared a common bond in a fraternity of depravity.

"You are a disgrace to the SS! You well know the rules. You do not have 'fun' with my workers, and you do not report to your duty station intoxicated. March yourself to the administration building, and wait for my arrival. *Schnell*!"

He gathered his helmet and weapon and headed out. I looked to Tzivya, who was collecting herself.

"I am sorry. He grabbed me. I tried to stop him. Thank you, thank you!"

"He'll not bother you anymore. Just finish your shift, and get back to your block."

I met with Osten on the matter. He was in his usual state, maybe more so that day. He shrugged his shoulders and said that the guards were away from their sweethearts and deserved a little leeway with the girls. Pressing the matter was useless. I saluted and left.

There was always paperwork and staff meetings and lectures from the Berlin faithful. It occupied too much time. I couldn't be everywhere, and I certainly couldn't protect everyone. The machinery ground on. Maybe some of the guards knew the end was coming and let up, but not all of them. Not Horst. I made it clear to the officers and NCOs that he was not to be assigned to the women's factory.

A week or so later, I came across Tzivya in a panicked state. Her face was scratched and her clothing torn. Amid the din of sewing machines, she pointed to a storage room. Rabbi Yitzchak stood there, holding a large pipe wrench. An SS guard lay sprawled on the floor, motionless. It was Horst. The story formed readily in my mind. The details were supplied.

"He's come at me several times. Smiling, leering. Today, I told him to stay away, but he laughed. I said I was only twelve, but that only made him crazier."

The rabbi spoke up, his hands shaking in anger. "He was fondling her, then pulling her to the floor. I came from behind and brought my wrench down hard. He turned suddenly, and the blow hit him right on the forehead. He writhed for a moment or two. No more. If someone comes to kill you, rise up, and kill him first."

Horst's head had a deep gash from hairline to nose. His eyes were lifeless, and there was no pulse.

"I did it. I'll confess and face the inevitable. No harm should come to anyone else," Rabbi Yitzchak said in steady voice.

"I'll handle it. Back to work now, both of you."

I barked at the Aufseherin to run to the infirmary and tell Dr. Tauber I wanted him here. There was an important case that required his help.

Hans arrived very fast. He breathed heavily as I pointed toward the body on the floor.

"I found him like this, Hans. Alas, no one saw what happened. I think he had an accident, but I, of course, defer to your expertise."

Hans leaned down and made a cursory examination. "Ah, poor fellow. Yes, I think you're quite right. An accident. The cut on the forehead suggests a hard fall to the floor."

"He was known to drink while on duty. Perhaps that played a role."

"I do smell schnapps, now that you mention it. I'll have to write up a report."

"Ach, so much paperwork. Sorry to call you away from the infirmary."

"I'm here to help, Johan. You know that."

"Indeed."

Osten read the report and sent it up the chain of command. He asked that the part about alcohol be removed.

9

The Birds

The Reich opposed, rounded up, imprisoned, and killed millions. Most were Jews, but the Reich also wanted to rid itself of other people—Gypsies, Jehovah's Witnesses, the handicapped, and homosexuals. They all came through the main gate at K XII.

Fritz and Bruno were brought in from Munich in a group of prisoners who'd been through a judicial process—not a fair trial but a procedure run by Nazis or by judges who felt obliged to follow the Reich to the letter of its laws, no matter how wrongheaded or murderous they were. The two men had been in the main camp but were sent to K XII.

They were assigned to the same block and work detail. They were cheerful and inseparable. It eventually became clear that they were homosexuals. Today, we'd use the term *gay*, but it was never used in that context back then. Some inmates might have detested them for their sexuality, but I don't think it was widespread. They were all in the same boat. As for the guards, most of them despised all prisoners, regardless.

Fritz and Bruno were especially humorous and obliging, so maybe that helped them get along. Tzivya got to know them. The men both had been college students at one point and enjoyed sports, especially football and hiking the foothills to the south. Tzivya told me of a conversation she had with them before lights-out.

"We were never accepted back in Munich," Bruno said, "not by our families or fellow students."

"Same with our church," Fritz added. "They wouldn't let us inside, once they found out. What about your religion, Tzivya?"

"Same-sex relationships are not allowed. But the Bible states that David and Jonathan loved each other to the end."

Bruno and Fritz felt they had a great deal in common with Jews and Gypsies. They were all misunderstood and hated by the mainstream culture.

They attended Rabbi Yitzhak's prayers and listened to his thoughts on the Talmud, Christianity, and life in general. They shared stories of their lives before Dachau, the loss of loved ones, and plans for after the war. They gave hope.

Many inmates warned them to be careful with how they behaved around guards and kapos. If they weren't, they might be killed on the spot. That was true of everyone, of course, but more so for those two.

Bruno was a bird enthusiast. He put together a makeshift feeder near his block and stocked it with seeds he found near trees along the fence or with crumbs from his rations. Two pigeons became regular diners. They'd show up not long before roll call—very punctual, those two; brown and white and rather rotund.

"The two are a couple—male and female," Bruno explained. "They will stay together their entire lives."

After a month or so, the two birds would eat out of Bruno's hands. It was quite a sight. We didn't have movies, but we had the miracle of the birds.

I heard shouting about a hundred meters from me at an evening roll call. A guard was berating and hitting a newly arrived inmate; judging by the sound, the incident was escalating. One could develop an ear for such things. I headed over to break it up. Halfway there,

I saw the guard draw his pistol and aim it at the cowering man, who was old and feeble and bleeding profusely.

Another inmate broke ranks and stood between the guard and the fallen man, shielding him, pleading for calm. Before I could do anything, the guard shot the brave inmate several times. He fell dead. My warning shot came a moment late.

"What's going on here, Soldat?"

"This old Jew refused to stand straight. And that one attacked me. In the name of order, I shot him."

The dead man was Bruno, the gentle keeper of birds. From the back of the formation came Fritz. He tackled the guard and wrestled with him. I saw no reason to intervene. Gaining the upper hand, Fritz got the guard's pistol and shot him.

He knelt near his friend's lifeless body and wept. "What will I do now? What will I do now?"

Everyone knew he had no future—not in that world. Several guards were on the scene, awaiting my directions. I could have tried to convince him to hand me the pistol, but what would his fate be? He knew what he was doing when he shot the guard.

Fritz smiled and put the pistol to his head. His fellow inmates groaned. He fired a round through his head and slumped forward near his friend.

I sighed silently. I had liked them.

I ordered the guards to march everyone to the mess hall for dinner. I stood there and said a silent prayer for them. I ordered two kapos to get a cart and take their bodies to the pit and place them side by side.

I passed the bird feeder every now and then but never saw the two pigeons again.

There were roll calls for inmates, of course, but also roll calls for the officers, guards, and kapos. One morning, a guard came up missing. I remembered him, if barely, as young and quiet. He did his job without the cruelty in which the others enjoyed partaking. I spoke with a few of his fellow guards, but no one had seen him since he'd done a perimeter patrol the previous night, which he'd done alone. Another insisted he had gone to his place of duty the following day.

I didn't worry. Soldiers headed into town for a drink or tryst and showed up later. A minor disciplinary procedure would settle the matter.

After a couple of days, the guard was still missing. Osten saw the notation and took interest. That meant I was to look into it. I ordered a thorough search of the camp and surrounding area, including the pit. Local police were notified as well. Was he in one of their jail cells after a night of revelry? The police all said no.

A week later, another man disappeared. This time, it was a young, zealous officer. There was another search of the camp and more calls to local police. Nothing. Osten forwarded a memo to Dachau. I knew what that meant.

Two SS officers, accompanied by three soldiers, drove into camp and asked for the rosters and names of the missing men's closest friends. They conducted their own interviews and beat around the woods outside the wire. They didn't find anything either.

I was summoned to the main camp for an unrelated matter. A junior officer named Kurt Hauser took my place and gave me a full account of what happened the following day.

The team attended the next morning roll call and said that unless someone came forward with information about the missing men, there would be fearful consequences. No one stirred. The warning was repeated but with the same result.

"As you wish," the officer in charge said with a dramatic shrug. He then looked over to his underlings. They picked out ten inmates at random, led them over to the side, and cut them down with MP-40s. Gasps and shudders came from the ranks.

The matter was referred to the Gestapo, and Otto Kaiser arrived.

"Johan, Johan, Johan, what is going on here? Two of your men vanish into thin air. It looks bad to the higher-ups. They worry; they call me."

"I have no idea yet, Otto. We searched high and low and talked to the police in nearby towns. No one knows a thing. Soldiers sometimes run off and hide with their families." I held off adding "until the war's over."

That was my suspicion—the two men sensed the war was lost and wanted no more of the SS. I couldn't blame them, but neither could I follow them. Otto stared at me and at my new rank. My superior height may have helped too.

"I'll give you one week to get to the bottom of this. After that, I'll have to conduct my own investigation. Higher-ups, Johan."

That meant dozens of people beaten and interrogated and more people shot down to show resolve.

"Your investigation is not to interfere with my camp's operation, Otto, old friend."

He stared at me again, this time with that familiar look of suspicion that I'd intermittently seen since I was a civilian in Berlin.

I breathed in deeply to expand my chest. After all, I was the second-in-command in this camp and with excellent reviews from Berlin.

Otto's authority deflated, though not entirely. "One week, Johan. One week, my friend."

I spoke again with the officers and men; no results. I asked Rabbi Yitzchak, but he had no knowledge of the matter. I sensed that even if he had, he would not have told me. At times, he saw me simply as another SS officer. I asked a few workers on the line, but they only shook their heads. Why would they care about a few missing tormenters?

A third young guard went missing. I didn't relay that information to Kaiser.

Hans arrived at my quarters with a bottle of cognac. "You need to relax." He poured two glasses and sat down.

"I'm getting nowhere, Hans. Three men can't just disappear without a trace for no reason. It hasn't happened in any other camp. I've checked. I thought they might have all deserted, but they don't fit the pattern of loners. Nor are their families in any special danger. Nor did they disappear at the same time of day."

"So none of them vanished at night?"

"Right."

"That means something happened to them during duty hours."

"Right again, Hans. If you're going to run away, you do it at night. And during the day, these men would have been armed. How did they get overpowered or killed while armed? And where are their weapons?"

"The only way someone can overwhelm an armed soldier is to pretend to be friendly or harmless and then strike. This leads us to two alternative scenarios. One of our people is doing it—"

"Or an inmate," I finished for him. "A clever, daring inmate."

"Soldiers have quarrels over girls and money, but it's hard to say three disappearances in so short a time are due to barracks tiffs."

"It seems, Dr. Tauber, we have a killer inmate in Kaufering XII. A clever, daring killer inmate. They all have the motive to kill us, save for a few. But most of them want us dead. So an inmate befriends or tricks one of us while alone; then, *wham*! The inmate strikes quickly and effectively, hides the body, and goes back to work."

"Johan! I think cognac has helped you think clearly for a change."

"The clear thinking came from you," I said. "Such detective skills are worthy of a *krimi*, a crime thriller. Perhaps you should transfer to the Gestapo."

"So much for your clear thinking. And no more of my cognac for you. One more thing, Johan. You should have the guards walk about in twos till you solve this crime."

"Come, come. I ordered that this morning."

I questioned the camp personnel from another angle and learned that two of the missing had raped women, and the third had killed one, probably for resisting. I focused on the women's plants. There were three of them by this time. I walked through each, alone but, of course, armed and wary.

The women went about their work, occasionally casting furtive glances my way. Nothing suspicious in that. Only a few knew of my occasional intermittent help. The rest saw my uniform and feared me. My increased presence continued for several days. There were fewer furtive glances but no leads.

In the back of a tunic factory was an area where one or two women folded the finished uniforms, packed them into boxes, and stacked them on a loading dock. A young woman was there whom I hadn't noticed before, not at the plant, roll call, or evening free time. Even in prison garb, she was strikingly beautiful. She looked my way and smiled sweetly. Something inside me awakened, and I decided to chat with her.

"Everything is moving along smoothly, young lady. Wonderful to see that. I don't remember you. And what is your name?"

"I am Luka Grunfeld." Another smile.

It felt as though we were in a coffee shop far away in an entirely different time. And in quite different apparel. I must admit I was attracted to her.

"A beautiful name and a most appropriate one." That came more spontaneously than I'd expected.

She cast her eyes downward shyly. "Are you an important officer? I don't understand much about the army and uniforms, but it looks to me like you are."

"I'm second-in-command here. You must have seen me in the morning. Where are you from, Luka?"

"Munich."

"A wonderful Bavarian city. I've been there many times."

"Yes, it is lovely."

"Carry on, please. Don't let me disturb you."

"I'm sure you'll see me again."

"No doubt, no doubt."

She looked at me invitingly and then returned to work. My vanity was in play. No doubt about that either.

That evening, back in my quarters, I thought about the encounter. She was happy in her work and alluring to an SS officer.

I watched roll call the next morning and looked for Luka. It took a while in the morning mists, but there she was. Off she went to the uniform factory. I leafed through the rosters, walked through a plant or two, and then headed for the loading dock—somewhat eagerly, I must add.

"Good morning, Luka. And how are things this morning?"

"Oh! Good morning! How nice to see you again so soon. I am doing well, thank you."

So much energy in the room. So many possibilities.

"I've brought you some bread in case you'd care for a nibble. I suppose the rations aren't all they could be because of the war."

"You are too kind," she said and then asked as leading a question as has ever been posed. "Are you this kind to your wife or girlfriend?"

My answer was ready. "I am married but, well, we are not getting along lately. The war, you know. Most likely, we'll separate soon."

"I was once married." She averted her eyes and became distant. She suddenly looked at me angrily. "Then all this came! My husband was killed—by your soldiers! We were herded from our house, and they shot him right there! How long were we man and wife? All of a month! A month!"

"I am sorry," I murmured as I pondered her sudden shift in emotion.

"Oh, you're sorry! How touching! How touching indeed! They were your soldiers—SS, like you. You drink with them and laugh with them. And more of us die from them."

She tossed a pile of uniforms into a box and calmed herself. It looked like she was stifling a sob. Serenity returned in an instant and with it, allure. "But those are old things best left out of things now. You're different. Much nicer, more charming."

We gauged each other for several moments. I was on to something.

"You know, Luka, we are not allowed to—well, it's forbidden."

"Yes, I know. But life goes on in between things and around things and underneath things. Special things." She took my hand and pressed it to her breasts—ample, despite the rations.

My eyes lifted from her breasts to her eyes. They were bewitching but crazed. I ran my hand through her hair and sighed. "Alas, I have some matters to attend to today. But we shall see each other again tomorrow."

"I'll be waiting."

"I'm sure of that."

"Hello, Johan! Nice of you to come by."

"Ah, Luka, dear Luka. I've brought you more bread. Let's take a break. I'm sure the Aufseherin won't mind."

"Ah, so you've put a spell on her as well!"

"I have that effect on women!"

"Come with me, then, my handsome soldier!"

She led me by the hand to a storage room, closed the door, and pressed her lips to mine suddenly, passionately, and, I must say, expertly. As we held our bodies close, I detected a flowery scent. Rather unusual for K XII.

"Where, dear Luka, did you acquire such an enchanting perfume?"

"A previous boyfriend brought me gifts."

Her lips returned to mine as I pieced it together.

"And who might that have been? An officer wants to know which of his men has courageously ventured out before him."

That did it. She knew I was on to her. She drew a cutting knife from her waist and thrust it into my side. I gasped as the blade drove home but was able to knock her down and draw my Luger. She tried to get up, but I kicked her back down, sending the knife to the ground a half meter away from her. She became strangely calm, resigned to what she must have been certain was coming.

"So it was you," I said.

Her eyes filled with defiance and hatred, though the rest of her was strangely still. She was about to speak her piece, and I decided to listen; nothing would surprise me at that point.

"Of course it was me. *You* killed my husband, my parents—everyone! *You* raped me too! Over and over. I'm pregnant now, and I don't even know which one of *you* is the lucky father."

"Luka, I'm not what you think."

"I know exactly what you are!" She grabbed the knife and plunged it into her abdomen repeatedly. Each thrust brought a weaker cry from her and more horror inside me. She fell back, with blood spreading rapidly across the floorboards. "I don't want this life anymore. This is my way out. The first man I killed raped me every day in this room. I pretended to enjoy the last one; then I plunged my knife into him at just the right moment. Ecstasy for both of us."

Life was emptying swiftly. She was cold and frightened. I shoved the knife away and held her hand. She looked at me forlornly. "Why is this happening? Are you a believer?"

"I was raised an Orthodox Jew."

"More lies!"

"It's true. Horribly true—one of many things I can never explain. I didn't want any of this."

She believed me. She held my hand as tightly as she could and continued looking into me. Pain, fear, regret, and need came across her face. "I always dreamed of dying with a kiss ... my husband ... or someone with good in him."

She trembled as life ebbed away. With tears in my eyes, I fulfilled her request. Her lips were warm and shaky. A moment later, she released her last breath.

Such a beautiful young woman. Her abilities, her possibilities, her passions, and her life had gone to waste. I wanted to shout as loudly as I could and kill every Nazi I came across, from that room to the gates of Dachau.

Instead, I sat alone and wept.

There was still work to be done on the case. There were three dead guards to find. I knew the culprit and the scene of the killings. Not far away was a decrepit barn from the days when the area was a farm. The stench hit me the instant I opened the door. The bodies were lying in disarray in a corner, covered with rancid hay and old planks. She'd had help getting them there. No doubt about that. I went to the infirmary for my wound.

Kaiser was impressed. He praised my detective work and wrote a glowing letter of commendation for my file. The final sentence read, "Would that we had more men like Johan Ludwig in the Gestapo."

A medal came my way. I stood at attention as someone from the main camp pinned it on and praised me. I hoped for a day when those SS and Gestapo monsters were lined up and shot. I imagined myself both in the firing squad and alongside the damned.

10

Fahrenzhausen

Kaiser and I established a degree of collegiality. He might've considered it friendship, but I never did. I despised him and his boorish anti-Semitism and idolatry of Nazism. Whatever unofficial interaction I had with him was based not on common interests or experiences but on the need to deceive him. By late 1944, I thought I'd been entirely successful and had no reason to fear him. I was also weary.

There were many moments of despair and self-loathing, when I was sure I'd be killed by Allied troops in a few months. That led to lack of caution and to bouts of self-destructiveness. A little drinking with Kaiser almost brought disaster.

"All's well at K XII, Johan. So well ordered. While other subcamps lag behind, yours leads the way. Discipline isn't as strict as we'd like, but as long as the matériel pours out, you'll get no trouble from Berlin. Ach, enough of this dreary talk. Let's have dinner and a drink or two. I know a charming place. My driver awaits."

Off we went down dark country roads to a tavern on the outskirts of a village called Fahrenzhausen, no more than ten kilometers from camp. The clientele were mostly officers and local women. Enlisted personnel had their own haunts. A gramophone played bouncy Bavarian tunes, which added to the jovial atmosphere. The owner knew Kaiser and led him to his usual spot. He ordered wine and roast pork for us. I'd had it before; I'd been playing my part for several years by then.

That night, my performance required me to be a convivial fellow officer—one of the boys. The first bottle went fast. Kaiser motioned for another and was promptly obliged. I doubt the vintage was available to all. I had a few glasses. More than a few.

"Johan, Johan, Johan. We should get to know more about one another. Your childhood and upbringing remain muddled to me. It's as though it all went up in smoke!" Kaiser chortled grotesquely.

I laughed too, perhaps a bit genuinely.

"I just don't know about you," he said. "Yes, yes, the camp is run well. It speaks of your dedication."

"I wish my fellow officers had my sense of duty."

"To the Reich!"

I raised my glass and silently toasted the Reich's demise.

"Since the records are incomplete, you'll have to tell me about your boyhood. Everything, Johan. Friends should not have secrets, should they?"

"So long ago. So much has happened since then that it fades into the mists of time."

"You were born in Austria, yes?"

I hadn't gone over my cover story in years, and the wine wasn't helping my powers of recollection. I was quite drunk and, worse, very cocky. "Yes, before it united with Germany. My mother was a housewife and my father had a business of some sort." My speech was slurred, my thinking unfocused.

"There's so much to know about you. Did you go to a regular school? Religious school?"

"A religious school, of course. An outstanding student, I was."

He charged my glass. "Girlfriend?"

"No. No girlfriend. Quite Catholic."

"So you had a dull childhood!" He appreciated his humor more than anyone else did, as is the case with most people in drunken states.

"You could say I was overly studious," I told him.

"And what is your most memorable event from those days?"

I sunk into reverie. My surroundings disappeared, and my judgment did the same. Dammed up thoughts and emotions began to trickle out to my inebriated fellow officer. "Oh, school, sports, reading, bar mitzvah."

"Ah, I see."

"I studied with a prominent rabbi. Rabbi Yechiel, by name. Old and wise."

"Old and wise, I'm sure."

"I had to show up at his house twice a week, exactly at five in the afternoon. He taught me my designated chapter from the Bible. I marveled at his distinctive phrasings. He moved his head from side to side and stroked his beard as he prayed. There was no one like him."

"I'm sure there wasn't." Kaiser was able to look at me but seemed barely conscious by the time the second bottle was gone. Very little was registering for me and Kaiser. He was completely drunk, and I could clearly see it by his incoherent eyes. As for me, I sunk into my own world of the past and completely forgot where I was.

"He was witty too. Not like many dour religious figures. Sometimes he'd nod off during lessons. Well, it's to be expected. He was ninety, give or take a few years."

"Yes. Give or take a few years."

"I admired his vigor at that age, but the naps!"

"Naps. Of course."

"I simply sat there, waiting for him to wake up. After a few minutes, he'd rouse, shake his head, and ask, 'Did you understand?' I'd of course nod and take on a look of respect."

"Ha! You're an excellent storyteller, Johan!"

"After I sang my parashah, everyone looked at me admiringly. Many predicted I'd be a fine religious scholar one day. Oh yes. My father and mother were happy and proud."

"I can imagine. Happy and proud." Kaiser, all of a sudden, stared at me with coherency. "What did you say, Johan?"

"I said that I didn't see back then how schul was good for me. I do now."

Kaiser seemed to be sinking again into his clouds of alcohol. He nodded and poured me another glass.

"You don't like Jews, Otto. You hunt them down. That's why they call you a bloodhound."

"Oh, I am that. I am that. You know, I don't really hate Jews as people. I just despise—oh, I don't know. I despise their ways."

"And so you became a relentless hunter!"

He raised his glass to his wet mouth and stared at me. "I have a nose for Jews. That's why I always thought you were one."

"And you were right, Otto, my friend. The hammer hit the nail on head!"

Before he could utter another word, he leaned forward and slowly slipped down to the tabletop, snorts and whistles issuing crudely from his nostrils.

I finished my meal as he snored across from me. Only when my head cleared did I realize my reckless blathering. I reached for Kaiser's smokes in an effort to think of what to do next and came up with a rushed explanation and practiced it. Evidently, I was speaking aloud.

"What did you say?" a muffled voice came from the face slowly rising from the tabletop.

"What did I say? I said you are drunk, Otto Kaiser! Here's to an unforgettable night in Fahrenzhausen!" I raised my glass toward him.

He reconnoitered the surroundings, slowly recognized them, and called for water. I flicked some of mine on his face, and he welcomed it.

He wiped his face with his dinner napkin and looked deeply confused. "Bar mitzvah? Did you say something about a bar mitzvah?"

I leaned forward. "I knew you'd like my little story, Otto. You fell for it, didn't you? I had you! I had you!"

He was still drunk and barely able to remember the conversation. What little he could recall was fragmented and absurd. It mixed in with past interrogations and passing thoughts of busty barmaids.

"Otto," I said in deep voice, like that in a radio mystery, "I am your Jewish nightmare! How much I've enjoyed playing on your fears! Otto, Otto, Otto. You and I have become best of friends this evening. Here's to many more of them. Alas, it seems we are out of wine just now."

"You are a superb storyteller, Johan. And while I too look forward to more nights like this one, I'm afraid I've reached my limit for the night. You have my word on that."

"I agree. When you begin to doubt your most-accomplished protégée, it's time to call it a night. I suggest you sleep this one off at my quarters. That is, if you don't mind the menorah."

I signaled the driver, who was waiting at the bar, and we helped Kaiser to the car. He slept the entire way back to K XII, snoring loudly, and later collapsed on my sofa. I thought of summoning Hans and asking him to inject Kaiser with something that would make his slumber permanent. It would have been fitting and far gentler than he deserved—or what he eventually got a few months later.

There were more like him in Berlin and in Buchenwald and Bergen-Belsen and a hundred other places. I understood this one. A replacement might prove difficult. Better the Gestapo officer you know, as the saying almost goes.

I covered him with an SS-issue blanket and headed for my room. How stupid I was to get so drunk and shoot my mouth off. Everything could have fallen apart. Over and over, I chastised myself and imagined hell coming down on me and my family. Fortunately, the wine I drank so recklessly in Fahrenzhausen put me to sleep.

The officers of the Dachau system gathered at the main camp periodically for lectures and meetings. We got to know one another's names, hometowns, and levels of cruelty. I was more aloof than the rest. Most thought this was due to an unwavering dedication to the war effort that precluded close friendship. I did nothing to let them think otherwise.

The truth, of course, was that almost all of them were devoted to Hitler and the Final Solution. There were exceptions, but most had little education, manners, or decency. In civilian life, they were ordinary people. In uniform, they were swaggering elitists. My limited contacts with officers of the regular army, the Wehrmacht, made me think they were better educated and more likable. They were by no means admirable; they just weren't sadistic wretches.

We are all social beings, so it was impossible not to have some friends, regardless of surroundings. Kurt Hauser was a young officer who had been at K XII for a year. He and I talked after meetings and at the mess hall, and we established a measure of amicability. One evening, he came by my quarters. His worry was clear. After some preliminary chatting, I asked why he'd come.

"I want your advice on a matter. Nothing to do with the camp. Well, not directly, anyway. It must remain confidential. Extremely confidential. If word spreads—"

"Kurt, please speak your mind. I promise the matter will remain between you and me."

He hesitated but eventually got on with it. "Johan, I have a Jewish girlfriend. I've been hiding her for more than a year now in an apartment not far from here."

I nodded in a manner that urged him to go on, but I had to hide my astonishment.

"There's another thing," Kurt said. "We just discovered she's pregnant."

A delicate issue in normal times, and we were not in such times. A dozen questions raced through my mind: *Has he been sent by Kaiser or someone of his ilk? If not, why is he here? Does he perceive my attitude toward workers as a sign I'm sympathetic toward Jews?*

"I know that you don't agree with what we do here," Kurt continued. "I know it. I need your help. What do you think I should do?"

I'm not sure how long I paused. "Kurt, this is a difficult situation. You know the regulations as well as anyone."

"Of course I know them. But I love her, Johan. I truly do. I'm a good soldier. I do my best. My plant is on schedule and often ahead of it. We want to live and have our baby."

"This isn't something that can be solved today, Kurt. Let me think of a course of action."

"Please don't disclose any of this to anyone. You are the only one I can trust here."

I looked for signs of deceptiveness on his face but saw none. Yet I had doubts. It could be a test. More of a trap, really. Friendship in those days could be both valuable and costly.

I told the story to Emilie on my next trip home. She suspected it was a trap and thought it could bring disaster. Even if I learned the woman was, in fact, expecting, it still could be a trap. We went back and forth as we ate, with our daughter beside us with a small fork and spoon.

"Can you get information about the woman's family?" Emilie suggested. "Parents? Schools?"

At breakfast in the mess hall, I whispered to Kurt, "I need to see your apartment."

Kurt sat back in his chair. No one was close to us. Nonetheless, we whispered and kept emotion from our faces. "Why?"

"It's best to see the situation and meet the young woman. It'll help me assess the situation and form a plan."

My words were defensible in the event of a trap. I was merely investigating the matter, as an officer should.

"I can't," he said after a long pause. "My girlfriend doesn't feel safe with anyone besides me."

"I am your friend, Kurt. That's why you came to me. If you want my help, I will need to see your apartment and meet the woman."

He dabbed artificial butter on a heel of rye.

"What's her name, Kurt? Let's begin with that. Surely you can trust me with that."

"Mila."

"Where is she from?"

"Berlin."

"Age?"

"Twenty."

"When can we go to your apartment?"

"I don't know. I'll have to ask her."

"You do that, and let me know. Soon, Kurt. Very soon."

A few days later, we met again outside the mess.

"I don't know, Johan. I don't know. She's frightened."

"I have to know more. What did her father do for a living?"

"Oh, I don't know."

"What does her mother do?"

"I only know her parents are from Austria, same as yours. They immigrated to Berlin many years ago."

"I see."

A dread fell over me. I'd never told Kurt that my parents were from Austria. I was sure of it. The only person who knew the story of my past in Vienna was Kaiser. Now I was sure Kurt was in league with Kaiser. Kurt wasn't hiding a Jewish woman. He was trying to ensnare a Jewish man.

"That's fine, Kurt. It's understandable. Let me think what I can do. I'll check with you as soon as I can."

I ran it through my head, over and over. I was certain it was a charade, and I knew how to prove it. Osten probably wasn't involved. Everyone knew as well as I did that Osten was an unreliable tippler and chummy with me. So I mailed a letter to Kaiser in Munich, referring to an urgent matter regarding the loyalty of an SS officer, and asking to meet him. He set up a meeting a few days later.

My role now required added dimensions. I rehearsed carefully. By noon, I was ready for the performance.

We lunched in my office in the administration building.

"Otto, how long have we worked together now? Four years, I think."

"That is what my notes say."

He barely looked up from his meal, but I kept a pained, earnest look on my face as I went on. "In the SS, we learn to respect our fellow officers. We share a common commitment to fatherland and Führer. The bonds of trust are powerful and enduring. Unfortunately, there are times when a fellow officer steps out of line, perhaps for personal reasons, and we must place duty ahead of friendship."

He kept eating as though I was discussing a minor detail about a factory or the weather. Was he expecting me to report Kurt and simply was uninterested in the process?

"I must reluctantly tell you of a transgression, a rather serious one, involving a fellow officer here. Sadly, he is a friend."

Apparently bored by the melodramatic preface, he motioned with his fork for me to get on with it.

"He has gotten his girlfriend pregnant."

His eyes rolled, and he resumed his meal. "Johan, Johan, Johan. You are too much the Catholic boy. This is hardly a serious issue, only a passing trifle. I've gotten a girlfriend pregnant, and the problem was solved in short order. Your friend may see the advantage in doing the same."

"There's more, I'm afraid. The girl in question is Jewish. He's been hiding her for some time."

He stopped cold. Disgust came across his face. "Who is this officer?"

"Untersturmführer Kurt Hauser."

He seemed to try to remember him but came up blank. "I don't know him. Are you sure of this?"

"Yes, I am. Though he's done something seriously wrong, I would prefer his punishment be limited. He performs his duties very well. It's just that those Jewish girls are able to cast spells on decent men."

"You've done the right thing, Johan. It's a difficult matter with a friend and an otherwise exemplary officer. You will never have to prove your loyalty again."

"Heil Hitler! For the fatherland!"

He saluted and left my office. I'd played my role well but an uneasy feeling suggested that the second act would not go according to my script.

Kaiser summoned me to the administration building two days later. There, in a sparsely furnished conference room, were Kaiser, two Gestapo agents, and Kurt. My friend was ashen.

"Untersturmführer Kurt Hauser, it has been brought to my attention that your girlfriend is going to have a baby. Ordinarily, such a thing is good for the Reich. It strengthens our Aryan blood. But the girl in question is a Jew! That dilutes our blood with that of inferiors and enemies, thereby weakening us. Hauser! You know this!"

Kurt managed to raise his head. He looked sick with fear. He nodded weakly.

"We are leaving now for this nest of yours. Untersturmführer Ludwig will accompany us."

Kurt looked at me with utter incomprehension and muted pleading.

The five of us traveled in two cars about eight kilometers to a row of houses in Vierkirchen. I sat in the back of one car with Kaiser, while Kurt was in the other car with two Gestapo agents. My insides were in knots the whole way.

Kurt pointed to his dwelling and opened the door. The two henchmen stormed in, and a young woman, heavy with child, screamed. Kurt pleaded to spare her. In despair, I couldn't move.

"Untersturmführer Hauser, because of the special considerations put to me by your superior officer, this matter will remain confidential. No court martial, nothing in your dossier, and no further shame upon the SS."

With that, he aimed his sidearm at the trembling woman. The first shot hit her in the forehead, sending her to the floor. Two more followed. I had difficulty breathing and had to make an effort not to pass out. Kurt seemed in shock.

"Now, Untersturmführer Hauser, you will return to your duties a better officer. I hope you have learned from this regrettable episode. Untersturmführer Ludwig, I suggest putting Hauser in the infirmary for the rest of the day. A little rest today and then roll call in the morning. A new day, a new man."

The return to camp was long and quiet. I couldn't think straight. Kaiser patted my shoulder.

"An ugly incident, Johan. You may feel a few qualms but nothing that a complete day of duty won't put behind you. You, of course, did the right thing. You know that."

I felt darkness falling upon me. I felt like a Nazi.

Hans was apprised of what had happened, and he administered a sedative of some sort before leaving us. Kurt lay on a cot, his face conveying anger, betrayal, and grief. If mine did not show deep self-loathing, I was a better performer than I thought.

"I trusted you. I thought you would help us. Why did you turn us in?"

I hoped my eyes conveyed sorrow, though I doubted they ever could. I repeated to myself the ancient commandment against murder, in Hebrew:לֹא תִּרְצָח. I thought of scores of passages from sacred texts.

"Kurt, did Mila have family?"

"Why do you want to know? Do you and Kaiser want to hunt them down too? You've already done your job!" His speech became more slurred as the pill took hold. "They were deported to Poland long ago. She had no one."

"According to the Jewish faith, someone has to say the kaddish for her." I doubted he knew the word. He certainly didn't know what I was thinking. "The kaddish is a Jewish prayer for the dead. It's said to elevate the soul to the heavens." I whispered the prayer I'd committed to memory in my youth, when grandparents and neighbors and my parents left the world. My head was bowed; my tears fell.

"What was that?" Kurt mumbled, almost incoherently.

"It was a Hebrew prayer for the souls of Mila and your baby."

"And how the hell do you know it?"

Guilt propelled me to divulge the story—a guilt that might bring proper punishment. Words were about to come. "I studied other religions in my university days."

The sedative took hold.

Back in my quarters, I realized my effort to save myself was making me one of the people I was eluding. I was wearing their dark uniform, making their weapons, being convivial with them at times, and helping eliminate the people they loathed, in one way or another.

I lay in bed with my Luger. I pulled the magazine and made sure it held bullets. I snapped it into place and loaded a round into the chamber. *Where was this bullet made?* I wondered. *Somewhere in the Dachau system? Or did it come from one of our newer sites in Poland? No matter, no matter now.*

One click—and it would be over. Yes, I'd be banished to hell, but no one seemed more deserving in all of Germany that day. After an hour, I thought of going home in a week, and I put my gun away.

Emilie noticed something wrong as soon as she opened the door. I sat in the living room, smiled briefly at Sophia, and stared straight ahead. I was often enough like that on arrival, as some dark incident possessed my soul, and Emilie gave me time. We had dinner, spoke about this and that, and retired early. Only then did I speak.

"I was wrong, Emilie. I was horribly wrong. Kurt did have a pregnant girlfriend."

Emilie covered her mouth as she began to imagine the rest.

"Kaiser shot her dead. Mother and child both. Kurt was there too."

Emilie wept and muttered "Horrible!" over and over.

"My fault. *Mea culpa*, as Catholics say. Mother and child. *Mea culpa, mea culpa, mea maxima culpa.*" We cried well into the night.

The tragedy hung heavy over us. I felt condemned. For the first time, I felt relief on returning to K XII, though only a small amount. Maybe I belonged there more than I thought.

The mother and child haunted my dreams for years, and they haunt me still. I know when it will end and accept the terms.

11

Dr. Roher

Typhus was spreading through the Dachau system, but there was little, if any, at K XII. Hygiene wasn't good, by any means, but it was better than elsewhere.

Berlin took note of flagging production and sent a team of doctors to our camp—not for the prisoners; for SS personnel. Exams were to begin right after morning roll call, and the first round would be over in less than two hours. More would come in following weeks. Officers first, as was expected.

We joked as we stripped down to our shorts and lined up for three stations. The first doctor asked me several questions about my medical history. The second listened to my heart and tested my reflexes. On to the third, who, to my astonishment, was a striking blonde woman with blue eyes—an Aryan ideal. Her hair was braided around her head in an unusual way that conveyed both professionalism and vanity. She looked familiar to me, and—apparently—I to her.

"Have we meet before, Johan Ludwig?" Her husky, cold voice contrasted with her looks.

I couldn't place her, but if she knew me, she knew Yochanan Berger, not Johan Ludwig. "No, I don't believe we have."

"I am Dr. Roher. Angelica Roher. I'll listen to your lungs and take blood samples. Have you had any rashes recently?"

"No."

"Fever?"

"No."

"Vomiting?"

"No."

"Diarrhea?"

"No."

"Dry cough?"

"No."

Then she looked intently at me in a disconcerting way before returning to the matter at hand. "I'll listen to your lungs now." She stood behind me and put a stethoscope to my back. Her hands moved along my back. My knowledge of medical practice was limited, but her hands didn't seem to be doing anything taught in med school. She had me cough and then turn to face her. Her stethoscope rested on my chest, and she told me to breathe in deeply. "Where are you from, Johan?"

"Berlin."

"I see. This concludes the examination for now. You appear well."

I stood and prepared to leave the station.

"You are a handsome young man, Johan. I'll see you next week."

Try as I did that night, I was unable to place her name or face. The whole thing was worrisome. Someone from my past. Someone who touched me sensuously. Well, another round of examinations was coming—Berlin's orders.

A week later, I stood in front of her again. She smiled professionally. "Any changes in your health? Fever? Rash? Cough?"

"Not at all."

She placed the stethoscope to my chest and told me to breathe in and out. Then she stood very close to me, her face inches below mine, her eyes looking into mine. "I'll be staying in the camp tonight and leaving tomorrow morning. I want to see you tonight."

"Sorry. I am married."

"A marriage isn't a mountain. It can be moved."

Those words! Everything fell into place. Terribly so.

My father's health had deteriorated. He was coughing blood, and the Berlin doctors were at their wit's end. They suggested a pulmonary specialist in *Frankfurt am Main* and gave us a last name and address.

We drove a few hours and arrived at the practice. Forms, waiting room, and then into the doctor's office. The highly regarded doctor, as it happened, was a woman—blonde, blue eyes, and quite fetching. That was highly unusual in 1930s Germany. Her gaze fell upon me immediately, and, in the course of the examination, her gaze returned more than once. Even my parents noticed.

Not long thereafter, she gave a prognosis. "I am sorry to report that there is nothing I can do."

My father cast his eyes downward. My mother was near tears. I asked for clarification.

"Exactly what I said. There is nothing I can do. His lungs are in poor shape and beyond the help of our medical knowledge. He'll not live long. Six months at the most."

After a few moments of cold silence, my mother and I helped my father to his feet and head toward the waiting room.

"Oh, young man—a moment please."

My parents continued down the hallway.

"Young man, would you like to see me at my home tonight?"

The question was shocking, unprofessional, and rude. She'd unfeelingly told us my father's death was assured, and now she wanted to strike up a little romance with his son.

"I have a wife," I said, hiding my disdain.

"A marriage isn't a mountain. It can be moved. You are a handsome man. Do us both a favor, and think about it. Here is my address. It's not far. And it would be very nice."

I thanked her and joined my parents. I disposed of her address in a waste bin.

Years later, here she was at K XII. If I remembered her, she might do the same with me. And if she recalled my family's name, the curtains might come down on my performance.

Try as I did to avoid the next round of examinations, order were orders. So there I stood, in front of Dr. Angelica Roher, formerly of a private practice in Frankfurt am Main.

"Any changes in your health?" She was professional and distant. I wondered if she'd forgotten me or relegated me to a lower category after finding a more eager officer. Maybe an enlisted man. "Pull down your underwear."

That wasn't expected. I'd been through the turn-your-head-and-cough routine countless times, in the service and beforehand, but never with a female doctor. There was the complicating matter of circumcision, which was then rare outside my faith, at least in Germany.

"Pull down your underwear," she repeated.

I reluctantly complied. I'd had an explanation since my days at the Berlin academy.

"As I thought."

"My father was a doctor. He insisted on it for medical reasons. Aren't you going to conduct your examination, Dr. Roher?" I asked coldly and in triumph as I pulled up my underwear.

"I don't need to examine you any further." Her voice was stern and foreboding. "I remember now where I saw you. Yes, I'm sure of it. Perhaps six years ago, a woman brought her husband to my office. An advanced lung illness—a terminal one. There were three people in my office. The husband, his wife, and you. The man's name was Benjamin. That's a Jewish name, isn't it? In my profession, we see many remarkable things. Now I've seen a Jew serving in the SS. A rare case indeed. Something for the journals."

I had to struggle to keep a calm appearance. "You are mistaken, Frau Doctor. I am a proud officer in the Schutzstaffel—a highly respected one. As for your invitation during our last examination, I must say that I'm deeply flattered, but my honor and duty require me to decline, albeit highly reluctantly."

"No, no. I'm not mistaken. In fact, I can prove it, if you like. The paperwork is in storage at home. My record-keeping is at least as impeccable as this honor you claim to have. From there, we can look for your name—your *former* name, that is—in Berlin hospitals. Ah, wait! In the hospitals of Friedrichstadt!"

Hospital records could indeed undermine me. Rudolph had scrubbed my existence from many sources, but I could not be certain of the hospitals. I could be tied to Benjamin Berger.

"I am staying tonight in the guest quarters," she went on. "They are adequate, even comfortable, but I want a little company tonight. Your company. You owe it to yourself to think it over. That will be all for now. Dismissed."

I went about my duties the rest of the day and tried to come up with something. I had to accept her invitation. After that, I'd have to use my resourcefulness.

I arrived at eight o'clock, and she motioned me in. She was dressed casually, even invitingly. I was in uniform. We were both sending signals, though very different ones.

"Would you like something to drink, Johan?"

"No, thank you."

"Well, please have a seat."

She poured herself a glass of white wine and sat next to me on the small sofa. She was even lovelier in casual attire and comfortable surroundings—full lips and softly scented shoulders. A line of sacred text came to me: "Nonsense of the beauty and the lie of the charm" (שקר היופי והבל החן). Nowhere in my life did those words seem more appropriate. Her smile suggested danger; her body, deadliness.

"You know, many men would be more welcoming of this. They would consider it a delight. A very special delight."

"I am a happily married man and an officer with a sense of honor."

"Oh, Johan, please! We have been through that. But I know your secret. And now you and I can have a secret of our own—something not a soul outside this room need know. Not even Ernst Osten. He believes your story about being a devout Catholic and a proud German. And he'd be very angry if he discovered he'd been deceived.

Deceptions can be intriguing, can they not? They can also be fun, Yochanan."

I must have flinched when she spoke my Jewish name. She slowly removed her blouse and skirt and lay back, completely naked.

"Now, kiss my feet."

I couldn't find a way out—or words for that matter.

"Kiss my feet! I'll not say it again."

I knelt and complied. A natural response came more swiftly than I'd have thought.

"Now my knees ... yes, and now my waist. ... And now, dear man, your lips to mine."

I looked into her eyes and was drawn in. I pressed my mouth to hers. The kiss went on. The line of sacred text flew from my mind.

I skipped the next trip home, although out of guilt rather than lust. Angelica made weekly trips to K XII, and the quarters were practically hers. I had to see to it. She convinced superiors that her calling required her to spend additional time there, but it was more a matter of a convenient place for trysts. I was the deputy kommandant and her subservient lover as well.

The iron mistress's knowledge was power, and power was central to her sexuality. She ordered me about, looked mockingly into my eyes, even at intimate moments, and laughed as she called me "Jew boy."

As much as I resented those moments, I confess she was beautiful, alluring, sensual, and artful. Yes, there were evenings when I looked forward to seeing her.

Mornings, I wondered just who I was. I felt sickened by waves of self-loathing and a yearning for an end to it all.

Kurt Hauser and I had professional interactions. It was unavoidable, as he was a junior officer. Orders were given, salutes exchanged—little else. We avoided each other at the mess hall and informal gatherings. Things were broken between us, understandably so but not irreparably so.

He approached me at the mess hall one evening. "Johan—"

"Oh, Kurt. Sit down, please. Have some coffee—or what passes for it these days."

"I thought I'd stop to see how you were. You don't look well. You haven't in a long time."

"Kurt, I want to say—"

"Ach, I don't want to talk about it!"

"I've earned a lot of ill will, and I can understand lasting hatred toward me."

"What's in the past is in the past. We all have to do things we don't want to do. I understand why you did it."

"Actually, Kurt, you don't." I sensed he once again felt the need for friendship here. I felt the same, though I also might have wanted an accomplice. "I want to talk with you about something. Can you come to my quarters tonight?" He stood up abruptly and picked up his hat. "Kurt! Can you please come to my quarters?"

He weighed the notion for a few moments and then nodded.

We sat in the cramped living room and sampled a bottle of cognac that Osten had given me. Neither one of us was a connoisseur, but it was clearly a step above the schnapps and beer we were used to drinking. Neither one of us wanted to revisit the dreadful events of months past, but that hung heavily over us.

"I know you don't want to discuss that day, but it's relevant to why I asked you here. Also, I'd like your forgiveness."

His eyes flared. I expected a thunderous response. A softer one came. "I can't forgive you, Johan. I wanted to marry Mila when the war was over. No, I can't forgive you, not yet anyway."

"There's something I need to tell you. It's related to that. You have to promise me that you'll not tell anyone."

"That sounds familiar. Oh, all right. I promise to keep everything confidential."

I believed him. Or maybe I wanted to believe him, or maybe I didn't care anymore and felt I was due retribution. I finished my cognac and poured another. A few more gulps, and I was ready.

"You probably don't know that Hauptsturmführer Kaiser has long suspected that I'm Jewish and is always looking for ways to prove it."

"Since we're speaking confidentially, I think Kaiser's a bloodthirsty wretch. Everyone does. But why doesn't the bastard believe you're a Catholic?"

I exhaled and closed my eyes. The second round of cognac was gone and a third needed. "The records are—well, incomplete. And they're incomplete because they've been falsified. I was born in Berlin—to Jewish parents."

"You called me here to make light of me? To make fun of Jews?"

"No, no! Not at all! I indeed was born into a Jewish family and raised in the Orthodox branch."

"That's difficult to believe. But all right, all right. Maybe so. How does this relate to what happened?"

"When you told me about Mila, I thought you were working with Kaiser to trap me. If I were Jewish, I'd help or at least be far more receptive to helping. So I called his bluff and went to him with the story. I thought for sure he'd simply chuckle, admit he was behind it, and that would be the end of it."

Kurt thought it through, looked at me long and hard, and tossed back a cognac. I recharged both glasses. With nothing more to add, I gave him time before continuing.

"Instead, Kurt, a tragedy came about. A grotesque tragedy."

"There are so many tragedies unfolding these days. So many unwilling actors."

"I have a wife and daughter. My wife truly is Catholic. If Kaiser finds out about me, he'll kill me and, in all likelihood, my family too."

"Your family's done nothing exceptionally wrong, though your daughter is an *Untermensch*, according to him and his laws."

"He'll kill them for spite, no matter what the laws say."

He nodded somberly and then stood. I thought he was about to leave, so I stood too. Instead, he came over to me and, to my astonishment, hugged me. We cried for Mila and the unborn child. We cried for all the tragedies going on in the world and for the ones around us and involving us.

In the morning, however, I donned the uniform and marched to the administration building. Roll call was coming. A selection too.

Emilie sensed something awry. "You don't come home as often as before. There's distance between us, and it makes me feel terrible. Please tell me what it is."

I lay back in exhaustion. Yes, the drive was longer, owing to damaged roads, but the truth was I felt out of place at home. My list of sins now included routine infidelity.

"I know that terrible things go on down there," Emilie said. "You've always told me about them, at least in general terms. Tell me now."

"The camp is becoming harder on me. Too many bad things recently. It's a burden."

"It feels like there's something more now. Anyway, the war will be over, and all this will be behind us."

"I don't think this will ever go away, Emilie. The killing machine is too big, too monstrous, too effective. I'm part of it. An actor can play a role so well and so repeatedly that he loses a sense of who he is."

"You are not part of it. You are not one of them. You are just trying to protect us. Do you hear me?"

Looking into her eyes and feeling her warmth and love, I felt unworthy and dishonest. It's said that confession is good for the soul, but I'm not sure that's always true.

"There is something. Something that's been bothering me for some time. I've been reluctant to tell you about it."

"You don't have to be afraid. We can get through it. We are one." She started to hum a melody, "Carol of the Bells," the song she was singing when she won my heart an eternity ago. The honesty of her soul pushed me ahead.

I told her of the initial examination by the doctor, my recollection of her in Frankfurt am Main, and what happened from then on—blackmail, trysts, right down to the "Jew boy" routine. She listened silently, her consternation slowly growing.

"If I don't comply, I'm doomed. We all would be doomed."

She lay there numbly for an agonizing few minutes and then left to spend the rest of the night with Sophia. It was the first time she'd ever done so. The rest of my stay was painful.

Not long after returning to camp, the iron mistress summoned me again. To my surprise, I felt an immediate yearning. I knocked on the door gently, and as soon as she opened it, I took her in my arms.

She broke free and glared at me. "What do you think you are doing?"

"I thought you wanted—"

"You thought I wanted you to take me in your arms and drag me into the bedroom like in a tawdry Hollywood movie? No! You do as I command! Klar? Do you think we have a budding romance here? Think twice before acting so rashly, Jew boy!"

"I have received a solid grounding in the race laws of this country, and I will remind you that having sex with a Jew is a serious crime."

That silenced her for a moment. Then, "I'll say you attacked me."

"And just how many nights have I been attacking you now? Several dozen in the last two months? The men in charge will not believe you."

"You are a Jew, and you will be put to death for dishonoring an Aryan woman. You and all your family. I am blameless here. It's the old story—a sad, trusting soul, led into shame by a conniving Jew."

Now I was the one silenced. The scenario was more than plausible.

She suddenly burst out laughing. "Our first spat! Exciting, no? Time for some fun now, Jew boy."

She shed her robe and led me to the bedroom.

Afterward, we lay listlessly and talked as I caressed her soft hair.

"Do you love your family, Yochi?"

"Yes, of course."

"It must be hard to live this double life. You have to do things against your beliefs. We kill Jews in accordance with the directives from above. You push parts of it through every day."

"I have to protect my wife and daughter."

"You are a remarkably strong man, Yochi." She knew the implicit power she had by using that name. "Your wife is Lutheran? Catholic?"

"Catholic. We met at her church and fell in love in a trice."

She lit a cigarette and exhaled in my face. Her face became cold and determined. "That Catholic wife of yours—I want you to leave her."

"What?"

"You heard me! You have to leave her. I want this Jew boy all to myself."

"Oh, Angelica, I have a daughter."

"A *Jewish* daughter. It's only a matter of time until that little secret comes out. And then? *Whoosh!* Off to Auschwitz. Ha! I can keep your identity confidential. I can do that for my precious Jew boy. But I want you to myself. No wife, no daughter. Oh, Yochi, I'm afraid they simply have to go."

"Not possible."

"You're a clever man. Find a way to get rid of them. I don't care how. Send them to another country if you want—Switzerland, Sweden. Who cares? I just want them out of the picture. I'll give you one month. That's reasonable. Very reasonable, I'd say. After that, I'll have them arrested. Your home address is on file somewhere not far from us right now."

"Angelica, please."

"No! You are an SS officer. They don't belong in that life. Face facts, Yochanan. You are a Nazi now, and you belong to the Third Reich and to me, though not always in that order."

"My daughter is four years old. Do you have the heart to murder a child?"

"She is a Jew! I too have received a solid grounding in the race laws of our country. She has no place in today's Germany. And neither will you, if you do not do my bidding. One month."

Sometimes we had to play for time, and this was one of them. I pretended to ponder the idea for a few minutes. "Very well, Angelica. You're right, as always. I'll find a way to get rid of them."

"Good! You'll be happier with me, Yochi. I'll see to it. But do not play me for a fool, my dear. The address is on file."

She pointed in the direction of the administration building.

Kurt and I spoke in low voices, even though we were in my quarters.

"So she's truly deranged, eh, Johan?"

"Deranged and evil—a product of our time, the Aryan ideal in female form."

"I presume you've come up with a plan. Like she said, you are a resourceful fellow."

"Oh, thank you."

"Well, our times force us to do extraordinary things, and the present situation calls for something extraordinary."

"Kurt, I want her out of my life. I want—"

"You want her dead. I see that, even if you don't yet. I have no fondness for these people, as you surely know. I am at your service."

Those words locked us into a silent pact, and we ran a number of scenarios through our heads. Kurt thought faster than I did.

"We can take her outside the camp and arrange an accident. The north road to Haimhausen passes through a wooded area. Invite her for dinner in town. Use her car. Then stop in the woods for a little naughty-naughty. I'll lie in wait."

"Kurt, I'm not sure about this. There is a vast difference between what I want to do and what I can do."

"Don't worry. I can do it if you can't."

I wanted out of an absurd, sadistic, potentially deadly affair, and Kurt wanted vengeance. But on whom? I studied his eyes and concluded that it was not on me, understandable though that would have been.

"I don't have enough words to thank you."

"Don't then. At least not yet. We shall plan it carefully, like good officers. We should try for the coming week. I'll reconnoiter for the right spot. Meanwhile, you must convince her that you have agreed to her plan. Not too quickly and not without qualms. She must feel she's got you in the palm of her hand."

We shook hands. I again searched his eyes and again felt I could trust him.

As he opened the door, he turned to me. "I hate Hitler. He and his detestable system are responsible for the death of Mila and our child. I hate the whole goddam Third Reich!"

I had a soul mate and an accomplice as well. I thought of the renowned commandment but also of the Talmud's wisdom: "If someone comes to kill you, rise up, and kill him first."

I played a new scene in the ongoing performance and convinced Angelica that I saw she was right about my family and accepted my place as her loyal and obliging lover. My words didn't make her happy. She was incapable of that. She did, however, feel power.

One afternoon, I suggested we get out of the dreary camp that night and dine at a small place in Haimhausen. She was delighted and readily agreed.

"Your car, Angelica?"

"Sure."

"There's a secluded area on the way. It's in the woods!"

Her eyes lit up.

I met her a short way outside the checkpoint at the main gate. Darkness was coming as we drove off toward Haimhausen, like two teenagers out on a date. She was at the wheel, of course. We neared the place Kurt and I had decided on.

"Let's pull over for a while."

"You can't wait for tonight, eh?"

I ran my hand along her thigh. "Appetizers come before the main course."

She giggled and pulled over. We kissed aggressively from the start. I peered out occasionally, looking for Kurt. Long minutes passed.

Suddenly, the driver's door jerked open, and Kurt hurled her onto the ground. I hopped out and stood next to him, staring down at her. She realized what was up.

"No, Yochi. Please don't kill me! I'll not do anything! I swear!"

My reluctance made me think of the small amount of fondness I had for her. She lay there like a frightened girl, probably for the first time in years. Her mastery of power and men had fallen apart in a dark woods.

"She's a liar—and you know it," Kurt snarled. "Hurry, Johan!"

The plan called for me to bash her head in with a shovel Kurt brought from camp. Then we'd put her back in the car and run it into a tree. Accidents happened on dark roads. I picked up the weapon.

"No, no! Please, Yochi! You can't do it! It's murder!"

I'd planned my part. I visualized her killing my family and then deployed my anger on her. But even those images couldn't propel me. I steeled myself by telling myself I was an SS officer, but my soul resisted. I'd never killed anyone; I couldn't do it. Maybe it was years of studying the Torah; maybe it was the Ten Commandments that were in front of my eyes; maybe I just couldn't do it. I even thought of the cat.

"Bah!" Kurt spat.

He kicked her flat on the ground and beat her repeatedly with the shovel. Blow after blow fell until her cries ended, and her breathing stopped.

Kurt leaned on the shovel and caught his breath. "Be strong, Johan! Help me finish this."

We put the body behind the wheel, poured gasoline inside and on the engine, and pushed it downhill until it crashed into a tree. Kurt lit a cigarette, walked down to the car, and flicked it into the car. Flames erupted with a soft boom; smoke billowed skyward. There might have been a few screams since she probably was still alive when we set the car on fire.

We drove back in Kurt's car. Very little was said. He dropped me off at my quarters, and with the help of a sleeping pill, the evening was done.

The next day, the officers' mess was abuzz with word of the accident.

"Unfortunate."

"Good doctor."

"Bad luck."

"Easy on the eyes."

I apprised Emilie on my next visit. She was distant. My home was no longer a refuge. Sophia was the only source of emotion for Emilie and me. We took pleasure in seeing her learn and grow, unaware of the personal and political turmoil all around her. How I envied her. I wanted to live in a world innocent of National Socialism and war and camps and doctors and accidents.

My sleep was repeatedly ended by dreams of falling into a dark, bottomless abyss.

12

The American

The cruel medical experiments went on and on at Dachau. By mid-1944, the notorious head of that section, Sigmund Rascher, was gone. He'd been discovered to have falsified his fertility research, and Himmler had him shot. Had he not, the Nuremberg trials certainly would have found him guilty and sent him to the gallows.

Hans continued to rescue handfuls of people from Dachau. One of the fortunate was a black woman. She was covered with bruises and welts and in a bad way. She went in and out of comas but eventually came back. Strong woman!

Her name was Marjory, and she was born and raised in the American South. We came to know her as Marj. Initially, she was reluctant to speak with Hans or me, but in time, she sensed we were different. That was gratifying. We were especially curious as to how she wound up in Germany before the war. Her German was quite good.

"I worked for a German family, Klaus and Agnes Mayer. They did business in South Carolina, where I hail from. They must have done all right in their business. They were rich and hired me to take care of the kids and teach them to speak English. The boy must be about twelve now and the girl maybe ten.

"When the Nazis came out with all those decrees, the Mayers

decided to help Jewish kids. They had a Christian daycare place and hid Jewish children there. They saved them. We must've had twenty of 'em, ages three to five. All their parents were taken away to one camp or the other. Mr. Mayer bribed a few government people. Quite a few.

"We all lived out in the country, far from the city and the police and all. It was a big place, a farm or estate, you might say, maybe fifteen miles from Hamburg. We heard about the war, but thank heaven, we were far away from all that. It was good for everyone, especially those kids.

"Sometimes soldiers came by—trucks and dogs and such. One day, they came right up to the house. We hid all the Jewish kids in the basement. When they asked about me, the Mayers showed them paperwork, saying I was a household helper. They knew damn well I wasn't Jewish! Anyway, they came back a few days later with Gestapo people. They said they knew the Mayers were hiding Jews. Someone they bribed had turned them in. That's what I think. But Mr. Mayer knew they were coming 'cause someone in the government told him. So he took the kids away to another place.

"Didn't matter that they didn't find any kids. They took the Mayers in anyhow. And they took me to some place where they hit me and hit me and kept asking me where the kids were. I said I didn't know. I guess they believed me 'cause they sent me down to Dachau. They beat me more down there. Raped me too. Kept asking about the kids. But I never said a thing. Never would and never will. At first, I worked in one of the factories, till one day they sent me for the medical experiments. It was bad, I tell you. And I thank you for getting me outta that damn place."

She was occasionally in tears but usually was bravely calm. Hans and I told her that we tried to help people where we could. She recovered well enough to be put to work in the women's factory. Such an unfortunate set of circumstances had brought a poor black woman from America to a Nazi camp.

I imagined people all around the world were being uprooted and sent to places they'd never heard of or never dreamed they'd see. For some of them, they'd perish far away from home and family.

Visits from Otto Kaiser were never welcome—not by me or anyone else. He summoned me to the admin building, where he sat with two Gestapo hoodlums. He told me to close the door and got right to it.

"Johan, Johan, Johan. I need your help with a problem that Berlin has placed in my capable hands. They are looking for a woman who has knowledge of where a group of Jewish children are hiding. Probably in the Hamburg area. It seems the woman was mistakenly sent to Dachau or one of the subcamps. This woman is unusual. She isn't Jewish. She isn't German or any other European. She is an American Negro."

"Otto, my old colleague, many people come and go through my gates. I do recall seeing a few Negroes, mostly from France or its colonies, though. Maybe from our old colonies in Africa. I cannot be sure. Naturally, I will look into the matter."

"Very good. It is an important matter. My two men will come again within the week. We want this woman, Johan. There was a blunder in sending her into the camp system, and it must be corrected. Such things—well, they look bad."

"I'll make a thorough search and have the results in forty-eight hours."

The war was going badly, yet Berlin was still allocating resources to hunting down children.

Kurt and I immediately deleted Marj's name from the rosters and placed her in a secluded station in one of the smaller plants that made insignia. I went there to tell Marj of the Gestapo visit and found her busily at work, humming an unrecognizable melody with a forlorn look on her face.

"Why did you move me here, sir? I'm all alone in a small room the livelong day. I was making friends at the old place."

"The Gestapo came to me. They're looking for you here and at every other Dachau camp. They want to know where the Jewish children were hidden."

"Well, I ain't telling! They can beat me all they want. I ain't telling!"

"That's very courageous of you, Marj. But we're going to hide you here for a while. You are to stay here. You are not to go back to the block or to the mess hall. Food and water will be brought here."

"Okay. It's your camp."

There was an underground, of sorts, at K XII. Hans, Kurt, and I led a resistance in uniform. Tzivya and Rabbi Yitzchak were with us. No high signs or midnight meetings, just a silent understanding. It was the rabbi and Tzivya who snuck food from their own meager rations to Marj and kept her spirits up. The three became friends and found sustenance in each other's courage and perseverance. They prayed together and talked about their beliefs and hopes for what peace would bring. Marj became much admired for helping those children. Much loved too.

I admired all of them and warned them to be ever on the lookout. Guards, kapos, and informers were everywhere.

Loud knocks woke me at my quarters. It was well after midnight, but that wasn't terribly unusual. After all, I ran the place, and there were always unexpected events, though usually minor ones, such as a broken generator at a factory or frozen plumbing in the dead of winter. Sometimes there were fatal car crashes. That night, it was Kaiser and two lowbrow henchmen.

"You are under arrest! And be so kind as to hand over your pistol!"

"It's not on me, Otto. I was asleep. What's going on?"

Off we marched to the administration building. Inside my office was Marj, tied to a chair. She'd been through it, yet she looked determined. Hans was there too. He was ashen-faced, but I could not discern anything more.

One of the henchmen spoke. "We found this *Schwarzerin* in the back of one of your factories, not so much in hiding as having been hidden. There were morsels of food and a cup of water nearby that did not get there by itself. Who has been helping her?"

"Johan, Johan, Johan," Kaiser said in his familiar taunt, "why didn't you report this woman to me immediately? Did this woman tell you where she hid the Jewish children?"

"No, she did not. I don't know anything about Jewish children."

"Why was she in your factory? Who was bringing her food?" the henchman barked.

"I use every available space for the war effort. That is well known in Berlin. Well appreciated too."

"Why didn't you report her? There aren't many *Schwarzerinen* here!" the goon continued.

"I have thousands of prisoners here. Many North Africans with grimy faces. Take a look around!"

The goon and I glared at each other.

Otto broke the tension. "It has been noted in the higher offices of Berlin that Ludwig, here, is dedicated to the war effort and delivers excellent matériel on time."

"It's not an easy matter to know every face in a camp with such a transient workforce," I added. "Yes, many inferior people with dark faces come through here. Hard to tell one from the other!"

The henchmen were put on the defensive. I thought the night was over, but one of them suddenly wheeled and punched Marj square on the jaw. She let out a sharp cry.

"Tell us where the Jews are!"

Gasps and groans were her only reply.

"Keep her awake!" the goon ordered Hans.

I understood then that Hans was there to keep her from slipping into unconsciousness. He wiped the blood from her face, revealing a swollen eye and lip.

"You will tell us where the Jew children are, or we will beat you all night long."

"Let me take care of this," I interrupted. "I'll find out what she knows."

"What makes you think you can get her to talk?" one of them asked.

"I deal with these people every day. You forget that I convince them to work hard for National Socialism. I can see this one will be a hard nut to crack. My professional experience tells me that she will not give up the information to you, and your methods will simply kill her. She'll die, and you'll get nothing. Really, you people back in Berlin can be so thick-headed! We out here in the field know far more."

Part of my professional experience was that these Berlin hoodlums were indeed thick-headed louts and could be put on the defensive by articulate condescension. They looked to Otto for guidance but got none.

One of them became frustrated. "You have one day to get the information from her. We'll be back tomorrow evening."

They put on their hats and stormed out.

Kaiser offered a word of caution. "Johan, I truly hope you know what you're doing. These men are serious. You better deliver the goods."

Hans and I took Marj to the infirmary, where he treated her wounds and administered a sedative. She looked at us hopefully as she fell asleep.

"Well, Johan, you are a most crafty fellow. We all know that. What's the plan?"

"I don't have one."

Hans's disappointment was clear. "Then we'll have to think of one. Until then, we all need sleep."

Sometimes ideas come to us while we're asleep. I had no such luck that night. But in the morning, a plan began to gel, and I headed to the infirmary. Marj looked at me hopefully, though I might have detected resignation lurking in her as well.

"We have only two options," I told her. "First, we get you out of here and claim you escaped."

"But then all hell's gonna come down on you," Marj noted quite astutely.

"Perhaps, perhaps. Second, you tell them the hiding place—an actual place but not the one where the children are. When the hoods come up empty-handed, you can swear the kids were there at one time but must have been moved. Of course, they might not believe you. Then they'll return to their standard methods, or they'll just kill you."

Marj listened then shook her head.

"No, no. I appreciate your help—believe me, I do—but let's not kid ourselves. They ain't gonna believe me. Worse, all this is gonna put you at risk. They'll kill you *and* me!"

The gears in Hans's head were turning, but it took a while for him to speak. "I suggest the second alternative but with an additional dimension—a very unpleasant one, though. If they believe the story of the children having been moved, that's good. The story is, after all, plausible. People who are being looked for keep on the move. The Gestapo surely knows that. If they do not believe her, then yes, they will return to beatings or, as you suggest, simply kill her." Hans turned to Marj. "I can offer you a glass of water. It will contain a certain drug that will end the punishment. You will simply fall asleep."

Moments of silence ensued.

Finally, Marj said, "Just fall asleep, huh? And no more of this mess?"

Hans nodded. "Correct. Not a pleasant choice, but who of us has had a pleasant choice in the last few years?"

I was saddened by the thought. She deserved better, but as Hans said, ideal circumstances were in short supply. "No drugs!" I told Hans. "That's out of the question! I'll smuggle her out of the camp." I turned to Marj. "You can hide in the woods until the Allies get here."

Marj smiled serenely. She seemed to recognize that her end might be near but that good people were around her. "Now, you guys, listen—please. I'll do my best to convince them the place I tell them is right. I really will. But, Doctor, do have that little drink of water handy, if you please. I'll ask for it if I need it. My choice. Damn! Never thought I'd live in Germany, let alone die here."

"We'll do everything we can to see you return to South Carolina, Marj," I said. "There's still a few hours before they come back. Anything we can do?"

"Yes, there is. In fact, there is. I'd like to write a letter to my sister. Don't know if she's ever gonna see it, but maybe you can get it to her someday after all this craziness is over and done with. I know her address by heart. I think of the place at night a whole lot."

"We can give the letter to the Americans soon. I'll get you pen and paper."

Marj sat near a window and wrote a long letter. Her cursive penmanship was delicate and the lines straight.

Outside the window, inmates trudged to work, guards and kapos beside them—slaves of the Reich. Oppression and destruction seemed like the way of the world to me then. I didn't think Marj's gentle soul shared that view.

She finished the letter, kissed it, and handed it to me. "And you take care of the rabbi and girl for me too."

"I will," I assured her. "You know what I have to do now. Forgive me, but it's essential to our plan."

"I know what you gotta do. I've taken worse. Go ahead! You don't look so tough!"

When Kaiser and the hoodlums returned, Marj was tied to the chair. Her face and eyes were swollen, her hair in tangles and clumps, and her work tunic stained with fresh blood. As for me, my hair was untidy and my hand bandaged.

"Otto," I panted, "I tried everything. At first, I offered her better rations, but she refused my generosity and insisted she knew nothing. So I had to adopt tougher methods. Still nothing. Frankly, I don't think she knows anything. If you must ask her a few more questions, then by all means proceed. But good seamstresses are hard to find."

Kaiser showed no interest.

"I knew you'd fail," a goon said. He then hauled off and punched Marj across the jaw and began jerking her hair about violently.

I made one last try. "You gentlemen have your orders, but I have mine. And they include getting matériel to the fronts. Now let's get this over with!"

The goon was outraged. "This is the Reich's highest priority! We don't care about your priorities!"

"You don't? Well, let me assure you that the Waffen SS and Wehrmacht care a great deal about them. The generals know me and my work!" I sat down, feeling I'd made my point well. I looked to Kaiser for support; I was disappointed.

"Johan, bear in mind that Berlin places great importance on the matter of hidden Jews," Kaiser said. "It might make little sense to you, but it is Berlin's will."

"She knows nothing about hidden Jews. She knows a great deal about making tunics."

Otto stared at me; his suspicions might have returned. He nodded for the goons to proceed. I left the room. The sounds of blows and cries began again.

Hours later, Kaiser came to my office in the administration building, not long after I returned from the plants.

"Why did you do that, Johan? Why did you want to save her?"

My glare probably told him that we'd been through that. He was sizing me up again.

"What became of her? I have paperwork to do either way."

"The matter's done with now," Otto said. "A little more paperwork for you. That's all."

"Another worker lost. Well, I will note this in my report."

"Johan, the Gestapo needs to find these Jews and send them where they need to be sent."

I'd had it. I could dispatch him in a second and then go after the goons and anyone else in my path. But I calmed myself and redirected my fury into a tirade. "I don't give a damn about your goons and their obsession with Jews! The war isn't going well. Of course, we're forbidden to say that. All's well in Russia! All's well in France! What do you think is going to happen when they get here?"

"They'll never get to me, old friend."

"Are you Catholic, Otto? Are you a *fellow* Catholic?"

"I was raised as a Lutheran, though not in a strict manner."

"Then you have some morality dwelling in you. How do you justify this?"

"Do you mean Jews and the like? Come, come. They're insects to be eradicated for the betterment of all."

"You'd never have done this before the war."

"Yes, I would. That's how I first came across a resourceful young man in Berlin."

"And what will come after the war? I am prepared to pay the price. Are you?"

"Johan, please spare me the cheap theatrics and defeatist chatter. Your Shwarzerin isn't dead. She's in your precious infirmary. Tauber is looking at her now."

I was taken aback, not only by the welcome news but by my tirade.

"See, Johan? They're not such bad people. They made an investigation, came to a conclusion, and moved on to the next case. You must put your sanctimony away for a while. We are at war. No time for such nonsense."

"I think you showed her a little mercy, Otto. I commend you."

"You are quite mistaken! She is just another insect. Your line of thinking about the needs of war is quite correct and appropriate here, but your mind is clouded by sentimentality. When victory comes, everything will be reconsidered."

"May the Lord have mercy on your soul, Otto."

"Perhaps, perhaps not."

Marj returned to her workstation a few days later, bruised and battered but able to work. Hans said Marj looked at him pleadingly, and he was very close to handing her the potion, but one of the goons called the interrogation to a halt.

13

A Medal from the Devil

Although I stressed production, and Osten generally supported me, many guards and kapos became crueler. Beatings went up, as did shootings. I think they saw the end coming. They all had friends and relatives on the fronts. They heard of steady retreats and fearsome casualties. And they knew that German cities were being bombed into rubble. They exacted vengeance where they could.

Some of the staff, however—not only at K XII but throughout the Dachau system—began to feel uneasy about what they were doing. We knew what was going on at Auschwitz and Treblinka. We heard of fevered efforts to hide the gas chambers as Russian troops neared. It wasn't something that could be hidden. It wasn't something that could be forgiven. Open discussion of such matters was something the Gestapo did not overlook. But talk went on.

My relationship with Emilie returned to its former warmth, though slowly. She knew of the dreadful things I had to do and accepted me as a loving husband and father. Sophia was a beautiful child, walking and talking, reading and writing—or trying to, anyway. With each report I received of a bombing raid on Berlin, I worried that my family was gone, like so many others.

It was common for a small number of prisoners to form a micro-community and help each other get by. Marj, Rabbi Yitzchak, and Tzivya ate together and mingled with one another in the free time between dinner and lights-out. They talked of their religions, families, and the foods they enjoyed before the war. They also talked of the long histories of their people's oppression and discrimination and that they hoped the war would end soon and bring a better day.

Rabbi Yitzchak delivered brief lectures on the Torah and other Hebrew texts, especially those relating to the treatment of people with love and respect. He'd committed to memory many passages and was fond of the ancient sage Rabbi Akiva's words: "Love thy neighbor as thyself" (ואהבת לרעך כמוך)

I once asked him how to explain what was going on in the world. How could a loving God allow this? The question occurred to me on a daily basis. Actually, the question plagued me. I knew that I was not a murderer. I knew that I always would be on the good side and try to do the best to help inmates. Yet the fact that I was put in this circumstance always puzzled me, and I questioned how I got here.

What was the meaning of all this? I'd come from a very Orthodox family that accepted the Torah as it was written. All has a reason, even if we humans don't see it. As much as I tried to logically find answers to my situation, I couldn't find any. I remained in the dark.

Rabbi Yitzchak urged me to recall the exile period and the centuries of Greek and Roman occupation. I said that those periods brought oppression and death but nothing comparable to what was going on in the Reich.

There were moments between duties when I would look up at the sky and give thanks for the beautiful clouds and warming sun. As second-in-command, I naturally had to avoid appearing like an idealistic nature boy, but I looked for interludes and enjoyed them while they lasted.

Osten came upon me behind the admin building during one such interlude. He was a little tipsy but not out-and-out drunk. "Beautiful day, Johan."

"Indeed, it is. That's why I'm lurking back here."

I came to know and understand Osten, maybe even like him a bit. He was poorly educated and rather coarse. He much preferred women and liquor to paperwork and inspections. He had no regard for the prisoners, but his soul wasn't as dark as many others. He accepted my views on brutality and productivity and generally let me impose the regimen as best I could. He professed to dislike Jews, but he wasn't the sort of man to simply shoot one down for sport—there was no shortage of such men, and there had been one with him in the infirmary that night. The SS found such men, or they found the SS, and the machinery churned.

That day, Osten was observing a labor detail about fifty meters from us, which was unusual for him. The laborers were tidying the shrubbery and painting the trim of the admin building.

"Is an inspection coming, Ernst?"

"No inspection. My girlfriend said the place looked a little dreary. That's all. You know women."

"Orders from on high, then."

"Ja wohl."

As he walked away, my eye caught a sudden motion. A tall inmate was running toward us, brandishing a shovel and shouting, "You bastards killed my brother! You bastards killed my brother!"

"Don't do it! Don't do it!" shouted a fellow worker.

The work-detail guard raised his machine pistol but knew even a short burst might hit the kommandant and me. I drew my pistol and removed the safety.

"Halt!" I shouted.

When he got within twenty meters of Osten, I fired twice at his legs, and he fell to the ground. The guard ordered the other workers to lie on the ground, and a half dozen soldiers raced to the scene.

Osten was remarkably calm, more than would be expected, even though he'd had a few. "Thank you, Johan. I should have—" He stared at the wounded man and slowly filled with anger. He drew his pistol and approached him. Five meters away, he took aim at the man's head.

"My brother was only sixteen! Sixteen!"

Osten was no longer an aloof administrator. "And now, you too will die."

The anger on the wounded man's face spoke of years of humiliation and cruelty, of lost family and friends, and of a thirst for vengeance—or at least a determination to go out under his terms and with dignity.

Osten stood motionless. He began to reholster the Luger, and I thought I was right about him. But he again aimed at the man.

"Don't kill him, Herr Kommandant!" I called to him.

"This man wanted to kill us. I'll handle the matter."

"There could be others involved."

He paused, exhaled slowly, and reholstered his pistol. "No conspirators, Johan. This man is simply insane. That's all. Oh, take him to the infirmary for a day of observation. I'll think of what to do with him another time."

He motioned for me to follow him to the office. His eyes were strangely vacant. I sat on a chair in front of his desk. He unbuttoned his tunic and looked out the window, wistfully. "You know, Johan. I've brought my girlfriend here a few times."

I nodded. "I do see what goes on here, you know."

Osten was well known in nearby towns. The tavern owners knew him, and so did many women.

"Yes, yes. But this woman is different." He sat back in his chair and rested his boots on the desk. "I've fallen in love with her. Yes, I have. She's a good woman from a middle-class family. Better than mine; I can tell you that. A few weeks ago, I showed her around Dachau and told her how well organized it was and how vital the work was. And you know, she almost left me. She didn't want anything to do with a man involved with the place. Yes, I told her about the orders and the creed. She said it didn't matter. It was simply cruelty and murder with an official stamp on it."

I didn't know where this was going. Before I could form a nonrevealing question, he continued.

"She's right. I was too involved with the orders and creed. And with cognac. That too."

"Ernst, even if you and your girlfriend are right, you and I and every other soldier have no choice but to do our jobs."

"What comes after this, Johan? You and I know what's going on. Every night, we listen for artillery. It used to be that we'd listen only for bombers. But now the artillery is getting close. They'll kill us. Just kill us."

Sympathy for a camp kommandant sounded unusual, maybe absurd, maybe horrible. But a conflicted man was sitting across from me. I, of course, agreed with him. I'd thought the same since entering the gate years ago. As moving as the moment was, I was not going to bare my soul. Not to him.

"Ernst, my comrade, you need some rest after this incident. We can talk at length about politics another time. Perhaps a little cognac will take away the edge."

"Yes, a little something to calm me down. Oh, Johan …"

"Yes?"

"Thank you for saving my life."

"No need to thank me, Ernst. Now get some rest—and listen to your girlfriend more."

Hans said the man's wounds were not serious. One round went through his calf; the other missed altogether. He joked about my poor marksmanship.

A day or two later, I came up to Rabbi Yitzchak at the factory.

He was not amicable. "Why did you shoot Selig?"

"Instinct. Military training. He was coming at me with a weapon."

"He could have killed the camp kommandant," the rabbi said approvingly.

"That might not have been a good thing."

"And why not? He's in charge of this place! He has blood on his hands!"

"People have many aspects to them. You only see one or two. And besides, if he'd been killed, there would have been fierce reprisals.

You know that. A hundred? Two hundred? And who knows who'd take his place. It could be a worse person."

"Yochanan, his replacement would have been you. You are the second-in-command here. Have you forgotten who you are altogether? You do not belong to them. You are one of us—a Jew."

"You see more than one aspect in me. Osten is not as simple as you think. Trust me on this."

"Who are you, Yochanan? Do you even know anymore?"

"I have to continue my rounds."

"Yes, you do."

Osten called me into his office two weeks later. He was in an uncharacteristically jovial mood.

"Tomorrow will be a great day for K XII. An important visitor is coming to decorate one of our officers. It will bring great honor to us."

"Who is being decorated?"

"You are! I made it known to superiors that you saved my life, and Weiter was so impressed that he made a recommendation to Berlin. You are getting the Iron Cross! It so happens a high-ranking figure will be here to pin it on your chest."

"Weiter's coming here?"

"Higher than him. Let us just say a high-ranking figure. He was coming to inspect Dachau this week anyway and was so impressed by my report that he's honoring us with a personal visit to bestow the medal on my second-in-command! Ten a.m. in the courtyard out front."

That morning, I put on a recently pressed uniform and went to the admin building, where a handful of officers and guards stood at attention. We were on time; not so our august visitor. Osten assured us he'd be there soon.

In through the main gate came three escort vehicles and, behind them, a shiny black Mercedes with small Nazi flags streaming from the front fenders. It pulled up near us, and an officer in the entourage dutifully opened the car's back door. Out stepped Reichsführer Heinrich Himmler. Osten saluted and led him over to me.

Himmler smiled proudly. It was the smile of a sociopathic killer. "Obersturmführer Ludwig! You are a brave man and a source of great pride to the Reich. Your work here has long been valued, and to this you add heroism! Today, I give you this Iron Cross and my hearty congratulations for all you've done. Heil Hitler!"

"Heil Hitler," came the responses from all there.

I thought that would be the end of it, but he patted my shoulder and said, "You are welcome to visit me any time in Berlin. Well done, Obersturmführer!"

I could have shot him. I could have gotten a round off before his guards had time to step in. But there was no dearth of sociopathic killers in Berlin. My survival show went on.

"Thank you, Reichsführer."

In the course of a month, I'd shot a Jew, saved an SS officer, angered a rabbi and friend, and been commended by Heinrich Himmler. I didn't want to serve the devil, but I had no choice. I didn't want to participate in killing people, and although I didn't physically kill anyone, murderers were under my command. I felt detached from reality, like watching from the side; watching a horror movie in which I was not playing a part. I think that's probably the only way I could survive. As for answering myself, I had no answer as to who I was anymore.

On some mornings, I was present for roll call; on others, I was filling out paperwork or dealing with correspondence with Dachau and Berlin. When I wasn't at roll call, I told the officer in charge to get it over fast and send the people off to work. They knew my regimen.

One morning, while working inside, I listened to the routine barking of roll call. Two shots rang out—pistol shots, judging by the distinctive popping sounds. I cursed and stormed out.

Just as I'd thought, a recently arrived guard was standing over a prisoner, who was clutching a wounded leg. The guard was relishing the moment of mastery and was about to deliver the final shot.

"Halt!" I shouted.

Guards and kapos snapped to attention. The new guard had recently arrived from Sobibor, where anything went. Why he'd been transferred here, I never knew. He was at home at his former post. Perhaps Sobibor was being emptied out as the Russians neared. The same for Treblinka, Auschwitz, Belzec, and others. I mistrusted guards from there.

"Unless I'm mistaken, soldier, I gave clear orders to you on arrival about discipline."

"Obersturmführer Ludwig, I was just having a little fun. We get new ones."

"The camps in the east serve specific purposes. Those in the Dachau system, which includes my camp, serve other purposes. Each camp has rules unique to its purpose. When you injure a worker, you break my rules and ignore the function of my camp. As for soldiers who do not obey my orders, there are other camps for them. Disobedient soldiers are put to labor, as per the instructions of their former commanding officers. Klar?"

"Ja wohl. Is it not the Reich's policy to eliminate Jews?"

"Obey my orders. Because you are new, I'll let this incident pass. Do not cross me again. I warn you."

"But—"

"Silence! There is no discussion here! You'll obey my orders, or I'll send you to a disciplinary barracks. Dismissed!"

The inmate slowly stood, despite the wound. He was a short man with a short beard and an odd grin. His eyes were bizarrely mirthful. "I would like to thank you, Herr Kommandant. I'd like to further express my gratitude by offering you a meal at Shmuli's Deli the next time you visit Stuttgart. The food is strictly kosher, of course!" He tipped a nonexistent cap.

Well, many an inmate had gone mad at K XII. Many more at other camps. Why wouldn't someone choose to retreat into a world of fantasy and delusion?

He looked about at the others in his detail and the show went on.

"It is a pleasure to meet all of you this fine morning. I am Herschel the cobbler. I can fix any footwear you might have. A lady's slipper or a man's work shoe. I even work on army boots. It will be an honor to mend your shoes. The name again is Herschel; the trade is cobbling." He again tipped his hat.

Inmates and guards enjoyed the performance and gave him a brief round of applause.

"Herschel, I am not the kommandant, and you need to go to the infirmary. We'll need you back at your workstation."

"I promise you, kind sir, that I'll be at work promptly in the morning. I'm never late to work. Not at home in Stuttgart or here in this lovely spa."

More laughter.

"I'll be seeing all of you tomorrow in the lobby, where coffee and croissants will be served. Please don't forget your breakfast tickets. I believe they'll be serving eggs, sausage, and fresh fruit."

"Take him to the infirmary," I ordered one of the soldiers. "He obviously isn't feeling well this morning!"

"That will not be necessary," Herschel said. "I'll hail a taxi. One should be by any moment."

"The bullet didn't do much damage. Perhaps the guard wanted to just graze his leg," Hans reported to me.

"Or maybe he's just not a good shot."

"Marksmanship isn't very good here."

"Enough! I'm intrigued by the show that this Herschel fellow put on. Is he cuckoo?"

"I'm not a shrink, Johan, but I don't think he's cuckoo. His humor demonstrates creativity and independence. It gives him a measure of control in a place where he has none. He wants to laugh until the day he dies."

I wanted to talk with him. Down the sad, crowded ward lay the cobbler.

"How are you, Herschel?"

"Couldn't be better. Excellent doctor, lovely nurses, sumptuous food. Can I stay here and work for you? I can make you a first-rate pair of boots at a reasonable price!"

This was an extraordinary chap.

"Where are you from?"

"I told you. Stuttgart. A beautiful place. I invite you to Shmuli's Deli. On me."

"Sure. Why not. Maybe after all this is over. Meanwhile, where is your workplace in my spa?"

"In the boot works. I make boots for your bandit host! And by the way, if you need your shoes or boots repaired, I am your man. Don't hesitate to ask."

"I'll remember that, Herschel. How long have you been here?"

"I was in another camp, Buchenwald, for a long time. They moved me here."

"Why?"

"I demanded better conditions!" He bounced his eyebrows up and down like a music hall performer.

"Herschel, you have to be careful. If you joke with the wrong men, you'll be beaten or shot again."

His mirth vanished in an instant. "I know, I know. So I've been warned."

"Be well. Have a good night, Herschel."

"Have a good night, Herr Kommandant."

"I am not in charge of this place."

"For me, you are."

"Again, Herschel, a good night to you."

I learned that Herschel, though recently arrived, was becoming much admired and even loved. He brought humor and joy and a little hope. He clowned it up at roll calls. He'd mimic a pompous officer or thuggish guard, if only briefly and surreptitiously. When I saw him, I chuckled—surreptitiously.

One morning, he wore a lady's hat. I could only guess that someone had sneaked it in when arriving at Dachau. Another time, he wore his work attire inside out. Once, he stood backward during headcount. He was the center of attention at the mess hall.

Some thought he'd lost his mind. There was no shortage of such people. They reduced their contacts with those around them and retreated to a state of spiritual decay and indifference toward life—*Muselmänner.* The inmates didn't call them that to ridicule them; they knew it was a sign of a downward spiral that led to boarding the next train out.

I shared Hans's view that Herschel was a natural comedian. I speculated that he had been a class clown in school and might have done well in the Yiddish theater. Inmates told me of conversations with him that were coherent, interesting, and articulate. He recounted memories of schools and parks in Stuttgart. His favorite delicatessen was a frequent topic.

I impressed it on the other guards that Herschel's antics were to be accepted as part of camp life and morale. They naturally assumed I thought Herschel to have beneficial effects of production. True. But I also liked him.

I brought Herschel to the officers' mess one evening and introduced him to an astonished audience of officers and Aufseherinen. I told him to tell the stories he told his friends in the blocks and inmates' mess. He went right to work without further ado. The audience was appreciative and even fascinated by his stories, jokes, and quips.

We'd all heard the tales of King David, but they'd been told in school and church by stern authority figures. Herschel's accounts were lively and ribald. The camaraderie of the officers and a few drinks made the show all the better.

In the book of Herschel, David was a good king, but he had a weakness for women. "Who among us doesn't?" he asked in an aside. I don't think he expected a reply, but he got chuckles and hoots. We'd all heard of Bathsheba but not like this. He described her voluptuousness in intriguing detail and her habit of sunbathing in the nude. David noticed and appreciated her from a vantage point.

The crowd oohed and aahed uproariously. After that, there was a captivating account of David and Bathsheba's amorousness.

He went on to tell of Bathsheba's husband, Uriah, whom David sent to his death in battle in order to have Bathsheba for his own. But the deed did not go unnoticed. Samuel was sent to David in the form of someone telling a story and seeking advice. Here, Herschel played both roles, switching from king to prophet in a clever way. In the end, the king saw his wrongdoing and sought forgiveness.

Herschel was received well. One might say he was a hit. He came back for repeat engagements. Word spread to other camps, and officers packed into cars for the drive to Kaufering XII for the Herschel Show. We bent the rules and allowed NCOs and enlisted personnel to attend.

He developed an opening gimmick of bowing to his audience, pointing to his belly, and saying, "An army needs food to go on—and so do I." Someone would get the cue and bring him a plate of food and a glass of wine. He'd then savor his meal as though in an elegant restaurant and boast of his fondness for wine, women, and song.

A story followed, more often than not from the Bible. Moses saved by Pharaoh's daughter and leaving Egypt, Queen Esther and the miracle of Purim, and Samson slaying his enemies and bringing down the pillars upon himself.

The guards sat there, enjoying their dinner and the riotous, often bawdy entertainment. They'd give him more wine and bread. Occasionally, one would suggest that Herschel stay the night in the camp's guest quarters.

Herschel would refuse. "I appreciate the offer, but I'm spoiled. I prefer the flea-ridden mattress and moth-bitten blanket in my regular accommodations. Breakfast is free, you know!"

After the show, a guard, sometimes an officer, would take Herschel back to his block.

Word reached Kaiser down at the main camp, and he came up one evening. He enjoyed the show, and afterward, he approached me.

"I don't know how you do this, Johan, but it seems that you always come into contact with acceptable Jews. I don't know exactly what it is with you, but you have some sort of rapport with those people. Maybe because you're so damned religious."

He stared at me, seeking some sort of alarm or weakness, but I showed none. A man who received a medal from Himmler himself could handle it.

"Good evening to you, Johan. Splendid show. Keep up the good work."

The Herschel Show went on. One night, the joint was packed, maybe fifty or sixty people. The air was thick with smoke; the drinks flowed. It was like a stand-up comedy club today.

Herschel relished his fame. He chatted with the audience before and after the show. They'd ask for the name of a good restaurant in Munich or Stuttgart, and he'd give sound recommendations.

New guards were stunned. Conviviality between SS and Jew was unthinkable and verboten. But they soon felt out of step with the others and, in time, drank up and enjoyed a break from the tedium. There wasn't a lot of entertainment in those places, I assure you.

One evening, it was the book of Exodus, according to Herschel. He spoke of being away from home and of family members separated from one another. The audience naturally thought of loved ones far away. I thought of the roundup of Jews in recent years.

He went on in detail about Moses's mother, Jochebed, placing Moses in the basket along the Nile and how heartrending it must have been. A new officer was especially taken by Herschel's tale—no, he was moved. His name was Wilhelm, and he asked for elaboration.

"The Bible doesn't provide details on Jochebed's thoughts and feelings, but it must have been quite painful," Herschel replied.

"Yet she knew her son was being raised by a princess," Wilhelm noted.

"Every moment she wasn't holding him, nursing him, and expressing her love for him must have been painful. Who of us cannot relate to that?"

"No one. My mother died only last week. It was a long illness."

"I am very sorry to hear of your loss. That, I'm afraid, is another thing to which we all can relate. There is a special bond between mother and son. The Bible speaks to that in many places—Rachel and Joseph, Sara and Isaac, Rebecca and Jacob. The precious bond is always there. It's still there between you and your mother. She's always with you, young man, and always will be."

The two men embraced warmly. The war had a short armistice; the Final Solution, a brief pause. I hoped that more than one person in that room reevaluated his life and sense of duty and went about his job the next day the better for it.

Herschel and I talked briefly with a few others. Something baffled me.

"Herschel, how do you handle all this with humor and hope?" I asked. "Look where you are. Not two hundred meters from here is a mass pit. We throw bodies in there every morning. You've worked that detail."

All eyes turned to Herschel. He smiled and touched the tip of his imaginary hat. "I live in an imaginary world, kind sir, an imaginary world wholly of my own making. It protects me, stimulates my being, and keeps me from joining the ranks of the Muselmänner. I tell myself I'm going to a regular place of work, dining at a restaurant of my choosing, and wearing attire from my lavish and extensive wardrobe."

"But there are so many dreadful things."

"Oh yes. Truly dreadful. Sometimes it gets through to me. No doubt. I see good people beaten and killed for no reason. My stay will be short. All this will end in time. We all know that now."

Herschel's words caused considerable discomfort. It was late in the war, and many of the Reich's claims of invincibility and the inevitability of the Aryan world could no longer be clung to. And there was great concern over what defeat would bring to the Reich and to those who'd served it so blindly, completely, and brutally. Yes, there was doubt in the SS ranks—unthinkable only a couple of years earlier and forbidden to the very end.

A change crept across the camp, slowly and incompletely.

Some guards, officers, and kapos did their duties with less zeal and less appetite for cruelty. Roll calls were more straightforward and businesslike. We put greater distance between our camp and the others. Work went on, gears turned, and people died, but the creed had lost its certainty. Herschel introduced a small but welcome measure of doubt and decency.

One evening, the Herschel Show had an unexpected observer. Obersturmbannführer Kruger strode in, unannounced. Everyone snapped to attention, including me. He was a tall, imposing, prickly fellow from Berlin, someone who'd amounted to very little before becoming a Nazi. I dreaded the very sight of him. So did everyone.

"Well, well. What do we have going on in the officers' mess? I thought to stop in your camp for a brief inspection and didn't see the need to call ahead." He walked right up to a young officer. "Have you forgotten the protocol on seeing a superior officer?"

The young man saluted, apologized, and remained at attention.

Kruger paced around the room until he came upon the out-of-place sight of Herschel. "You! Jew! What are you doing here?"

"I am here to regale these good people with my storytelling and wit, Herr Kommandant!" He then saluted, though less comically than might have been expected.

No one laughed.

"Jews do not have sufficient dignity to salute German officers. They may kneel beneath us, however." He then struck Herschel on the face with a powerful blow that sent him to the floor.

We were dismayed to see him sent sprawling, but for all our numbers and years in service, we were powerless. The system was back on with full force.

"Who is in charge here?" Kruger demanded.

"I am! Obersturmführer Ludwig!"

"Ludwig, what is this? This Jew is here to tell you stories from the stock of Jewish lies? Is he convincing you the Führer is not what he claims? If so, please tell me now. Have all of you taken leave of your senses?"

"Obersturmbannführer, allow me to explain. This Jew provides—"

"No explanation can justify this disgusting violation, Ludwig! You are responsible for this! You are a disgrace to the uniform, and this will not go unpunished!" Kruger turned back to Herschel and began to pull his pistol but was stopped cold by the sight and sound of several pistols being drawn and trained on him. His look of astonishment was unforgettable. "Well, well. And what is this? I cannot believe my eyes. What has this Jew done to you that would have you threaten a superior officer?"

No one replied, but no one lowered his pistol either.

"Put your pistols away," Kruger ordered in a calm, official tone.

The order from a feared officer slowly took effect. Pistols were lowered but not put away. One stayed where it was.

"You well know the rules about Jews and their fate. It seems to me that this place has lost sight of its mission, and I must reacquaint you with it through stern disciplinary measures."

He aimed his pistol at Herschel. I held my breath, and I doubt I was alone.

"Halt!"

It was Wilhelm. His voice conveyed anger, commingling with youthful uncertainty. "Obersturmbannführer, lower your pistol! *Schnell*!"

Emboldened by the unprecedented challenge, a few others aimed again at Kruger.

"I'll not accept his. This is preposterous!" Kruger roared. He suddenly shot Herschel twice in the chest, and the poor man dropped to the floor with a surprised look.

Wilhelm rammed his Luger against Kruger's temple. Kruger froze and dropped his pistol, and Wilhelm spoke through gritted teeth. "You should not have done that! It was a great error."

"Put your gun away," Kruger ordered, though with fear in his voice. "Obersturmführer Ludwig, arrest this man! Arrest this man now. That's an order!"

No one moved, except Wilhelm. He shoved his pistol into the stunned superior's mouth and fired. Kruger's blood and brains splattered all about, and he fell hard to the ground. Wilhelm fired two more rounds into his forehead, though the first had done the job admirably.

Wilhelm and I tended to Herschel, who was leaning against the wall. I was glad he'd seen Kruger's blood flow across the floor not far from him. Each breath was more difficult for the poor man.

"We'll take you to the infirmary. The doctor will take care of you," Wilhelm said with a shaky voice. I assessed that Herschel's condition was fatal.

"No, no. No need, young man. I am just fine. This is my destiny. I want you to survive this. Promise me you will try."

Wilhelm nodded feebly.

Herschel leaned up as straight as he could. "I hope you enjoyed the show. I wish I could see you tomorrow night, but I have another engagement. Don't forget to leave a tip. Take care, and enjoy the rest of the evening."

With a tip of his imaginary cap, he was gone.

Silence and grief gave way to planning, at least for the officer in charge. What to do with Kruger's corpse? I sensed that yet another accident had befallen an SS man at K XII. Those fanatical types really should be more careful.

I had those present stand before me. They were not in formation, and I was not giving orders, but we were saving our necks.

"We all witnessed Kruger leave this room late at night. About eleven o'clock. Alone."

Heads nodded.

"We'll take his body to the pit outside the main camp. They burn the bodies every other day. One more will scarcely be noticed. The important thing is that we stand together in our position. *Kruger left here late at night.*"

"About eleven, I think it was," came a voice.

"Alone," proclaimed another.

Wilhelm and I removed Kruger's tunic and trousers and drove his corpse down to Dachau. I took his car; Wilhelm took one of the camp's. As we got within a hundred meters of the pit, the sickening stench of rotting corpses almost overwhelmed us. As we got closer, we could smell smoke, kerosene, and scorched flesh. Before us in the headlights was a field of human remains in a neatly dug pit, perhaps fifty by twenty meters. Men, women, and a few children lay in various positions and states of decomposition. Some had been burned. Some were naked; some in tattered pajama-like uniforms.

We took the half-naked body from the back seat and tossed it in with the victims. We left his car just outside a darkened town and drove back to K XII.

Investigators came to Osten's office a few days later. Kruger had not been seen or heard from. A few of us feigned surprise and gave the story about his unremarkable inspection.

"He left late. About eleven, I think it was," I said.

"Alone," said another.

That was it. The investigators left. About eleven, I think it was.

For weeks, I wondered if we should have taken the precaution of burning the flesh where Kruger's SS tattoo was. If his corpse were found amid the others, the mark would be easily seen, and the bloodhounds would be back. But the pit at Dachau was set ablaze regularly, by prisoners, and we never heard anything more of the matter.

Herschel's murder saddened me a great deal. He'd brought a little life where there hadn't been any. Witnessing his humor made me hopeful. Many others, I was sure, thought the same, both staff and inmates. We all enjoyed his imagination and defiance.

I didn't go to the officers' mess at night very often after that.

14

The Führer

There was a lot of absurd and petty bureaucracy in the SS—inspections and the routine motivational talks at Dachau. Officers often had to go to SS headquarters in Berlin for a week of seminars. Most of those sent had excellent, even distinguished, service records.

K XII's production was first-rate, and I'd been given prestigious awards, one from Himmler himself. In the fall of 1944, I was sent to the SS headquarters in Berlin. It seemed foolish and a waste of time, but it would mean being near Emilie and Sophia for a while.

Osten was sent up for a day or two as well. For him, it would be a couple of nights of revelry in a big city.

The seminars were the predictable stuff: Aryan blood, impure blood; endangered nation and relentless enemies; foreign conquest; excellent supplies. Once or twice, an officer would suggest the war wasn't going well. The response was swift denunciation. One guy was rumored to have been tossed into a disciplinary barracks.

One morning, the building and grounds were tidied up, and the lawn was mowed. The work had more than adequate supervision and seemed frenetic. We were told that our uniforms had to be meticulous and our grooming impeccable, more so than usual.

"What's this all about?" I asked the seminar chief.

"We'll have a very important visitor tomorrow," he said with great pride. "The Führer himself will be here!"

So, I was about to see Adolf Hitler in the flesh. His likeness was on the walls of the admin building and my quarters. Every memo and newspaper had his name. I'd heard idolatrous prose from doltish fellow officers. They thought he was bringing vitality, unity, and victory back to Germany. I thought of my pistol.

"Morgen, Adolf. Ich bin Jude." Bang! "Aufwiedersehen."

The following morning at exactly ten o'clock, he arrived. We stood in several ranks as he walked through, sometimes shaking hands and chatting. When not shaking hands or patting shoulders, he kept both arms tucked behind his back.

It was a revoltingly memorable event. I thought of the millions of people who had died and who would die because of him. So much horror and pain and mayhem because of this shabby man walking near me. If not for him, those murderous guards would be small-time thieves, robbers, and pimps. But he gave them dashing uniforms, weapons, and ideas. He also gave them a free hand. He gave them more opportunity to kill and rape than any Mongol warlord. The Mongols, Huns, and others had no Auschwitz or Dachau.

This man was coming toward me. He stopped and extended his hand. "Obersturmführer Ludwig, I've heard excellent reports about you." He actually smiled. His face was pale and sweaty, his hand clammy and trembling. I thought he was sick, physically sick. This was only a few weeks after the unsuccessful assassination attempt by Stauffenberg and others.

"Danke schön, mein Führer." I looked into his face.

History will record this man as probably the ultimate evil of the human kind, a psychopath of the worst kind, and a monster that no one could ever match. Yet I could see why an entire nation followed him. He was definitely charismatic. He radiated the ultimate power, not enforced by good but with evil. By fear. Yet his power was not doubtful. I could simply pull my pistol and kill him right here. A thought crossed my mind—*Where all others have failed, I could win. Yes, I probably will be killed, but I may save many.*

I sent my hand to my holster and felt the cold metal of my gun. *Tempting*, I thought. Then I imagined Sophia, giggling and laughing, and my hand went away from my gun. Ultimately, I was not able to kill a human being in cold blood, not even the Führer himself.

He smiled and continued down the line.

Later that day, Hitler came to the officers' dining hall and moved among us, giving words of encouragement and pride and receiving the same from the fawning officers. I'd had better dinner companions, so I ate quickly and excused myself. Hitler and Osten came upon me.

"Mein Führer, you may recall Obersturmführer Johan Ludwig from this morning's inspection. He's my right-hand man! Together, we've made our humble subcamp a model of productivity—the envy of Dachau!"

"Yes, of course I remember you." Hitler seemed genuinely pleased, though somewhat dazed.

"I'm honored you remember me, mein Führer. And Kommandant Osten, you are too generous in your praise."

And too generous with the liquor tonight too, I thought.

Again, I noticed Hitler's shaky hands, pallid face, and bloodless lips. Very sickly. I was heartened by the idea that he wasn't long for this world.

"Where are you from?" he asked me.

"I lived in Berlin before entering the SS."

"What did you do before the war?"

"I was a student at the University of Berlin, mein Führer. I studied electrical engineering."

"Very good, very good. Are you married? Do you have children?"

"Yes, mein Führer. I am married and have one daughter."

Mention of them caused a shadow of dread to fall across my soul, as though merely mentioning them in his presence cast a shadow over them.

"A family man, then! Splendid! What do you think about the war?"

A most unexpected question. My mind raced to find a suitable reply. "We must win this war—and I am sure we will. I promise you I will do everything in my power to see to it. I have one question, with your permission. How do you think the war will proceed?"

Where I'd found the audacity to ask that, I do not know. Perhaps his manifest frailty emboldened me. Or perhaps it was my hatred. In any event, his eyes darkened.

"We will win! Of course! The wrongs are being corrected. Jews and Communists are being dealt with. It's our war; it's our time." An oddly ecstatic look swept across his glazed eyes as he got caught up in his words, as so many Germans did back in the thirties. He went on about Aryan superiority and Germany's national destiny in the world. "Your thoughts, Obersturmführer?"

He looked to me intently, and I returned the look to him.

"Yes, we will achieve our destiny. I believe this with all my heart."

"Indeed! Splendid! Splendid! Excellent, young Obersturmführer!"

"An honor talking with you, mein Führer!"

Thankfully, he and Osten walked away.

Sweating profusely, I dabbed my forehead with a handkerchief and sat down at my table for the rest of the evening.

At the end of that week, I was able to spend a few days with Emilie and Sophia.

"I met Hitler this week."

She showed no interest.

"He visited the headquarters. I shook hands with him."

"I see. Are you well?"

"Yes, I am well now, but the week was a terrible ordeal. I also chatted with him in the mess hall. He's on death's door."

"Welcome news."

My shapeless, shifting identity was making me dizzy and ill. Soon enough, I packed up and drove south, back to the camp.

The camp was ever subject to unexpected inspections and visits from SS bureaucrats in Berlin, who vied with one another to curry favor and rise up the ranks. They knew nothing of production, warfare, or decency, for that matter. Their only concern was with regulation and obsequiousness and climbing over others. Nuisances, all of them, but running the camp entailed routine encounters with them.

Osten and I were having breakfast at the mess hall when in marched a Berlin functionary, briefcase tucked under an arm, and a pair of soldiers behind him. Osten recognized him. The look on his face revealed that he thought the guy meant trouble. He was SS all right, but his face and demeanor spoke of an office worker who wanted a larger desk and another medal—paradoxical, as shall be seen.

We were obliged to snap to attention, salute, and play our roles as deferent junior officers. Osten led the way.

"Obergruppenführer Darges! Guten Morgen! We met in Berlin last year. How may we be of help this day?"

Congeniality had no effect on the man. The closer I looked at him, the more hateful he seemed. Aberrantly well groomed; emotionless, save for arrogant eyes; a practiced furrow in his brow.

"I indeed remember you from Berlin. We will meet in your office at once."

Osten reached for his tea.

"Now, Osten!"

Breakfast was over.

We walked to the admin building and entered Osten's office. Darges motioned for his entourage to remain in the anteroom. I didn't expect any pleasantries, and he didn't offer any.

"I am sure that you two officers are aware of the paramount orders from Reichsführer Himmler."

Osten said he was indeed aware of them, but I don't think he knew exactly what Darges meant. I did, so I spoke up.

"Obergruppenführer Darges, you of course are referring to the elimination of the Jewish problem. Yes, we receive regular briefings and memos."

"I'm relieved. Are you both aware of its importance?" Osten began to speak, Darges cut him off. "Buchenwald, Stutthof, Mauthausen, and the others are in full compliance! Dachau and its satellites are in compliance, save for one—Kaufering XII! Your camp is not in compliance! The numbers you send to our facilities in Poland are disgracefully low!"

Osten and I wanted to state our case, but Darges's tirade was just beginning.

"Our duty is to systematically eliminate the Jews of Europe. The purpose is noble, the directives are clear, and the camps and transportation networks are in place. Your numbers show utter disregard for the Reich's policy. We understand fully that yours is a labor camp, but nonetheless, the process must be carried through without further delays or demurrals."

A back-and-forth ensued about meeting quotas and aiding the war effort.

"Yes, yes. Indeed, your camp gets high marks when it comes to production, and that pleases me. Yet the Reich has its priorities, and those priorities are ours. Your manifest shows many old people and youths. Surely they can be sent off without too many problems on the assembly lines. Now, I want you to send more people to Poland, klar?"

Osten and I saw no more room to argue.

"You have one month to increase your deportations to standards. Go over your manifest carefully, and see to it. We have to get cracking on this Jewish problem!"

With that he picked up his briefcase and left.

"What to do, Johan, what to do? The orders are specific, and this fellow is on us. The consequences of failure are unspecified, though I think we know them in general."

Osten was annoyed less about the lives than about the disruption. The routine we'd established would be upset by a meddlesome functionary whose understanding of the war could be placed inside his briefcase. I thought of people out there.

"We have to meet other quotas, Ernst. That's clear too."

"If those quotas falter, too bad. We can lay the blame on the shiny boots of that Darges fellow. That could be interesting."

I imagined myself writing the damning report to Berlin. But I wanted a way around Darges. He was a denizen of a bureaucratic jungle with many dangerous beasts.

I requested an urgent meeting with Himmler himself. He'd given me a medal recently and might recall me. Unfortunately, the appointment secretary said he was far too busy. I requested that I be apprised when he was free. I didn't expect a return call.

Not long thereafter, Darges came by again, this time with four accomplices. Presumably, he thought this would double the pressure on us. He riffled through the paperwork and saw no increase in deportations. His disapproval was brewing into anger.

I assured him that procedures were underway, and he'd see results soon enough. We stared icily at each other until I thrust my chest out to better display my Iron Cross. Height worked to my advantage too.

"I am here to see that orders are executed, Ludwig!"

"As are we all, sir."

Still no word from Himmler's office. I looked for help from another bureaucratic beast. I called Otto Kaiser's office, and luck was with me.

Darges was obsessed. He came by again, and after a summary look through the rosters, he ordered an assembly of the young and old that evening. I knew how it would go. He'd shoot a few to make his point, at least as much to Osten and me as to the others. Then he'd deliver a lecture about racial purity and the Reich and this and that. Afterward, the unfortunate inmates would be forced to live out in the elements until the next Death Express pulled in.

Toward the evening, the work details left the factories and headed for the assembly yard. By then, most were gaunt and weak. Kapos and guards sent the young and old to the side. They knew what it meant. Darges and his MP-40–toting guards walked among them, inspecting them, enjoying mastery over them. Tzivya was in the ranks.

Ordinarily, the sight of a staff car coming in from the main gate was not a good omen. It certainly hadn't been with any of Darges's arrivals. But at that moment, I wanted to see one pull in—and for once, my hopes were fulfilled. A Kübelwagen came in, and out stepped Otto Kaiser, recently promoted Sturmbannführer.

"And just what is this gathering all about?" the Gestapo chieftain said to Darges and me, after a most cursory salute to his nominal superior.

"Welcome!" I said. "Obergruppenführer Darges, here, has come from his office in Berlin to instruct us on the proper running of a work camp. He feels that these people—several hundred of them, as you can see—are not needed for the war effort and can be sent to Poland."

As Darges walked our way from the inmates, Kaiser whispered to me. "You and these Jews, Johan. You and these goddam Jews."

"I am handling this matter, not the Gestapo," Darges said.

Kaiser was not intimidated by Darges's rank or demeanor. I sensed he knew him and, more important, loathed him. That was probably why he was there.

"Obergruppenführer Darges, do you people in Berlin understand the situation here? As much as we all would like to comply with orders, our soldiers need weaponry and ammunition. These workers can be of value for a few more months. After that, nature will do our work for us."

"Orders are orders, and we need to see results. This camp hasn't met its quota of deportations. There will be other inmates to replace these ones."

"They will not be as well trained."

Those were Kaiser's words that day, but they'd long been mine. He was playing a bureaucratic game quite well.

"I order you to deport these inmates to Poland now! A train will arrive in two days."

"I countermand your order on the grounds of their importance to the war. The Gestapo is charged with investigating any acts that harm the Reich. Reichsführer Himmler has authorized us to use our discretion on such matters. And I have an excellent record in that regard."

Darges was silent and motionless but enraged all the same. He weighed the matter for a few moments. "We shall have to get a decision on this question from the Reichsführer himself. He will determine who is right here—and who is very wrong. There will be consequences, I assure you."

"And I assure you I'll speak with the Reichsführer personally. And Obergruppenführer Darges, please remember we are all working for the Reich."

Darges, briefcase under an arm, stormed away with his guards. I ordered the assembled inmates to return to their blocks and prepare for work in the morning.

I calmed myself in Osten's office. He said we'd just have to see how it played out.

There's no telling exactly what happened in Berlin. Maybe Kaiser had more pull than I thought, or maybe he had some dirt on Darges. Kaiser, after all, was a masterful collector of dirt and undoubtedly had file drawers full of it. Perhaps the matter came to Himmler's attention, and at that moment, he and his staff felt that production was more pressing than deportation.

In any case, I pressed everyone to exceed quotas. They knew the alternative. And I hoped at least some of them knew I'd intervened on their behalf.

Some of them must have overheard the confrontation that evening. And word spread in the evening free time.

A week or so later, Osten called me in. He was in an unusually ebullient mood, yet his words weren't slurred, and his eyes weren't glazed.

"Johan, you astound me at times. I wasn't sure we would get away with standing up to Darges, but it looks like we did. I hear Darges is in a stew and maybe on the outs with Himmler."

"Welcome news."

"There's more. Himmler is awarding us medals. It's a good day for Kaufering XII!"

My eyes might have rolled. Whatever I did or didn't do, it caught Osten's attention.

"I don't like ceremonies, Ernst. They're a waste of valuable time. Yours, mine, the Reich's."

"Well, my unassuming, dutiful junior officer, there's one more thing. You may want to savor the moment with a shot of cognac."

"You don't mean Himmler is coming here again!"

"No, not Himmler. Wait and see, wait and see. In the meantime, drink up. This is a great moment of triumph—and this is good cognac."

A week later, Osten and a few other officers and NCOs stood at attention just outside the admin building. A staff car drove in from the main gate, and Darges got out. He took his place near Osten and me.

Kurt opened the proceedings. "Kaufering XII is honored to have Obergruppenführer Darges here to bestow special awards to our commanding officers."

Darges, eager to get things over with, schnell, picked up immediately. "Reichsführer Himmler himself has asked me to express his deep appreciation to the officers and men of this camp for their unswerving dedication to the war effort."

The mortified bureaucrat reached into his briefcase for the medals and brusquely pinned them on us. Salutes were exchanged. He noted a faint smile of enjoyment on my face and headed back to his staff car. His shadow never again fell on Kaufering XII.

Osten and I congratulated each other in front of the assembled staff; then we returned to his office for another round of cognac.

In a way, I'm proud of that medal. It had nothing to do with service to the Reich, of course. It had to do with preventing the deaths of several hundred people. I have the satisfaction of knowing I'd used petty rivalries within SS bureaus to force its machinery of death to sputter for a while.

I still have the medal stored away. Every few years, I take it out and hold it.

15

Escape?

Orders came on short notice to put up another factory. This one would manufacture parts for rifles. Civilian engineers looked around for a suitable location and found one a few kilometers away from K XII. I charged a younger officer to assemble fifteen men for a work detail with the engineers. One of them was Rabbi Yitzchak.

My presence wasn't really required, as it was a small, uncomplicated matter, but if a factory had to be put up, it was best that I have firsthand knowledge of the terrain and roads. The inmates rode in two military trucks, while the junior officer, engineers, and I rode in staff cars.

After a short drive, we came to a field near a farmhouse and got to work. The civilians set up surveying equipment and had the inmates clear brush with spades and shovels—dull work, but it was good to get out of camp. I looked around and noticed the flat terrain. I took notes on trees that needed to be brought down and on the condition of roads. I was making rough calculations on construction time when a commotion broke out.

An inmate was clubbing the officer with a surveyor's tripod. Other inmates swiftly joined in. One grabbed a machine pistol, and the others went for the two guards. One guard got a rifle shot off before both guards were overwhelmed. The stunned civilians raised their hands. The alarmed officer in charge had his hand near his Luger as Rabbi Yitzchak approached him.

The rabbi was no longer gentle and spiritual. He was angry and armed. "We're getting out of here," he said to me. "Whose side are you on?"

I asked myself where this would lead. Hiding in the woods until the war ended? Heading south for Switzerland? Both too dangerous.

"This won't work," I said.

Rabbi Yitzchak glared at me.

"So then. You're not with us. Do you remember who you are? Or have you been pretending to be a loyal SS officer so long that you've become one?"

His words stabbed me. Better put, they reopened wounds I'd already made myself.

"Even if I get away, they'll kill my family," I said.

"No, no. You're one of them now. Yes, you help one of us to ease your conscience, but you, Yochanan, are a loyal officer in the SS—with medals. I don't believe you even have a family, besides those in the officers' mess."

Inmates surrounded me, armed with shovels and firearms. Was this how it would end? Beaten to death and shot by people I'd tried to help? Would I be eulogized poignantly by Osten and Kaiser just before a massive reprisal?

I began to recite the Morning Prayer in the Yiddish dialect that my family used in Friedrichstadt. I did so softly and fervently, my inflections and phrasings true and emotion-laden. No one spoke or stirred. The rabbi was taken aback; those around him were baffled.

"I hope the Lord will forgive you and us," Rabbi Yitzchak said. "For now, give me that pistol."

I complied. A blow fell from behind, and I fell into darkness.

I came to an hour later with a fierce pain in my head. I looked around and saw the civilian engineers had been killed and were lying not far from the SS corpses. *Why did they kill the civilians?* Judging by the position of power that Rabbi Yitzchak had held at that moment, he'd probably ordered it. *Sheer vengeance?* As I walked uneasily to the bodies, it dawned on me. The civilians had seen me offer a Jewish prayer, and the rabbi wanted no one to attest to that. So convoluted, so maddening, so absurd.

A search party came in the early evening and found me. I ran a hand over my skull and said I didn't recall much. Hans bandaged me and told me to take a few days off. First, however, I had to give an account to Osten and the people sent up from Dachau. The young officer and guards had been lax. The absence of dead inmates proved that. They never should have been overpowered so easily. The family probably got a medal anyway.

In a week, I was well enough to drive north. I told Emilie the story, and she was horrified by how close I'd come to being killed and by the paradox of the attackers being fellow Jews.

"It will only get worse. I know it," she cried.

"The war will be over in a few months. Then my charade will be over too."

I pondered the hell that was coming down on us and was determined to do something decent. "We need to save Tzivya," I whispered.

"Could we hide her here?"

"I thought about that. I can schedule my departure for late at night and take her with me. I can edit the camp's manifest. It may work."

"There's grave risk. What if that Kaiser fellow pays us another late-night visit—henchmen in tow?"

"He's mostly in the south these days. He'll be very busy over the next few weeks, hiding his crimes and hiding himself. The war is almost over. I don't think he'll visit us anymore. Nonetheless, I suggest preparing a hiding place in Sophia's closet. A blanket and a container of water."

The following Monday, I did my rounds in Tzivya's factory. She asked for word about Rabbi Yitzchak and the other escapees, but I had none.

"I want you out of here, Tzivya. I fear the worst for this place when the Americans get close."

"What do you mean? How?"

"Never mind. I'm going to smuggle you out and hide you in Berlin until the war ends. No more than a few months from now, as best as I can judge."

"But the others!"

"I cannot help everyone. That's been made quite clear to me over the years. Now, on Friday you are to stay here after work ends. Do not go to the mess hall. Do not go to evening assembly. I'll pick you up here at nine o'clock in my car and drive us out of here."

She nodded and smiled. I think she wanted to give me a kiss.

I went through the week, doing my rounds, filing reports, and talking with Osten about routine matters. I was nervous. I'd done risky things before, but I felt chaos coming upon us, and that brought uncertainties. However, impending chaos also meant things were getting lax. Guards were thinking less about their duties and more about their necks or about heading for the hills.

There was one thing I did that was out of the routine. I deleted Tzivya's name from the rosters of both her workplace and block. As far as K XII was concerned, she no longer existed. Sometimes bureaucracies can be outwitted by internal rivalries, sometimes by a simple stroke of the pen. She joined Yochanan Berger in the mysterious realm of non-people who roamed the land.

On Friday night, I went through a pile of correspondence and looked at the clock every ten minutes. Just before nine, I packed it in and drove to the women's factory. Tzivya was sitting on the floor in a back room. She looked at me trustingly. Out we went.

"Into the back seat, dear. We're going for a little drive tonight."

"You're silly!" she said nervously.

I covered her in a blanket and put a small suitcase on top of it. On the way to the checkpoint, a uniformed figure waved me down. It was Osten.

"Heading home, Johan?"

"Yes, I thought I left word."

"You did, you did. I'm meeting my *Schatzi* in Fahrenzhausen tonight. I need cheering up—and a ride too!"

"But of course."

We drove through the checkpoint, receiving salutes from the guards. Tzivya knew what was going on, and I could rely on her to keep still. But I needed to occupy Osten for the ten-minute trip to Fahrenzhausen. He lit up a cigarette in his holder and started the conversation rather unexpectedly.

"It won't be much longer now, will it—I mean, the war. It's over. We're not supposed to say this, but you and I are not sticklers for rules."

"No, we certainly aren't."

"What comes will come. We'll be taken prisoner—thankfully, by the Americans, not the Russians."

"Do you feel bad for what we've done?" I asked him. "Do you hate Jews?"

"Hate them? No. Not the way others do. I don't like them, but I don't hate them. My parents are religious, but it didn't take hold on me. I liked girls and beer too much. When my father learned about the camps, he stopped speaking to me. His own son. So drinking helps me get by. Numbs me. Helps me sleep. Tauber gives you pills to sleep. You didn't think I knew about that, did you? We all need to take something to get by."

"What are you going to do after the war?"

"Johan, I'm not sure we have much of a future. When the war ends, we end. Someone will see to it." He chuckled nervously and cynically.

The lights of Fahrenzhausen came into view. I stopped next to a tavern and bade my front-seat passenger a pleasant evening. He assured me it would be and entered the joint. It wasn't as lively as it was when Kaiser and I had raised a few glasses there a year earlier.

I eagerly got back on the road to Berlin.

"Are you all right, Tzivya?"

"Yes, I am. Is someone going to kill you when the war ends?"

"I hope not. Let's get you to Berlin, and we'll worry about that another time."

We arrived early in the morning. Emilie greeted us with hot soup and good cheer. Afterward, she showed Tzivya to her room—and to the closet sanctuary. I slept a few hours and headed back to K XII. In the daylight, I could see that large parts of the city had been reduced to rubble. People looked gaunt and fearful. It was early 1945.

Official reports and obligatory optimism could not hide the fact that the lines were pulling back, and the Allies were closing in. The most dutiful propagandist in Göbbel's employ couldn't hide it. So each report ended with rosy promises of new weapons and robust offensives that would turn the tide. People believe what they want to believe, and many Germans held fast to the faith. Military people knew about casualties and logistics and were less given to false hopes.

Most people I knew, including Osten, thought the end was coming. We made plans about what to do. A few were determined to face the end manfully, either by going down fighting or putting a bullet through their heads. Others accumulated civilian garb and money. As Osten had pointed out, we were relieved that we'd face the Yanks, rather than the Ivans. The maps suggested they'd be here by spring.

Emilie and I had long discussed the coming day. Almost no one knew of my prewar life; almost everyone knew of my wartime service. There were a few inmates who'd speak up for me, I hoped. The rest knew me as an SS officer with an excellent record and a medal from Himmler. Perhaps there were photos in Berlin of Hitler commending me.

If I told the SS who I was, maybe they'd imprison me, and the Americans would know my story. Or maybe the SS would shoot me. Or maybe the Americans wouldn't believe me and would put me up on the gallows with the rest.

Maybe order would break down in the camps, and reprisals would come. A handful of inmates would tackle a guard, get his MP-40, and then kill another guard and get his—and so on, until every officer, guard, and kapo was dead. Rough justice. The inmates were probably planning this, most likely since the February day they heard artillery fire from the west and cheered right in front of us.

We stopped receiving new inmates. The same held for the whole Dachau system. Guards and officers were sent off to combat units. Every night, I listened to war news on the BBC. One morning, I looked up and saw a military plane. Not one of ours. It was small and flew overhead at a medium altitude, probably taking reconnaissance photographs. I wondered how much the Allies knew about the camps.

Kurt and I discussed the end one evening in my quarters. The beer was flowing.

"No matter how much we've tried to help here and there," he said, "there have been many thousands of deaths. There's a reeking pit not far from here."

"And they'll see how emaciated the people are and how many die every day from malnutrition and typhus."

"It's worse at the main camp. Far worse at the places in Poland. The Russians have already taken them. But no one will come here and say, 'Well, it's not so bad here. These Krauts are okay.'"

"No, they certainly won't. They might just shoot every goddam one of us."

We paused a minute or two before finishing the beer.

A cluster of SS officers arrived toward the end of April 1945. Those of us still there were assembled in a training room. The speaker deftly avoided words like *lose* and *surrender* but pointed out measures we should take in the event that southern Germany, including Dachau, came under Allied control. Everyone knew what he meant. Some knew where he was going.

The speaker was a portly, oafish major. Like many of his peers, he came from humble origins, and education had eluded him. He was an excellent speaker, for what that was worth. He took on a pleasing demeanor as he spoke, looking comfortable, thoughtful, and even jovial.

He began with high praise for K XII. He ran down a list of statistics and noted the camp's tidiness. He detailed the supply needs and transport schedules, as he would have two years earlier. He then turned to the business at hand. The room became still.

"We are in need of officers and men who are in excellent physical shape for an extraordinary undertaking. They will escort inmates from the Dachau camps to a new location in the south. This undertaking is being done for logistical purposes."

Well, that sounded like nonsense to me, and I became more suspicious.

The next day, the major was present at roll call and walked about the camp. About noon, he summoned me to the admin building. He began with compliments, something I've long thought signaled bad news.

"Your inmates are in good shape! I understand that you are concerned about production, but did you receive instructions about reducing the numbers of undesirables?"

"Yes, of course. I attended the lecture put on by superiors and read the follow-up memoranda. However, I use my judgment to help win the war. It seems not all my peers have had the same priority—at least, that is what I gather from the news."

He was surprised by my frankness. "Of course, of course. I was merely asking a question between fellow officers. It seems I will not be selecting any inmates from K XII for the march to the south. They will be taken from other camps. There's no shortage, as you know."

"Allow me to understand the purpose of marching prisoners out of Dachau. They are malnourished and sickly, and spring is late this year. The march will take a toll."

"Well said, Ludwig! The march is in keeping with the directives concerning undesirables. You have your priorities; we have ours. We want as many of the weaklings—well, out of the way. Somewhere else. Far away from us. Therefore, they will be taken on a brisk walk." He seemed to marvel at his wording for a moment; then he leaned forward to finish his thought, enunciating each word for dramatic effect. "We want to have as many of the weak inmates dead as possible. That is what's going on here."

I feigned a look of sudden realization, as though something had at last been cleared up in the mind of a junior officer.

"I see, I see. Since the Third Reich is about to fall, it wants to eliminate those it's been starving and overworking."

He was pleased by his pupil. But the pupil was angry and saw little force in the school's administrative machinery at this late date. The teacher was shocked, even frightened.

I went on. "The Reich wants to hide evidence of its nature. Berlin is being too modest. Its actions have been too bold, too daring to be obscured by a brisk walk in the countryside. Its actions have been made across all Europe, and the Allies have taken note. They know! And what will you say to the Allies when they take you in?"

The officer was dismayed, unable to form a reply. One eventually came—it was dull-witted bureaucratic drivel. "It appears you have forgotten your sense of duty, young man. And you have also forgotten that when they take me in—*if* they take me in—you will be in the same situation and face the same consequences."

"My father always told me to be the man that does his best. I've done my best here. I'm not sure others can say the same."

The dolt couldn't tell if I was denouncing the Reich or underscoring my devotion to it.

Kurt, three enlisted men, and I were ordered to report to Dachau. We were to serve as cadres for the march. The Dachau guards assembled a few thousand prisoners in the main yard. They were far worse than anyone at my camp and far worse than my recollections of Dachau only two months earlier. Their eyes were sunken into the sockets. Their faces showed little vitality or hope. Their arms and legs looked like brittle sticks. The few without shirts looked like skeletons. Paper-like skin covered their ribcages and pelvises. Some didn't even have the clogs they'd been issued. I later learned that last winter, many of them had marched from Auschwitz to Dachau.

"They'll hang us for this," Kurt whispered.

"If they don't just throw us to those who survive," I replied. "What sort of mind came up with this?"

"A high-ranking mind. You can be sure of it."

An officer stood on a platform and announced the inmates of the impending march, which he said would last a week. The inmates looked about furtively at friends, perhaps for the last time.

Officers and men were assigned to specific groups. We were told to march along with the condemned in shifts of six hours, after which we would be relieved. We would then board vehicles, which carried food and water, before taking on another shift.

Orders went down to group leaders and then to inmates. We marched out the south gate and into the country. After only a few hours, many marchers were exhausted. By late afternoon, the orderly formations had broken down into a dismal mass of ragged, struggling, ghostlike humanity. People were dropping every thirty minutes or so. If they didn't look dead, they were shot. Most guards did their work as a matter of routine. A weapon was unslung, a shot fired, a weapon reslung.

We walked into wooded areas that had a rustic beauty that contrasted with the nightmarish legion of the dead. We came to villages, where simple people stood along the roads and watched. Some wanted to help the marchers; others saw them as enemies, getting what they deserved.

The group to which I was assigned withered away and combined with another that also had lost many. I didn't know what I was doing or thinking. I simply marched along until my shift ended and I could eat and rest.

In the morning, a few more groups merged. The operation was working as planned. On we went. I considered telling my superior that I was sick and needed to get back to camp. The medals I'd deliberately put on the day before would vouch for me. But I performed my assignments.

Men staggered and limped everywhere. I deliberately avoided

looking at faces, but one man's profile looked familiar. I moved closer. Yes, it was Rabbi Yitzchak. We spoke surreptitiously as we walked.

"What happened?" I asked.

"Oh, it's you. They caught us a few days later. Most of the men were beaten to death. Some were shot on sight. The rest of us were sent to Dachau. Crematory kommando. Hauling the dead to burn. This will all be over soon."

"Not soon enough for many. You know the reason for this march."

"We all do. I am ready. Tired … sick … I've seen enough of this world."

I furtively handed him an apple. "Hide this until we stop. It'll give you strength."

"Too late. My body is gone. I'll not survive this."

He dropped the apple. Another inmate snatched it and devoured it.

"A few more days, and this will end," I said.

He looked straight ahead.

"I know the war news. The Allies will be here soon."

Still no answer. A hundred meters later, he spoke. "Yochanan, I am sorry for what I said about you that day. Hard time … anger. I'm truly sorry."

"Not necessary. I want you to get through these next few days."

"They'll shoot those who survive. We all know it."

"No word of that. Think of Tzivya."

Her name brought life to his eyes. "How is she?"

"I took her to my home in Berlin. She lives with my wife now. She'll survive this, and so will you."

"I haven't heard welcome news in years. This is wonderful. I'd like to see her again, but I don't know. I don't know. Where are they taking us?"

"Somewhere in the south. I don't know exactly where, and neither does anyone. I'll get you food and water when I can. Keep walking. If you fall, they'll shoot you."

I returned to my duties and looked at the endless column, stretching as far as I could see in both directions of the rural road.

"Keep moving!" I shouted angrily. "Keep moving!"

I walked near him again in the evening darkness and handed him a slice of ham and a morsel of bread. He didn't mind, but his pace had slowed and his shoulders slouched forward. Those in that position were soon to stumble. Some marchers would help another back up. Others couldn't spare the strength.

"Rabbi Yitzchak, what do you plan to do after the war?"

"I used to think about that. No more, no more. I can barely keep up now."

"One foot ahead of the other. That's all there is to it. You must have some hopes for the future. We have to."

"My synagogue. I want to return there and pray for my family. I need to say prayers for *all* the dead. How many do you think, Yochi? Hundreds of thousands? Maybe more."

"Many, many more."

"I would like to put Tzivya in a good school. She'll need friends."

"Excellent plan."

"Then, maybe I'll plant a garden behind my little house. Tomato plants, flowers, an olive tree. The olive tree is one of the seven species mentioned in the Torah. It's found in Palestine, the land of Israel."

"A garden. Perhaps in Palestine. That sounds lovely!"

It was chillier on the third day. Spring was in no hurry that year. The poor, emaciated bands, with no food or water and wearing very little, were not faring well. When someone fell, others pulled off any clothing. I wanted to give Rabbi Yitzchak a military coat, but he'd be noticed within an hour, accused of theft, and shot on the spot. No jury, no appeal, no chance. One less marcher.

In the evening, I stripped a corpse of its tunic and gave it to the rabbi. His shoes were torn to bits, his feet discolored and numb. He wasn't eating much of what I brought him. Nonetheless, he made it through the next day.

On the fifth day we were along a road overlooking the Tegernsee, a picturesque lake in sight of the Alps. People hiked the adjacent foothills on vacations and took pictures of the Bavarian landscape. Whatever thoughts of beauty occurred came and went in an instant.

Rabbi Yitzchak fell that morning. I was the only guard in sight, so I helped him up.

"You have to keep moving. One foot out, then the other. This is the last day. The last few hours. Please, keep going."

"My time is at hand … I can feel it. No more of this … no more of any of this." His face was gaunt and sallow—cadaverous. Thoughts of olive gardens in the hills of Palestine had left him. "Take care of Tzivya, Yochi. She is all alone. … I saw her as my daughter. … Do the same. … Do the same."

I promised I would.

"You are a good man. … You are a good man. … May the Lord bless you … and give you life." He managed a brief smile and then looked straight ahead and walked precariously. No more than a minute later, he fell again. The stillness told the story. I marched on as my eyes teared, and I tried to hide my sorrow.

"Keep moving! Keep moving!"

Within three hours, we arrived at the Tegernsee, and the survivors were allowed to rest. Some water and food arrived. Most of the SS personnel were driven back to Dachau and the subcamps. I was one of the first to get away.

16

The Liberation of K XII

The end had come. The signs were clear, and no one was denying it any longer, not even those holed up in the Berlin bunker. The artillery was closer. The dull booms in the distance were now like cracks of thunder in a summer storm, though unceasing. The roads between camps were lined with trucks and troops. Some columns maintained order, but most were uneven lines of dispirited men with haggard faces and dirty uniforms. Many wore bandages and limped.

The radio reports from Berlin continued, though the signal came in and out. The Russians were on the outskirts. The lines were bending in places and giving way altogether in others. The streets of most cities had soldiers foraging for food and trying to find a place to hide from the military police.

I feared for my family but could not join them. Even if the roads had been clear, I'd have been shot as a deserter or hanged by patriotic zealots on the loose. I couldn't sleep at nights, thinking what could happen to my family. I knew that when Germany was liberated, there would be serious anger toward the people of Germany. When our death camps were liberated and the atrocities exposed, there would be no mercy.

A lot of our guards already had taken off to the fronts, leaving us with only several dozen guards and officers. Some slipped away at night. I didn't blame them, nor did I try to stop them. Many times, I thought to escape myself but hesitated. I was afraid that something bad would happen to my family if I were discovered. I was pretty much recognizable in the camp. I was also afraid of being shot on the spot when the Allies took over the camp. I figured I'd have a better chance if I waited to be captured and then exposed who I really was. I lost track of Hans and Kurt just before the end, and I hoped they got away, though I later learned different.

Osten and I had made our decision a few days earlier. We'd stay to the end and surrender K XII to the Americans. Our camp had the best conditions in the Dachau system—or better put, the least abysmal.

Kaiser decided to come to our camp for the end. He said the supply trucks to the main camp hadn't arrived in a week. Army units were disintegrating or surrendering en masse. Everything was breaking down. Dachau had lost contact with Berlin. I had lost interest in Dachau and Berlin. He said the "Amis" would be here in a day.

On the third day of creation—as recorded in Genesis—the passage on the Lord seeing his work as good is mentioned twice. According to Jewish tradition, Tuesday is considered "twice good." For all I knew, that meant I'd be shot twice. I was half right.

On Tuesday morning, May 1, 1945, we heard the rumble of armored vehicles just down the road. Osten, Kaiser, and I sat in the office and waited, occasionally glancing out the window until the gunfire got close. Kaiser's swagger and smugness were gone. He was worried. So was I.

Osten used the occasion to indulge in his favorite pastime. "Well, gentlemen, we shall see what will become of us now," the kommandant murmured as he poured another glass of cognac from a nearly empty bottle and slowly squeezed his cigarette holder.

"Drunk again, it seems," I said solemnly.

"Yes, I am. This is the best way I can think of to face the end," he chortled.

Kaiser sat quietly and nervously. I thought he might put pistol to head; there was a lot of that during those last few days.

"Otto, why did you come here?" I asked. "Why not Munich or Berlin?"

"I don't really know. Your camp always had a good feeling to it. I don't know how to define it. It's … clean."

Well, K XII had plenty of filth and criminality all the same. Could I convey what a handful of us tried to do? Would I be given the opportunity? I despaired as I thought I'd never see Emilie or Sophia again.

The gunfire became quite close, less than a hundred meters away. Tank guns and machine-gun fire were destroying guard towers and the main gate. The half-tracks had the white star of the American army. A few of the stalwarts shot back, but they were quickly killed or taken prisoner. GIs went from building to building. We heard the cheering.

We put our pistols on the desk and walked out with hands raised. A young captain ordered us to lie down with arms stretched out and faces down. There was shouting and intermittent gunfire all around. The guards were being summarily executed—shot or beaten to death.

The captain paced above us, a .45 in hand. "You goddam Kraut bastards are going to pay for this! By God, I'll see to that! Which one of you sons o' bitches is top man?" His German was fair and comprehensible.

Osten raised a shaking hand.

The captain ordered him out with a sharp, "*Raus!*"

Osten complied. He yelped as the butt of an M-1 struck his head like a baseball bat. He fell not far from me, his face bleeding from a deep gash.

"It was like this at Dachau too, you sons o' bitches! You goddam Kraut sons o' bitches!"

I expected to hear his .45 settle the issue.

"You two! Stand up!"

Kaiser and I began to obey, but the blows came fast and hard. I fell to my knees as the pummeling continued. Punches and rifle butts came down on us. My hope for unconsciousness and more was not granted. I weighed the matter of allowing death to come or trying what I'd planned. In between blows, I managed to get a few practiced English words out.

"I am a Jew! I swear to you I am a Jew!"

The captain held a hand up, and the beating stopped. He had a look of incredulity mixed with anger. "What the hell did you say, you lying bastard?" A powerful fist crashed into my jaw.

"I am Jewish! I was forced into the SS! I had to protect my family! I swear to you I am Jewish."

Blood splattered from my mouth as I spoke. The captain didn't believe me, but a compelling witness spoke up—Kaiser.

"I *knew* it! I always knew you were a filthy Jew! Well, in the end, a Jew wins out against me! Think of it!" Kaiser spat out the words and then fell into deranged laughter that welled up from his dark, emptying soul.

A GI translated for the captain. His .45 remained at the ready.

I welcomed the opportunity to tell the truth, even if only Kaiser believed me, even if I was going to die any moment. I wanted to see Kaiser's face.

"Yes, you bloodhound! Your suspicions were correct all along." I shifted to the Yiddish dialect. "My name is Yochanan Berger. And I am an Orthodox Jew."

"Ha! You killed your own people, then!" Kaiser snarled.

"I helped where I could but failed many times, and my soul is stained."

Osten looked up from the ground, and two M-1s quickly were pressed to his head. "Ach, so. It makes sense now. Realization has come late."

I hurriedly spoke in Yiddish-German about a friend in the records office, my new identity, and my family. The translation went on among several puzzled faces. A handful of inmates stood not far away—a jury, of sorts.

The captain asked a handful of them about me. Had they seen me kill anyone? No one could attest to my story, of course, but neither could anyone say I'd killed anyone.

"You are all filthy Jews! One day, we'll finish the job! Heil Hitler!" Kaiser stretched his arm out in salute, and the captain shot him in the head. He crumpled to the ground with a moronic look on his face.

Scores of inmates cheered the GI justice. I felt no satisfaction. I'd seen so many killings that I could no longer feel anything over one more. Kaiser was just another corpse for the pit.

"Lift him up," the captain ordered the men behind Osten. "What about this guy?"

No one spoke.

"Anyone?"

"He didn't kill anyone," I said. "He was just a drunken office worker."

"He goes to the MPs," the captain said.

As Osten was hauled away, we gave each other a quick glance that conveyed a wish of good luck.

"And what of this supposed Jew?" the captain asked. "Anyone vouch for him?"

Again no one spoke—at least for a few moments.

"Yes, he killed many of us here. I saw him."

"No!" I cried.

An emaciated, sickly man stepped forward. I'd never seen him before. "You did! I saw you!"

He spoke clearly, and his eyes showed intelligence. Was he confusing me with someone else? Did he just want to see us all die?

The captain aimed his pistol at me. "The SS in Dachau put on prison uniforms. They had a way of trying to fool us, and you have yours."

Bang!

It took me a second to realize I'd been shot. Blood flowed from my abdomen onto my shirt and tunic. I felt weak and slumped to the ground. My strength drained onto the cold earth. Emilie's sweet voice came to me. The crescendo of "Carol of the Bells" was to be my requiem.

I began to recite the Morning Prayer. I was reasserting who I was and felt decent once more. The captain let me finish.

"What bullshit!" he said and then aimed his .45 at my forehead.

"No!" someone shouted in Yiddish. An older man stepped from the crush and stood next to me. "Only Jews from Berlin use that dialect."

"Yeah, he's right," said a GI in heavily accented Yiddish.

"I might have seen this man in a Berlin synagogue!" the inmate told the captain.

"You have no idea how good it is to see you again, my friend." With that, I lost consciousness, half expecting never to see this world again.

I heard rumbling from far away and thought it was a tank coming at me. I couldn't see anything. Slowly, the fog lifted, and my vision and other faculties began to function, if barely. I made out lights and people. I was in the infirmary, and trucks were rolling by outside. Large American ones. Scores of them.

I felt weak. Someone gave me water, and I drank it slowly as I tried to make out the face. It was the GI captain. The man who had shot me. He began to speak in broken German.

"I'm Captain Miller. Oh hell, call me Mitchell. Good to see you coming around. The medics say you're going to make it. Looks like, for an officer, I'm a lousy shot."

"So am I."

"Look, I feel bad about that. We'd just come up from Dachau, and after seeing that place, my patience was pretty damned limited for Kraut bastards—no offense."

"None taken."

"You know, I looked around this place, and a few spoke up for you, especially one or two who came from Dachau."

"Good to hear. Truly so."

"You know, Yochanan Berger or whatever the hell your name is, someday you'll have to write all this down. A Jew in the SS? Sounds like a Jack Benny movie I saw."

"Maybe I'll do that someday. A hundred years from now."

"Should do well. Make you a rich man. Be sure to mention old Captain Miller from Chicago. Just don't say anything about his marksmanship."

"I want only to be with my family."

"Same with all of us. Is there anything I can do for you?"

"I want to keep all this secret. I don't want it out. Please. All this stays between you and me."

"I get it, I get it. I can pull the paperwork on you in the main building and burn it. You'll be another liberated inmate, one of thousands of people without birth certificates or IDs or dog tags or anything but the clothes on their backs. New threads, courtesy of a famous tailor named Uncle Sam."

"I cannot thank you enough."

"I'm keeping your Luger."

"It has no further use. I need to get to my family in Berlin. Is there still fighting going on there?"

"It's almost over now. The Russkis are mopping up. I hope to be back home pretty goddam soon."

"I hope you get the next boat back."

"I hope so too. Meanwhile, my battalion's moving out tomorrow morning. They say Germany will surrender any day now. Did you hear Hitler's dead? Shot himself in the head, according to the BBC. I'm glad *he* wasn't a lousy shot. Anyway, Auf Wiedersehen."

"Auf Wiedersehen."

Most of those in the Dachau system were placed in Displaced Persons camps that the Allies set up to deal with the huge numbers of liberated inmates and refugees. There were scores of such camps in the western half of Germany alone. Some were in old SS camps, some in hard-hit army installations, and at least one in a former summer camp for the Hitler Youth. They were cramped and crowded, but the barracks were clean and the rations generous. The more emaciated had to eat small portions for several weeks so their bodies could adjust.

I did some work around a camp for a few weeks until my wound healed. I no longer had any uniform, pistol, or ID card. I even shaved my head. I processed in as a liberated inmate named Yochanan Berger of Berlin and received an ID card to that effect. I couldn't wait to go back home but had to wait until I was able to move after my injury. I also wanted to make sure that I was clearly identified as a Jewish survivor.

Just as I'd had to hide my Jewish identity over the last few years, I now had to hide my SS past—and my tattoo. They were looking for those distinctive markings, but I avoided showing my arm in showers and delousing procedures. I'd loathed that mark since the day I got it, and now it was a danger to me. One glance, and I'd be whisked off to a prison camp for interrogation or worse.

Most of the former inmates tried to find loved ones who'd also been rounded up and sent to one place or another in Nazi-occupied Europe. We were only beginning to understand the scope of the Final Solution. So many people would never know their loved ones' fates, except, of course, in general terms. Millions simply vanished.

I knew where my loved ones were. The Red Army took Berlin in early May and was not gentle with the population. Naturally, I was desperate to contact Emilie and Sophia. How? No phone or mail service. All I could do was put Emilie's name on a list and go through the camp's process.

Two months passed. Berlin was divided up between the Russians, Americans, French, and British. That was good. With some sort of administration there, things would begin the long return to daily life. There'd be electricity and water. Mail would start back up. People could go home.

Trains were running better, including one from Munich to Berlin. I was in good health by then and had a place to go. I had enough for a train ticket to Berlin.

We chugged along north, not far from the roads I once traveled on regular visits home. The roads and railways were once clogged with German soldiers and vehicles. Now GIs were everywhere. Some carried weapons. Most were out on the town and waiting for orders home. A pack of smokes went a long way.

I walked the two kilometers or so from the train station. Berlin was in ruins. Whole blocks had been reduced to rubble. People rummaged through the piles for sellable items, including intact bricks. Former soldiers begged on street corners. They got very little, even the crippled ones.

I knocked on the door of my apartment. Sophia opened the door and bounded into my eager arms. Emilie and Tzivya were just behind her. We'd all made it. Through luck, perseverance, and painful circumstances, we'd all made it.

As much as we wanted to simply relax and inch toward normalcy, we couldn't. Emilie and Tzivya told of looted stores and rapacious Russians. They stayed inside as much as possible, going out only in groups to barter for food. No one tried to break in. We had to do that for several more weeks until the streets were safer and food distribution more stable.

Even though there was a shortage of men, it was not until the fall that I found a job. The radio shop where I'd worked before the war gave me my old job back. Not long thereafter, I re-enrolled at Berlin University. It was disorienting to do the same troubleshooting and soldering, to enter the same classrooms and library. As much as I wanted to get on with things, memories persisted and haunted and stabbed. I no longer worried about the Gestapo hunting Yochanan Berger; I worried about the tribunals hunting Johan Ludwig.

A cover story would be needed. I developed some of it in the DP camp. I was taken from my home in Friedrichstadt and sent to Dachau, where I was assigned to the K XII subcamp and put to work making ammunition. I could tell you about every building and what it manufactured, what roll calls were like, and what sort of meals the mess hall served.

One weekend, we borrowed a car and drove out to Emilie's

parents' house. Both parents had made it through the war. Many bombing raids had come within a few kilometers. One night, the house suffered light damage from the concussion of an errant bomb.

We walked to the cabin, shovels in hand, and with little effort found the place where Johan Ludwig had buried the Berger family's Judaica. My prayer book, menorah, a painting of the rabbis, and a few other items were intact, though a little moldy. They'd survived the Nazi years too.

I retained a few articles from my past—some material I'd read at the academy, a few photos, and a medal or two. There was no point in destroying or burying them. I packed them in a small box and put it in the back of a closet.

I completed my electrical engineering degree in a few years and found an engineering position with Siemens. I went on to work there for many years, developing television, radio, and military products that the new Germany was making for the world, restoring the country's image.

Over the years, I tried to locate Kurt and Hans, my friends and fellow conspirators. The West German government had a database that helped people find people scattered by the war. I made inquiries and left messages, but nothing came of it. It was the same with Osten, though I had little interest in seeing him again. I'm certain that most former SS personnel made an effort to remain unknown. After all, not everyone wanted to find them as old friends. I hope they made it and lived good lives.

Everyone followed the Nuremberg trials. I didn't know any of the prominent names, like Göring or Frick or Keitel, but I'd encountered some of the lesser figures. The kommandants of Dachau were tried and executed locally, or they cheated the hangman by killing themselves.

Would any of those investigations look for Johan Ludwig? Unlikely. He was not as significant as the others. Captain Miller had set a match to Johan Ludwig's personnel folder at K XII, and Allied bombers had done their work on many parts of Berlin. I nonetheless worried that, somewhere, there was file, or a photograph, or a compelling witness.

My wife and daughter and Tzivya told me over and over that I was a decent man. Their words were as loving and well intended as any that humans have ever spoken, but I was never convinced.

In 1952, Tzivya's uncle in the United States tried to learn what happened to his relations in Germany. Most everyone had perished, but he found his niece with us. He came to visit and convinced her to move to Brooklyn. She tearfully said goodbye to us but corresponded for many years from her new home, where she thrived.

Emilie, Sophia, and I observed Christian and Jewish holidays but in a secular manner. Out of a firestorm of intolerance, we came to respect all religions but never joined any of them. Over the years, Sophia chose not to join either.

My religiousness had declined when I'd married Emilie, and I'd made concessions, as had she. It fell away during the war years as I played the role fate had so perversely assigned me, and I had to profess to be a Catholic. I memorized Catholic prayers and doctrines and strategically placed its paraphernalia in my home and quarters. But I witnessed such large-scale cruelty and hatred that the idea of a providential entity hovering above seemed out of place, obsolete, childish, and absurd.

I could never be at home in my former community because I had betrayed it. I had betrayed it by denying it and playing a role in trying to exterminate it. The role was unwilling, and I deviated from the script where I could, but there's no mistaking it: I took part in the Final Solution.

Yes, Emilie and I observed many religious holidays. I observed the most important one in silence, isolation, and despair. Every fall, I yearned for atonement.

EPILOGUE

Yochi and his family lived in Germany for a few more years, until they decided to immigrate to the state of Israel. They settled in a small, enchanting town called Zichron Yaakov, where they built a new home and raised Sophia. Yochanan worked for one of the most well-known military firms in Israel and excelled in his job.

Yochanan kept his life story a secret and pretended to be a Holocaust survivor.

When Sophia was sixteen, Yochanan and Emilie told her about Yochanan's past. She didn't grasp the meaning until later in life, at which time she developed anger toward him. Only many years later did she confront Yochanan with a very crucial question: "Why didn't you refuse to serve in the SS?"

Yochanan explained the reasons, but she didn't seem to be convinced. She held anger toward her father and only let go after many years of therapy. Sophia graduated from Tel Aviv University and moved out of the family home. She got married and has two children, all living in the state of Israel.

Yochanan and Emilie decided to move to the coastal city of Netanya for retirement. They enjoyed living near the beautiful Mediterranean and creating new memories.

Yochanan and Emilie went to visit Germany, where they used to live, and they even paid a visit to the person who had saved them, Rudolph Weber. They learned that Weber had saved more people in the same way as he had saved Yochanan—by faking their identities as non-Jewish in the population records.

They also paid a visit to the Auschwitz and Dachau memorial sites. It was a very emotional time for Yochanan, as he recalled the Kaufering XII camp. He and Emilie visited the Yad Vashem Holocaust Museum, and that left them with a deep emotional impression. Although Yochanan received numerous requests from Yad Vashem to share his life story, he consistently refused to do so and kept his secret.

Yochanan searched to get back to his origins, the Jewish faith, which he lost after the war. After befriending a synagogue rabbi in Netanya, he returned to his beliefs and found happiness in that.

Surprisingly, he met his friend from the camp, Dr. Hans Tauber, as he visited Israel. It was a very emotional reunion, as Hans never had learned the story of who Yochanan really was.

Emilie passed away at the age of eighty-seven from an illness, and Yochanan remained alone. When he met new friends who were Holocaust survivors, he decided to tell his life story, which he'd kept secret for more than fifty years.

Shortly after he completed telling his story, he was found dead on his doorstep from natural causes.

APPENDIX

Yochanan
(Portrait by Emilie, ca. 1953)

Emilie
(Self-portrait, ca. 1953)

Sophia (later, Sofi)
(Portrait by Emilie, ca. 1952)

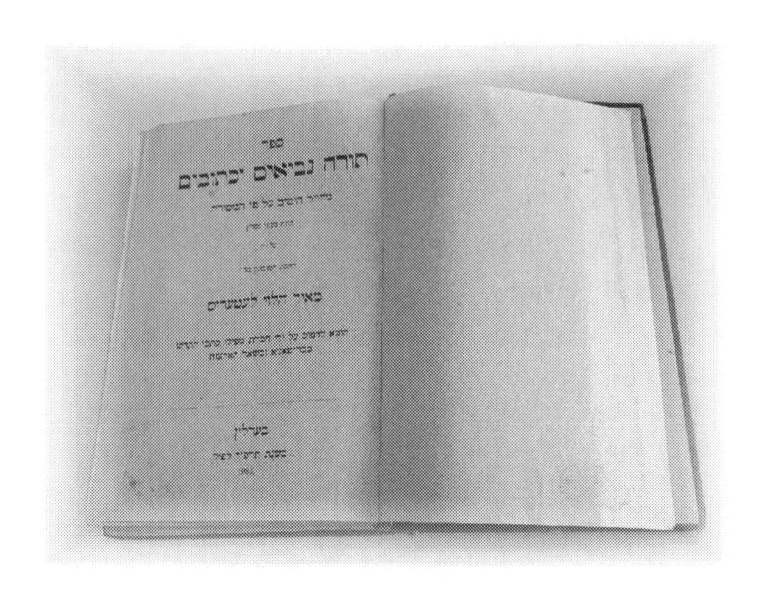

A prayer book given to Yochanan by his father, ca. 1934
(From Yochanan's personal belongings)

The synagogue on Fasanenstraße in Berlin-Charlottenburg before it was destroyed on Kristallnacht in 1938
(Source: Wikimedia commons)

Berlin Catholic church
(Source: Free photobank)

SS and Gestapo headquarters, Berlin
(Source: Wikimedia commons)

Gate at the main entrance to Dachau, 1945
(Source: Wikimedia commons)

A Kaufering subcamp near Landsberg
(Source: Wikimedia commons)

A selection on the platform at Auschwitz-Birkenau
(Source: Wikimedia commons)

Dachau prisoners' barracks, soon after liberation, May 1945
(Source: Wikimedia commons)

Yochanan's rank, Obersturmführer (1944)
(Source: Wikimedia commons)

The Iron Cross given by Heinrich Himmler
(From Yochanan's personal belongings)

Medal given by Obergruppenführer Darges
(From Yochanan's personal belongings)

Obersturmbannführer Ernst Osten
(From Yochanan's personal belongings)

Unterdrückte Wahrheit

Der Stürmer

Deutsches Wochenblatt zum Kampfe um die Wahrheit

HERAUSGEBER: JULIUS STREICHER

39

1943

Das Geheimnis des Blutes

Unsere Jugend

Aus dem Inhalt

Die Juden sind unser Unglück!

Die große Enttäuschung

Das Judenproblem in den USA.

Newspapers Yochanan received while in SS training

(From Yochanan's personal belongings)

Heinrich Himmler in Dachau
(Source: Wikimedia commons)

88 mm shell—shells like these were produced in K XII
(Source: Wikimedia commons)

Survivors of Kaufering I—April 1945
(Source: Wikimedia commons)

Reprisals against SS guards at Dachau
(Source: Wikimedia commons)

Plaque on the front of the New Synagogue in Berlin. It states that the old synagogue was burned by the Nazis on Kristallnacht and destroyed in a bombing raid in 1943.
(Source: Wikimedia commons)

Haifa, Israel, 1960
(Source: Wikimedia commons)

Jerusalem—the Western Wall and Dome of the Rock
(Source: Wikimedia commons)

The Ohel Yaacov synagogue in Zichron Yaacov, not far from where Yochanan lived
(Source: Wikimedia commons)

Netanya, where Yochanan and Emilie lived in retirement
(Source: author's collection)

Printed in the United States
By Bookmasters